INTO THE VOID

TAYLOR GREGORY

Copyright © 2019 Taylor Gregory
All rights reserved.

Cover and layout by ebooklaunch.com

Chapter 1

Mist swirled and timbers creaked as the ship carved its way through the calm waters. Goros tried his best to peer through the thick fog, but it was no use. Visibility was nonexistent. He was having difficulty seeing from one end of his vessel to the other; trying to see anything past that was futile. The helmsman could close his eyes and do as good a job as he was doing now, with the wayfarer guiding his hands.

Goros knew that there was no real point to his being on deck, but he was always too nervous to stay in his cabin. At least on deck he could fool someone into believing that he was calm. Alone, he would be pacing the floor and drinking rum by the bottle. Out here, in the eyes of his crew, Goros was forced to maintain some composure. When he had been coming up through the trading company, he had scoffed at his father's ideas of how a captain should comport himself. Now that he had been in command of a vessel for years, he knew that there was value in that composure. It kept the men calm.

And they needed it.

Even though almost all his crew were veterans, there was something about sailing the ways that had an effect on a man. Maybe it was the ever-present, clinging fog that frayed the tempers of even the hardened sailor. Or the idea that they were somehow outside of reality. Or it could be the fact that they were forced to rely on the pseudoscientific art of the wayfarers to pull them through.

Personally, Goros believed that it was the tales they had all been told since they were youths. Every single child raised in a coastal town had been regaled with the tales of ghost ships floating into port, their crews missing. Rumors of what happened to the men varied. Some claimed it was the enchanting song of the sirens that lured them to their deaths, others that demons lived in the mist and fed on human flesh. Others swore they had sailed too close to the void and been swallowed up.

It was easy to dismiss those as simple ghost stories and children's tales when you were in port, with the sun warming your bones. It was much harder to explain away when you were plying the ways. The chill and the ever-present fog cut through any false bravado a man might carry. Goros had been a sailor his entire life, and he'd still never managed to acclimate to the sensation.

Despite the unease in his heart, Goros forced himself to maintain an outward air of disinterest. He'd found that it was good for the men if they could fool themselves into believing that their captain was unperturbed. Even if deep down, they knew it wasn't true. So Goros stood with his feet planted beside the helmsman and wayfarer, his hands braced behind his back.

Men meandered about the deck lethargically. There was not much to do while moving through the ways. The younger sailors were cleaning the deck under the directions and sharp eyes of the more experienced hands. Anyone who did not have to be on deck generally avoided it. Most of the men would be below deck, trying to keep warm in the galley or huddled around in the crew quarters telling ghost stories.

Goros had no idea where the tradition had originated, but it was said that telling such stories while in the ways would keep spirits at bay. And perhaps it worked. Goros had never been on a voyage where the tradition hadn't been upheld, and he had never seen a spirit either. He believed the stories had a different purpose. By giving the men something to look for as a warning sign, it helped to calm their nerves when the signs weren't present.

"That's odd," Marscan said.

The sudden words made Goros almost jump out of his skin. After his heart had settled somewhat, he turned his head to look at the wayfarer. The man stood beside the helmsman, guiding the route they would take. Marscan was a wisp of a man, though tall. His face was pale, and despite the chill in the air, it was beaded with sweat. His eyes were half-closed, and his face was scrunched together in concentration.

Goros had never been able to feel the ways, but he held a sailor's respect for those who could. Many who had never been aboard a ship thought of wayfarers as odd recluses who hid below deck until it was time to enter the ways. Though that depiction was somewhat accurate, Goros had seen through the years the strain that detecting the ways and guiding a ship through them put upon a man. A good wayfarer was the difference between reaching your destination on time and not reaching it at all.

Marscan was a good wayfarer. He had been aboard the trading galleon *Highcastle* for almost as long as Goros. The man was an odd one, but he had never led them astray. Goros could see the hint of concern on his face, and it worried him.

"What's odd?" Goros asked.

"The way…wavered."

"You lost it?"

"No, not exactly. I…it's difficult to describe. It sort of jiggled."

Goros had no idea what the man was talking about. He had not been blessed with the gift of sensing the way. Though there was a lot of intellectual thought and a pseudoscience surrounding wayfaring, there was still much that was unknown. Those who possessed the gift could hardly put it into words. There was still as much magic to the craft as there was science.

"Is that bad?" Goros asked after a moment.

"I don't know," Marscan replied. "I've never felt anything like it before. It's grown still now."

"Let me know if anything else changes."

"Of course, Captain."

Goros settled back into his place, even though the hairs on the back of his neck were standing on end. This reeked of one of the tales that might be told over a bottle of rum in a tavern. Goros recounted every story he had ever heard an old sea dog tell the new blood to put the fear of the gods into them, but none matched what he had just been told. Still, Goros knew that he would not be able to relax until they were safely out of the ways and sailing into a port.

• • •

"Are we there?" Akos whispered.

"Aye," Vibius replied. "We'll be upon them in moments."

"Good. Get below deck."

The man nodded and trudged down from the aft castle toward the crew's quarters. Akos waited until he was safe below to nod to his first mate. The large man nodded and moved between the men, whispering instructions as he moved. Akos stood next to the helm, adjusting his belt as he waited. The sword on his hip was a short and sturdy cutlass, though he hoped he would not have to draw it. Things always went smoother when swords weren't drawn.

There was no way to know that they were on the right course. Akos could barely see the prow of his oversized sloop as it sliced through the still waters of the way. The likelihood of any regular sailor finding another ship in this fog would be like finding a needle in a haystack the size of a city. Akos had full confidence in Vibius's skills, however, and the crew had a secret weapon. It wouldn't be the first time that the man had put them directly on the mark. Wayfaring was an art, and Vibius was a master.

Despite the lack of visibility, the lanterns on the *Mist Stalker* had been doused. Akos wasn't one to take unnecessary chances. He wanted his prey to be as shocked by their presence as they could. If they were shocked and terrified, they would be much more likely to surrender without putting up a fight.

That didn't mean his crew wasn't ready for a fight. Every man was armed with a mixture of cutlasses, pistols, and boarding axes. Some of the cannon crews even stood at the ready, though Akos had no desire to see them put to work. Their prey and her cargo would be worth a good deal more whole than they would be if he damaged them, but he wouldn't hesitate if it was necessary.

For several tense minutes, there was almost no sound. Akos's men waited anxiously. He could feel his heart pounding in his chest. His hands were braced behind his back, but he could feel his knuckles going white from his fists clenching. This was the most critical part of the whole endeavor. The *Mist Stalker* needed to spot its prey and attack before the prey even knew they were there. If the ship they were following somehow caught wind of them before they could get into position, the fight would be much harder. The element of complete surprise was crucial to taking a ship without a fight.

Without warning, the mist parted enough that Akos could make out the outline of another vessel in the fog. He glanced over toward his helmsman, but the man was already correcting their course. Akos felt some of the tension drain out of him. The most difficult part of hunting through the ways was finding prey. Once that was done, the rest seemed easy by comparison.

Dozens of men waited on the deck, and Akos could tell they had also seen the shape in the fog. Men steeled themselves, ready to attack at a moment's notice. Akos saw his first mate, Leodysus, with his sword already in one hand and a grappling hook in the other. Leo would likely be the first one onto the other vessel. Akos would prefer it to be him, but several of the ship's officers had insisted that he take fewer risks.

It was an odd feeling, knowing that he would have to sit and wait for the boarding party to give the all clear. Akos didn't have some bloodthirsty desire for combat. But he had always believed that if he was going to ask men to put their lives in danger, he should at least lead from the front rather than the rear. His friends disagreed. Akos had ignored them at first, but over time they had worn him down, and he had agreed to give a different style a test run.

So, he would sit by the helmsman's side and call out orders, trusting that Leo would deliver them victory if the enemy resisted. If it were any other man, Akos would have refused and been right there among the boarding crew. He had complete trust in Leo, however.

As the ships drew closer together, Akos felt his breath catch in his chest again. The ways were so still that even a cough or a sneeze would be enough to alert the foe to their presence. As the soft glow of the lanterns on the other ship guided their approach, Akos could not help but wonder whether this ship had bothered to keep lookouts. It was rare to be attacked in the ways, so most merchantmen allowed their men a break. Only the paranoid and those with foreknowledge of a possible attack kept the watch while in the ways. Akos knew that the other ship couldn't have any foreknowledge of their attack, but the other captain could very well be a paranoid man.

Rather than allowing his nervousness to show on his face, he put on the mask of calm he'd developed over the years. Akos tried to project an air of unimpressed focus. He had no idea whether he was fooling anyone, but it helped him to feel better. Akos took a moment to make sure the brace of pistols to the back of his belt were loose and would come free of their holsters quickly if necessary.

Once that was done, Akos turned his attention back toward the rapidly closing distance between the ships. It would be only a few moments now before they were upon the merchantman. He could almost make out the name painted on the back of the vessel now, but the fog was still distorting it. There were shadowy figures moving about the craft, but none of them seemed to be looking in his direction. Akos hoped that luck would hold long enough for them to get a little closer.

• • •

Goros thought he heard something other than the creaking of the planks beneath his feet and the water lapping against his vessel. He glanced over his shoulder, sure he had heard someone moving about. There was nothing there but the fog, however, and he berated himself for being a fool. He was letting the ghost stories and Marscan get to his head.

The glance over his shoulder shifted his weight enough for him to realize how stiff his legs had become. Goros sighed. He was no longer a young man, and his body took every moment to remind him. His knees creaked and complained as he stepped aside. The helmsman shot him a questioning glance, but he waved the man's worries away.

"I need to take a quick walk around the deck, that's all," Goros said.

He stepped back from the railing by the helm and strode over to the port side of his ship. The fog gave up no more secrets as he took a good long look into it. He chided himself for letting Marscan get into his head. He knew that there was no such thing as sirens or any other sea monsters. And here in the ways, it was highly unlikely that anything else was likely to find them. In his forty years of sailing, he had never so much as encountered another ship while in the ways.

Into the Void

Goros continued his walk around the aft castle, looking behind his vessel as far as he could. Below him was the sea, so deep blue that it was almost black. Frothy-white wake spread out behind them as they plowed steadily forward. Goros followed it with his eyes from the base of his ship to where it disappeared into the fog.

Goros blinked for a moment, sure his eyes were playing tricks on him. It looked as if his wake was mixing with the wake of another vessel. After several blinks he was sure of what he was seeing. His mind raced to decipher the information that his eyes were giving him. The only way that such a thing could be possible was if there was another ship beside them. He glanced starboard, but he couldn't see anything.

Then, hardly shadows against the mist, Goros could see a trio of masts rising next to him. He rushed to the starboard railing, looking down as he did so. Goros could feel his heart fall into his stomach as he recognized what he was seeing.

Below him was a sloop. The surprise of seeing another vessel so close in the ways was hard for him to fight past. Shades moved amid the deck of the vessel in silence. Goros realized that his jaw had dropped, and he snapped it shut as he realized that the smaller vessel was about to try to board them.

Goros looked over toward the helmsman, realizing with his foggy mind that no one else had come to the same realization. Goros took a shaky step toward him, raising his hands to his mouth to amplify his voice.

"Sound the alarm!" Goros yelled. "Prepare to repel boarders!"

• • •

"Damn," Akos cursed under his breath.

The alarm went up right before the men were preparing to throw their grappling hooks. Half a dozen men appeared at the rails, peering over to confirm the call. A few shots rang out, sudden thunderclaps in the silence. *I suppose that's out of the bag*, Akos mused. To be fair, the call had been to repel boarders, not to strike the colors. Akos had been hoping to get the ships hooked together and then fire a shot across their bow with a pistol to announce their presence and intentions, but he could not fault his men for firing.

It didn't appear that any of the shots had hit home. There were no screams or bodies flopping over the railing. Akos knew that few of his men could be called expert marksmen, but he'd armed those few with rifled muskets and stationed them up in the rigging. A pair of shots rang out from above him even then, and this time the shots were rewarded with a scream of pain.

So much for doing this without a fight. Akos sighed. At least the cannons might not have to come into play. That would at least keep the value of the prize high, which might balance out the ransoms he was about to lose. Leodysus shouted an order, and the grapnels flew out, finding purchase on the railing and in the lines of the other ship. Men heaved with all their strength, and the lines snapped taut. The ships were inexorably drawn together by the combined effort of his crew.

A few axes flashed out in the gloom and tried to hack away the lines. There weren't enough men on deck ready to repel, however, and soon enough the ships were close enough for his men to throw their boarding planks down. As Akos had predicted, Leo was one of the first men over the side, his pistol firing and his sword ready in his hand. Akos wanted nothing more than to join them, but he had promised to wait this one out, and he was not one to go back on his promises.

Once again his hands clenched into tight fists behind his back. Akos did not like feeling useless. He knew that most captains acted this way, but it wasn't something he had ever intended to do. He'd never been scared to put himself in harm's way. Now, as he watched other men clamber over the railing of the enemy vessel ready to fight in his place, Akos wondered how anyone could do this on a regular basis.

Fortunately, he did not have to wait long. Mere moments passed before the enemy captain realized his position was hopeless and struck his colors. It was difficult to see in the fog, but the flag was descending. As soon as the flag began to waver, all sounds of fighting ceased. Despite knowing how well trained his crew was, Akos still let out a breath of relief. Men could get carried away with bloodshed, and when that happened surrender was a foreign term. Within moments, Leo was leaning over the side of the railing to wave to him that it was all clear.

Relieved that he was finally moving, Akos stepped down from the aft castle and toward the boarding ramp. The merchantman was much taller than the low-slung sloop, but Akos had no trouble scaling one of the grapnel lines. A glance was all he needed to take in the situation as he cleared the railing. His men were busy relieving the merchantman's crew of their weapons and piling them in the center of the deck. Only one man among the enemy crew still had a weapon, and from the looks of it, he hadn't even been wearing it when the attack started. He was holding an unsheathed cutlass in his hands that looked as if it had been forced there by someone else.

Akos took a moment to scan the scene for any casualties. There appeared to be a pair of men bleeding on the deck, but neither of them were his. At least one man lay dead, probably the man picked off by his marksman. Akos was grateful that none of his men had fallen. There was nothing he hated more than telling the families of his crewmen that they had been killed in action. Krallek would have his hands full for the next few days keeping the injured pair alive long enough to reach port.

Akos stepped across the deck toward the man who was holding the sword. The man was older, clearly a veteran sailor. Even with all his age and experience he hadn't expected anything like this to happen. Akos couldn't really blame him. No one could be expected to anticipate an attack while they were traveling the ways. Vibius had told him it was like trying to find a needle in a haystack that was in constant motion. Akos stopped before the group, the man stepping forward with his hand outstretched with the sword.

"I am Captain Goros," the man said. "I surrender. The *Highcastle* is yours."

"Your vessel is now my prize," Akos responded. "Your crew is under my protection and shall be treated as prisoners of war. Once we reach port, you will all be ransomed. Now, which one of you is the wayfarer?"

A spindly man begrudgingly stepped forward.

"We are going to tow your vessel back to port," Akos said. "You will remain aboard the *Highcastle* as a safeguard against any difficulties. If such difficulties arise, my crew will instruct you where to go. If you go anywhere except the instructed destination, your life is forfeit. Do you understand?"

"Yes," the man said.

"Good." Akos turned to Leodysus. "Get these men in the brig, and make sure they are taken care of. Then select a prize crew and ready the ship for towing."

"Aye, Captain." Leo nodded.

The man turned and began to bark orders, with the men leaping to obey them. Akos returned to his own ship, striding directly to his cabin. Once inside, he closed and latched the door, settling down into his desk chair with a heavy thud. He popped the cork out of a bottle of rum on his desk and took a heavy swig. He was glad to be done with this hunt. Sitting and watching had been much more stressful than any sword fight he had ever been in.

Chapter 2

The sights and sounds of port were nothing new to Akos. He had been a sailor all his life and had been to almost every port in the realm of man by now, and many of the ports of the other realms. The only thing that changed among them was the language being yelled by the longshoremen as they worked.

This port was no different in that regard. The sound of men working and seagulls crying filled the air. This port was particularly busy. Cargo was being moved between dozens of ships and the shore, including the cargo from the vessel he had captured.

Akos would normally be on deck, overseeing the transfer of both the cargo and his prisoners. But while this port was no different than others in terms of sights and sounds, it was the closest thing that Akos had to a home port. The *Mist Stalker* and her crew spent more time in this port than any of the others scattered across the realms.

It wasn't because Geralis held some sentimental value for him or any of his crew. Many of Akos's crewmen were Macallian, some of them even from Geralis, but not all of them. Akos himself wasn't. The rulers of the port city, the Empire of Macallia, had very favorable privateer laws and had been the ones to issue Akos his letter of marque. But even this was not the reason that he spent so much time in the port. There were many other ports in the empire that he could have visited to take his prize to court.

Akos heard the door open behind him as he finished lacing up his boots. He turned to find Vibius standing behind him. The man was almost too tall for the cramped cabin. Akos's wayfarer had pale skin that belied the amount of time he had spent aboard a sailing vessel. Vibius laughed when he saw how his captain had dressed himself.

"How do I look?" Akos asked.

"Like you think they are going to let you in the front door this time," Vibius replied.

Akos tended to dress the same as any other sailor. Trousers, boots, and a loose-fitting shirt were enough for him. This was a special occasion though, and he had decided to break out his best. He was wearing his finest boots, the pair that matched the black trousers he was wearing. His shirt was a flowing scarlet thing that might have made its way straight out of a nobleman's closet.

"Maybe they will," Akos replied.

"What in all the realms makes you think that this time Lord Varrie will let you stride through the front door?" Vibius asked.

"He has to realize at some point that if they don't let me in, I'll sneak in anyway. At least if he lets me through the front door, he'll be able to keep his eye on me."

"Well, you've no doubt cracked the code to worming your way into his heart. Have you ever considered finding a woman whose father isn't demanding a small mountain of money in exchange for her hand?"

Akos ignored the question and continued to make small adjustments to his outfit in the mirror. Lord Varrie was not known for welcoming his daughter's suitors. Even the ones with the proper status to call upon her were turned away. Under usual circumstances a lowly privateer captain like Akos would never make it past the outside gate. Fortunately, Akos had an advantage that none of the other suitors could claim.

Anastasia Varrie had already chosen him. They'd met at a ball Akos had not been personally invited to. It had been open to any captains in service of Macallia. The only requirement was that he'd seen action against one of Macallia's enemies. It had even been decided that the invitation would extend to privateers, because they helped Macallia to dominate ocean shipping.

Lord Varrie was an ardent supporter of the navy, having several sons serving as captains and even one who was an admiral. His whole family had attended, including the beautiful Anastasia. Much like half of the men in the room, Akos had been drawn immediately toward her. Luckily for him, she had been drawn to him as well. Though her father would never allow the two of them to have a formal courtship, Akos had grown to know her quite well during his frequent calls to Geralis.

"You ought to be more careful," Vibius said. "One of the guards might mistake you for a common thief and shoot you on the spot."

"What thief would attempt a robbery in this much damn frill?" Akos said as he scowled at the shirt. "Honestly, whoever thought this should be the style should be the one shot on sight."

"I'm sure that the household guards will consider your state of dress before firing. Perhaps when they see you scaling the walls they will provide you with a ladder so that you won't soil your clothes."

"That would be very thoughtful of them."

Vibius rolled his eyes again, but Akos took no heed of it. Vibius only wanted him to be safe. The wayfarer was right; if the guards caught him sneaking into Lord Varrie's daughter's room, they would most likely believe him to be a thief or worse and shoot before asking any questions. Fortunately, Akos was an expert at not getting caught.

"I'll be fine, Vibius," Akos assured his friend.

"I'm sure." Vibius sighed. "Just be careful."

"Am I ever not?"

Akos held up a hand to forestall any retort as soon as the words left his mouth. His crew considered him to be too careless with his own life. It was one of the many reasons they had cited for asking him to not join in the next boarding action. If the recent boarding action had been any indication, Akos would much prefer to take risks than sit to the side and do nothing.

"Just have a little faith," Akos told him.

"I have all the faith in the world," Vibius replied dryly. "Now if you'll excuse me, I must—"

There was a trio of sharp knocks on the door, followed by a dull thud. Akos was instantly alert. That was the signal that things were not well. Vibius moved away from the door as Akos snatched up his sword belt. He fastened it quickly around his waist and made sure that the blade was loose in its scabbard.

"Visitors to see you, Captain," Leodysus called through the door.

"Let them know that I have a prior arrangement," Akos called back. "But let them know I will be more than happy to schedule an appointment."

"I'm afraid they insist."

Akos shot a questioning glance at Vibius, but the man shrugged. Whoever these visitors were, they must have arrived mere moments ago. And to get aboard the vessel without his permission, they would have to be on official business. Akos couldn't think of any reason why he might be arrested, or why any of his cargo might be seized. That didn't mean that there wasn't a reason, but it would be odd for the authorities to wait all day before coming to arrest him.

Akos unlatched the door and stepped outside. The short hallway that led to the deck had a pair of doors on either side, one for Vibius and one for his sister, Vibia. Vibius ducked into his own room as Akos met with Leodysus.

"Who are these visitors?" Akos asked. "And why did you allow them on my vessel without my permission?"

"They say they are here on behalf of Lord Hailko," Leodysus explained.

Akos froze right before the door to the deck, one hand already on the latch. He turned and raised an eyebrow at Leo. The large man shrugged in response. Leo wouldn't have let them on board unless he was sure. Still, Akos couldn't imagine what Lord Hailko could want to talk to him about. He'd given him a sizable portion of every prize he'd taken over the years in return for his continued patronage and letter of marque.

Akos took a moment to compose himself and put on his captain's mask before stepping out of the cabins. The deck was a swarm of activity, with men carrying out their different duties. A pair of serious-looking men stood still, observing the organized chaos around them. The two were so similar that Akos imagined they had to be brothers, if not twins. Both were of middling height, slender as rails, and had small spectacles perched on hooking hawk noses.

"Can I help you gentlemen?" Akos said as he approached.

"Are you Captain Akos?" The first of the men asked.

"I am. And who might you be?"

"Beralin and Lusalin Carralt. We represent your business partner, Lord Hailko."

"Was there something wrong with the notice I sent Lord Hailko when I landed?"

"No, everything was perfectly in order. I'm afraid that I have some truly terrible news. Lord Hailko passed away while you were at sea."

That was terrible news to Akos. Though, the hooked-nose Beralin didn't seem terribly distraught. The man seemed as if he were discussing a facet of the weather, rather than talking about a man's death. The man went on without so much as allowing Akos time to offer condolences.

"His oldest son, Halis IV, has taken up his mantle as Lord Hailko. When he received your notice this morning, he made arrangements for us to bring you to his mansion for a meeting."

"I would love to meet with Lord Hailko," Akos lied, "but I'm afraid I am already engaged for tonight. Perhaps we can schedule this for another time?"

"I'm afraid that won't be possible. Lord Hailko stressed that this meeting was to take place at the earliest possible occasion. We've a carriage waiting at the end of the dock to take us there now."

Akos took a moment to consider his options. None of them looked particularly good. Lord Hailko had been a generous and understanding man, but Akos had never gotten that same impression from his son. Hailko held much of the power in their business relationship, though he had never thought to flaunt it. The new Lord Hailko might not be of the same temperament. It might even be that he was waiting for a chance to yank the leash of one of the many privateers that he now sponsored. And it wasn't as if Anastasia could be expecting him, as much as it would pain him to spend another night away from her.

"Well then," Akos said. "Let's not keep him waiting any longer."

• • •

The Hailko mansion was well appointed. Akos had visited it several times over the course of the years. It wasn't quite as familiar to him as the Varrie estate, but he recognized it once they were close. Not much had changed since the last time he had visited several years before.

The estate sat a short distance away from the bustling town of Geralis. It was a one-hour ride by carriage from the edge of town. By the time they drew near, the sun was just beginning to set. Akos cursed the timing. If he had left for the Varries' mere moments earlier, he might have avoided this trip, at least for a few days.

Despite his trepidation, Akos had to admit that he was curious about what Lord Hailko might have to say. It was obvious enough that the young man was, at least in part, flexing his newfound power. From what Akos remembered, Halis was only a few years younger than he was. And though Akos was not sure of his exact age, he knew that he was still a few years shy of thirty. A young man given that much power so suddenly was bound to try to show it off.

But that couldn't be the only reason. Certainly, there were captains who were more impressive to bring in if all he wanted to do was show off to his new peers. Akos was well known among the ranks of privateers, but he didn't have the same high birth as some of the others. In the eyes of the people Hailko was now calling his friends and peers, birth was one of the few items on a short list of things that mattered. The man must have wanted to make some alteration to their contract.

Akos frowned as he thought of the contract he had signed with Lord Halis Hailko III over a decade ago. The man had been generous to him, much more generous than Akos had deserved. It wasn't as if he had a reputation back then; nor did he have the pedigree that would usually warrant the deal the man had cut him.

Though they had never been anything resembling friends, Akos still owed a great debt to the man that he didn't think he'd ever be able to repay. Now, it seemed that he would never get the chance. The thought saddened him much more than it seemed to sadden either of the Carralts.

They might as well have been carved from stone for all the emotion they betrayed. During the entire ride through town and the countryside, they had said a combined fifty words. Any question he asked was met with a terse answer that told him nothing. Akos resigned himself to not knowing the entirety of what was going on until he was able to speak to Lord Hailko himself.

After what seemed a near eternity, the carriage turned off the main road and onto the immaculately upkept driveway to the Hailko estate. The mansion that sat at the end of the driveway was enormous. Several stories tall and sprawling, the main house seemed to go on forever. Akos couldn't imagine what one would do with all that space, not to mention the multitude of side buildings. Many of those would be the servants' housing, but he was sure that others served a myriad of purposes.

Akos noted that the guards at the door still wore black armbands around their house uniforms. Lord Hailko's death must have been recent. Akos wondered how long it had been since the lord passed. He would have asked one of the Carralts, but he was fed up with trying to get an answer to anything out of them. He wasn't sure why it mattered so much to him at all. Still, the thought nagged at the back of his mind as he stepped down from the carriage. They'd never been much more than acquaintances and business partners, but Akos owed Lord Hailko a great debt for his patronage over the years.

"This way." Beralin gestured toward the front door. "Please."

The way the man said please left a sour taste in Akos's mouth, but he followed him into the mansion, nonetheless. He'd made it this far; there was no point in being a rude guest now. Akos wondered if the men had been hired based on their grating personalities or if that was an affectation for their jobs. Either way, he would be glad once he could wash his hands of both.

Akos recognized the way that they were going through the sprawling mansion after a few moments. The late Lord Hailko had always liked to do business in his library, and it seemed that his son had inherited that habit. That might also be a show. The Hailko mansion library rivaled many universities for sheer number of books. Though every building on the estate was a study in grandeur, the library was the crown jewel. Akos knew that Halis III had loved to read and to be near books. Halis IV might as well, but if Akos were to place a bet, he would imagine the young lord knew that it was his best chance to awe visitors.

The hallways the group strode through were covered in priceless pieces of art, but Akos paid them no mind. He'd never been a man of expensive tastes. He'd also always assumed that the practice of buying art was something nobles did to show that they could waste money on things that served no purpose other than to look pretty. Akos had always thought that once he had money to spare, he would buy some art as well. Since he'd met Anastasia, he had always assumed that once they were married she would take care of it for him. It didn't matter to him what they put on their walls, so long as she was happy.

Akos had to shake the thought of his love from his mind. He didn't want to anger his new business partner, and he was much more likely to say something stupid if he was preoccupied with the thought of how he could have been in her arms by now but for this meeting. Instead, Akos knew he needed to stay focused on the matter at hand. *Which*, Akos mused, *might be easier if I knew what the matter at hand was.*

As they made their way to the door of the library, Akos supposed that he would know soon enough. The heavy wooden doors swung inward, revealing the rows upon rows of books held within. The library was well lit, despite the setting sun outside. Several very comfortable-looking reading chairs were arranged around the center of the room. Beralin motioned for him to take a seat in one of them.

"Lord Hailko will be with you shortly," the man droned.

Akos nodded and turned, but Lusalin cleared his throat hard enough to turn him back around.

"We'll take your sword," Lusalin said. "For safe keeping."

Akos wondered if the man knew that his tone made it clear that he had no concern for his guest whatsoever. If he did, no sign of it showed across his face. Akos considered refusing just to see what the men might do. He doubted that they would try to force him to give it up. But instead Akos unbuckled his belt and handed it over to them. There was no point in making petty shows. Akos was growing more convinced by the moment that Lord Hailko would soon put on enough shows for both.

Once his sword was secure within Lusalin's hands, the men took their leave. Akos was left to wonder exactly what they had been hired for. Neither man seemed particularly diplomatic, nor did they strike Akos as bodyguards. They certainly seemed a little too grim to keep around as errand boys. He shook his head as he turned back toward the library. *Some things*, Akos thought, *are better left as a mystery.*

Instead of sitting and waiting in one of the many chairs, Akos decided to have a look around the library. As he made his way around the stacks of books, he didn't recognize any new sections. It didn't surprise him. Akos couldn't imagine that there were many books of note that the library didn't already contain. Within its stacks it held everything from treatises on the ways to sappy romantic novels. Akos had always wondered if those had been for the late lord or if they were there for his wife or daughters.

Akos pulled an old tome down from the shelves to inspect as he walked by. It was a heavy thing, bound in leather and gilded. Its face read *The Lost City of Namoa and Other Sailor's Tales*. Akos could imagine that some of his crew could recite the contents of this book from memory, despite never having read it. He'd never read it either. There was no need. He'd learned the stories the way they were meant to be learned, hunched over a lantern in the dark belly of a vessel plying the ways, told by a grizzled old sea dog to keep the demons at bay.

"Every seaman who's spent time here has found his way to that particular book," a voice said from the doorway.

Akos turned to see that Lord Halis had joined him in the library. The man was much as he remembered. They stood more or less eye to eye, though Halis might have been a hair or two shorter. He had an unruly mop of shoulder-length dark-brown hair that he had tied back away from his soft face. There was nothing soft about the cold blue eyes set there, however.

"If you like it you may have it," Halis continued.

"Thank you, but my men would laugh me off my own ship," Akos said. "Besides, I'm sure I've heard all the tales before."

"That is the same response I've gotten from every seaman I've made that offer to. I know we've met before, but I don't believe we've ever been properly introduced. I am Lord Halis Hailko IV."

"Captain Akos. A pleasure to formally make your acquaintance."

"The pleasure is all mine, though I'd say we are more than mere acquaintances. We are business partners after all. And though I wish I could say that all I wanted is to meet the men my father issued letters of marque to, it is business that brings us together tonight. Shall we?"

The young lord motioned to the chairs in the center of the room. Akos slotted the book he was holding back onto the shelf before joining him. Akos sank into the chair across from Halis, and within a moment of sitting down there was a servant at his shoulder. The man had a bottle of wine and a pair of glasses. Akos was about to refuse but remembered at the last moment that was considered a rude thing to do among nobles. Vibius often chided him for his lack of table manners, but nobles took these sorts of things much more seriously than sailors.

Akos waited until Halis had a glass of his own, and then the two took a sip. Having traveled to many nations and even spent time among the different races of the other realms, Akos had often wondered how the various traditions of different people had arisen. Though the details might have been specific to the region, he'd found that the realms universally tended to settle major business over a drink or a meal. Here in Macallia, it was a glass of wine; in the dwarven realm, deals were made over mugs of hearty ale; and in the orc kingdoms, there was a feast. It had always amazed him that such diverse peoples could develop such similar traditions.

"To your ventures," Halis toasted. "May they continue to be as lucrative as they were under my father."

That was something that Akos could toast to wholeheartedly. He sipped at the red wine. He was no lightweight, but he knew that if this were to become any kind of negotiation, he would need all his wits about him. Akos also wasn't very fond of wine in general, though in Macallia that was borderline blasphemy. He did his best to put on an appreciative face as he sipped.

"One of the best vintages," Halis said. "A fine Vanocian red. The bastards might be backward at everything else, but they know how to make a fine wine."

If Akos was correct, the last vessel he had captured flew a Vanocian flag. Macallia had all but put out a bounty on any vessel bearing Vanocian colors. Since it stacked on top of the normal prize money and ransom, it was one of the easier ways to make money. Overall, it didn't cost the Macallian Empire much once one factored in how it cut into their competition. That brutal efficiency was one of the things that had allowed Macallia to rise to a position of power in the waves of their realm.

"But enough small talk," Halis said after Akos didn't respond. "I brought you here to discuss your arrangement with my father, not have a wine tasting."

"I take it you are familiar with the agreement?"

"Quite. I've been poring over all the various contracts and agreements my father made, to make sure nothing surprises me."

"Was there some particular point you wanted to amend?"

"No, overall the agreement is quite fair. I was instead hoping that I could ask you for a personal favor."

That was unexpected. Akos had been ready for demands. He'd been prepared for the man to attempt to strong-arm him into less favorable terms. What he hadn't been bracing for was a request for a favor. Not that it was much of a request. Halis now held his letter of marque. If he chose to rescind it, Akos would be little more than a pirate. Any prize he brought back would be invalid, at least in the ports where there was any semblance of law and order, and he would be an open target to any vessel. That was if he made it out of port at all, since he had a prize vessel in the harbor currently.

"What kind of a favor did you have in mind?" Akos asked as he swirled the wine in his glass.

"Have you ever met my younger sister, Calia?"

"I'm afraid I haven't had the honor."

"Few have. She tends to keep to her studies at the university. All that interests her are her books and her studies. She's even written several scholarly papers and submitted herself for a professor's position at the Geralis Royal University. Unfortunately, they have informed her that she would need some field experience in order to be considered for such a position."

"I'm afraid I don't see how this connects to me. I do not sail a sightseeing vessel. My ship engages in combat, and only a thankfully small number of the men who sail under me do not come back home. I don't believe that is a setting for study, unless she intends to become a naval officer."

"Calia's particular area of study involves the ways. I've happened to hear that your vessel is the stuff of legends among those who sail the ways. I must admit that to a landlocked nobleman such as myself, her thesis makes no sense to me. But perhaps to someone somewhat more familiar with the ways, her thesis might be understood. Calia, would you care to explain?"

Before Akos had a chance to protest, a young woman stepped around the chairs and into view. She must have entered the room while Akos was focused on Halis speaking. She had the same soft face as Halis, though it was much more becoming on her. Her hair was about the same length as his as well, though a few shades lighter and much more well kempt. Her eyes were the same blue as her brother's, though hers seemed much warmer.

"I would love to," Calia said as she seated herself. "I have long noted that sailing too close to a realm without actually entering can cause a wayfarer all sorts of problems. This…distortion can cause all sorts of problems for wayfarers, even causing them to go insane in some rare cases."

"I am familiar with this madness," Akos said.

Vibius and Vibia had always described it as something clawing at the back of their minds as if it wanted in. They said it was unpleasant, but nothing to worry about if they kept a decent buffer between themselves and a realm or turned directly toward one. No one knew the reason for the madness, though many theories had been proposed. In true sailor fashion, the theories ranged from demons to sirens and everything between.

"I'm afraid I like my wayfarer far too much to allow you to perform tests of his sanity, however," Akos continued.

"Oh, gods no, I would never suggest that," Calia said. She seemed genuinely taken aback. Akos noticed that she had a hard time meeting his eyes. He guessed that she did not get much social interaction outside of academic circles. There was also the chance that she was naturally shy.

"I have noticed that sailing to close to what is known as the void has the same effect," Calia said. "And I theorize that it is because there is a sixth realm located where we know the void to be. I'd like to prove my hypothesis."

INTO THE VOID

Those words made Akos consider standing up and leaving at once. It would take a while to get back to Geralis from here on foot, and he would run the risk of getting robbed along the way. But he knew how to handle himself, and it would be better than listening to any more of this insanity.

The void was the stuff of legend among sailors. Many others had theorized that it was the lost sixth realm as well. They claimed it was home of the fabled Namoa, a city made of silver and gold, with diamonds, rubies, and emeralds cobbling the streets. Even the greediest among those theorists were not so foolhardy as to sail directly into it.

No ship had ever crossed into the void and returned. Not even one in all recorded history. There was no telling what had happened to them. Some claimed that the void was a gateway to hell and that if you sailed into it, you forfeited your soul to the demons that lived there. Others supposed that it was the source of the ways, and that to go into it was to enter a maze with no end. Regardless of the truth of the void's composition, it was certain death to any fools who thought they knew better.

Akos *just* suppressed his urge to leave. Halis held his future in his hands after all. Perhaps if he explained the risks to him, he would see the foolishness of this and call the whole thing off.

But when their eyes met, Akos's objections died in his throat. Those cold eyes revealed that he knew exactly what his sister was asking, and he didn't care in the slightest. Halis clearly knew much more about sailing than he let on. Still, Akos knew that he had to try.

"That would be a foolhardy endeavor. No one has ever returned from a trip into the void. Most don't even survive brushing up against it. The madness, or something else, claims them all."

"I understand your trepidation," Calia said, "But I believe I have pinpointed the cause. And I also believe I can prevent it."

"See now," Halis said with a cold smile, "your fears are unfounded. If you need further assurance, however, know that I always repay my favors tenfold. In exchange for this small favor, I will not only fund this expedition, but I will pay you ten thousand marks upon your return."

23

Akos could recognize a carrot and a rod when he saw it. Halis was leaving him with very little choice. He could either do his bidding, and be much better off for it, or he could lose his legal standing as a privateer. Akos knew he could not afford to do either of those things, but the wheels of his mind were already spinning. There might be a way he could turn this hopeless situation to his advantage. Akos had schemed his way out of sticky situations before; he would have to do so again.

"Well," Akos said after a moment of consideration, "when would you like to depart?"

Chapter 3

Calia could hardly contain her excitement as her carriage bumped its way toward the docks. Normally she would have complained about the quality of the ride, but today was a special day. The sun was cresting up on the horizon. Through the open window of the carriage she could already smell the salt water and hear the call of the seagulls. The scent was not particularly pleasant, but that was all overshadowed by the pure giddiness Calia felt throughout her entire body.

Today was the day they had chosen. Today was the day she would begin to get the field experience that her peers were using to refuse her the place she had rightfully earned. It would be several agonizing weeks until the ship reached the void, but Calia was already plotting her triumphant return and how she would word her paper on the sixth realm that she was sure she would discover.

The bustle of the dock slowed their progress to a crawl. Calia tried her best to suppress the irritation that was building up within her. *Do these workers not realize that they are standing in the way of the greatest breakthrough in the science of wayfaring in centuries?* Calia thought. She shook her head and reminded herself that there was no way that the men carrying goods to and from ships could know. Not that many of them would be able to comprehend her thesis even if they did know what she was intending to do.

"You're tapping your foot," Valesa said.

"Apologies," Calia said and forced her foot to stop bouncing off the carriage floor.

"I know you're excited, but this is the first day of a long voyage. You may want to save some of that energy for when we actually reach the void."

"I just can't help it. I've been waiting for this opportunity for so long. Father never would have let me go on such an expedition."

The mere thought of her father dampened her mood. Halis Hailko III had been a very loving man and Calia knew that he had only ever wanted what he thought was best for her. But at the same time, she knew that he had never understood the burning desire for knowledge that consumed her heart. Her father had enjoyed learning, but in a more philosophical way. Calia did not care about the why of things. She cared only about the how. Still, her heart darkened every time she thought of him, knowing that he would never be around to share his wisdom or joy with her again.

It was also true enough that he never would have let her do something like this. But Calia had waited long enough. Safe or not, she had decided on this course. She hoped that if her father was watching her from somewhere, he could understand and come to peace with that.

"Your father was a wise man," Valesa said. "There may have been something to his worry. It isn't too late to call this whole thing off, you know."

Calia turned to face her maidservant. Valesa was tall for a woman, standing equal to or even taller than the average man. She was not beautiful in a classical way, but Calia had always admired the strength of her jaw and her emerald-green eyes. Her hair was black and cut much shorter than the fashion of Geralis. Calia knew that she did that to keep it out of her face when she was fighting.

Her father had chosen Valesa as her maidservant more for her skill with a blade than he had for her skill at the traditional tasks a maidservant might perform. Valesa had been Calia's bodyguard, confidant, and best friend for many years now. Calia often watched her fence and spar with the other guards in her family's employ, and Valesa's speed and skill with a blade was unmatched by any of the men she'd ever seen her fight. Valesa was a warrior woman, and Calia could not remember ever having seen her afraid before.

It made the fear she saw now even more surprising.

"You don't have to come along, Valesa," Calia said. "I can bring one of my other maidservants."

"You think I would allow you to go on a ship full of pirate scum without my protection?" Valesa replied with a snort.

"I believe they prefer the term privateer."

"They steal what isn't theirs for a living. I don't care what they prefer to call themselves; that sounds like a pirate to me."

In her mind, Calia knew that the minute distinctions such as the difference between a pirate and a privateer were the things that societies were built upon. Her heart, however, had a much harder time finding fault with Valesa's assessment. She knew her father had been a patriot as well as a shrewd businessman, but she could not imagine why he had ever associated with such disreputable characters. She had always known him to be such an honorable man, but he had issued several letters of marque over the years.

"Yes, well," Calia said after a long moment. "They are our hosts. We should at least try not to insult them to their faces."

"I'll do my best," Valesa replied with a grin that informed Calia that she would do no such thing. "To tell you the truth, I'm less worried about myself and more worried about Tomas and Sir Blackfur."

"I'm sure the cats will be fine without you there."

Valesa tilted her head to acknowledge the point and then returned to looking out the window. Calia turned her eyes back to the world outside the carriage, though her mind was elsewhere. She knew Valesa was worried for both of them as well, though she would never say it out loud. And Calia understood her fears as well. No one had ever managed to return from the void, but then, none of them had ever been she. Calia was confident that she had uncovered the secret to making the journey a successful one.

Instead of dwelling on that, Calia turned her mind toward their provisions. She had an extensive inventory of instruments that needed to be brought, and she had spared no expense while procuring them. There were at least two more carts full of her equipment trudging along behind her carriage. She had everything she would need to take any measurement she could ever want and the materials to safeguard themselves against the perils of proximity madness.

Calia continued to go over in her head every item she had brought. She had double- and even triple-checked the list before they set off, and everything had been in order. Still, Calia was not the type to be anything but thorough. She had mentally rechecked her list at least a half dozen more times before the carriage finally settled to a stop before the docks.

"Well, off we go," Calia said joyfully.

The pair stepped off the cart with the help of the driver and looked around. Calia had been to the docks only once before, despite having lived in Geralis her entire life. The port was so central to the city's wealth that very few other Geralins could say something like that, and the few who could would never admit it out loud. Calia had accompanied her father out of the city and farther down the coast once when she was younger, but she had been much too young to remember anything of the trip. She hadn't remembered the smell. The stink of salt water, rotting fish, and unwashed men at work filled her nose, and it took everything she could do not to pinch it closed to ward off the stink as she got her bearings.

As Calia watched the bustling commotion, she wondered why so many of her peers spoke of the docks as if they were the place to be. Hundreds, if not thousands, of longshoremen were moving their loads from point to point. It looked as if it would be a dangerous affair simply getting to the correct boat. There had to be some form of organization to the chaos, but Calia would have to study it for a while before she could be confident that she had discovered it.

It didn't seem she'd be given the time for that today, however. Almost as soon as they were out of their cart, they were being whisked away toward the wharves. Calia had barely managed a glance back toward her equipment before they set off. A team of men was already unloading her luggage and the instruments off the cart.

"Be careful with that," Calia managed to yell as she was herded away.

It did not seem that any of the men heard her, or if they had, they were paying no mind. It took almost all her self-control not to march back toward the carts, but a firm hand clasped her arm and kept her going. She glanced down at the hand and back up at Valesa. The stern woman gave a quick shake of the head, and that was all Calia needed. If Valesa thought they should keep moving, she would.

Before she knew it, they had picked their way through the crowd and to the wharves. Dozens of ships sat in their berths, forming a swaying forest of masts. Vessels of all shapes and sizes surrounded her, though their types and purposes eluded her. Despite her interest in the ways, she had never concerned herself too much with the methods of transportation through them.

That would all change very soon, however. Calia was nothing if not prepared. She had included in her luggage several nautical manuals covering everything from the basics of seamanship to the nuances of maritime. Since she knew that she would have a great deal of time to spend doing nothing more than sitting around, she might as well learn something useful about her situation.

Soon enough she spotted their vessel. The name *Mist Stalker* was painted on it, though it was hard to make out. It seemed the wooden planking of the ship had been lacquered a dark shade, most likely to make it harder to see at night. There were few enough reasons why someone might paint a ship in such a way—either to sneak past someone or to sneak up on someone. From what she knew of the *Mist Stalker* and her crew, it was most likely the latter.

Men moved about the deck, performing their tasks and getting the vessel ready to leave. A pair of tall men stood near the helm, keeping a careful watch on the proceedings. One was a swarthy brute of a man, with a barrel chest and skin the color of a moonless night. The other was almost as pale as Calia and resembled a toothpick when compared to his companion. She didn't know much about sailing, but she couldn't imagine how a man could stay so pale working on a boat.

The pale one spotted her and nudged the other fellow. He turned his gaze toward their group and then began to make his way toward them. As he approached, Calia could see that his eyes were a light hazel, and that his skin was covered in swirling tattoos that were hard to see from a distance against his skin. And much to her surprise, he seemed to keep growing as he made his way down the ramp to greet them. Even Valesa looked like a child next to him.

"Lady Hailko?" the man asked with a gentle voice that belied his appearance.

"I am," Calia replied, holding out her hand to shake.

The man took it and offered a clumsy half bow. Calia realized that this kind of a vessel was not used to receiving guests of her stature. She decided to overlook the fact that he had not bowed quite deep enough, nor had he kissed her hand as he was supposed to. Not that she was sure that she could find the nerve to say anything reproachful to this giant, even if she wanted to.

"I am first mate Leodysus of the *Mist Stalker*," The man continued. "It would be my honor to welcome you aboard."

"Where is Captain Akos?" Valesa asked.

"The captain had some last-minute business to attend to. Please, allow me to lead you to your berths."

Calia took a deep breath before taking the giant's hand and ascending the ramp with him. She tried to remain dignified, but even walking was difficult with the way the ramp was swaying. Valesa followed behind them without anyone's assistance, but Calia noticed that even her surefooted maidservant was having some difficulty with the unfamiliar footing.

"Lady Hailko?" The pale man called to her once she had made her way on deck. "Vibius Antonius, a pleasure to make your acquaintance."

"Ah, the pleasure is all mine," Calia said.

This man had clearly been raised with at least some courtly training. He bowed low enough to show the proper respect without making it seem like he was groveling. His lips brushed her hand, hard enough to ensure she felt it but not so hard as to be improper. Calia raised an eyebrow. Despite thinking that all the courtly rituals were frivolous, Calia could admire someone who had taken the time to learn them so thoroughly. She'd spent a great deal of time learning them herself after all.

"I'd like to apologize ahead of time," Vibius continued. "I'm afraid your lodgings will not be up to the standard I'm sure you're used to. We are a military vessel, and our passenger accommodations are… sparse."

"Oh, it will be no trouble at all," Calia reassured him. "We didn't expect this to be a luxury cruise after all."

"I assume this lovely lady is your maidservant?"

Calia glanced back at Valesa, who had pursed her lips and raised an eyebrow. She stood only a few inches shorter than this Vibius, and he had stepped around Calia to shake her hand as well. Despite herself, she seemed impressed. Whoever this man was, he was very charming. Enough to crack even Valesa's defenses it seemed.

"She is," Valesa answered for herself. "Who exactly are you again?"

"I am so sorry. In my excitement, I seem to have forgotten my manners. I am the *Mist Stalker*'s wayfarer. Once you are settled in, I was hoping to speak with you about your research. It's been some time since I've been able to speak with anyone knowledgeable in the field, and I like to keep abreast of any new developments."

"I see," Calia said.

This was an excellent opportunity. Even though studying the ways was her life's work, she had not had much chance to speak to actual wayfarers. She had never seen the need to until her peers had demanded more hands-on experience. If her brother's tales of this vessel's exploits were to be believed, Vibius was likely to have a wealth of information on wayfaring. And it sounded as if he thought of it as a science rather than the art that most wayfarers insisted it was.

"I would love that," Calia continued. "I'll call upon you as soon as we are settled in."

"Please do."

• • •

Akos finished pulling his boots on and looked up from his chair to find Anastasia watching him from the bed. Her raven-black hair flowed down her back, and he could not help but think that she resembled some ancient statue personifying beauty and lust. She'd watched him dress without bothering to do so herself, which made it hard for him to remember why he was bothering with his own clothes in the first place. But every time he considered disregarding the task and rejoining her, he remembered that he was required elsewhere.

Akos knew that he would be cutting it close, but the Varrie estate was not far from the docks. He would have ample time to reach his ship before it was time to cast off. At least he would if he did not succumb to Anastasia's wish for him to stay. He'd always managed to resist that desire in the past, but it was getting harder and harder to do as time passed.

"You know," Anastasia said, "Losing your letter might not be the worst thing that could ever happen."

"Is that so?" Akos replied.

"It might force you to take up a…more sedentary profession. Preferably one near my estate."

Despite knowing that he would never love any profession as much as he loved sailing, somehow the proposition was so much more tempting when uttered in Anastasia's sultry voice. Akos had to remind himself that no matter what else he did after this voyage, he had already given his word. He was not a man to break a promise lightly. That thought was the only thing that helped him rise from the chair and not immediately dive back into the bed of his lover.

"I must say I'm shocked," Akos said. "A whole month of me, and you haven't tired of my company yet."

"I would never," Anastasia replied with mock indignity, bringing her hand to her chest.

Akos had to turn his gaze out the window, lest his eyes followed her hand and he became lost in his lust again. He knew that Anastasia understood the effect she had on him. Akos had begun to believe that this was something of a game to her. *Well, she won't win today*, Akos resolved.

With that he began to stride toward the window. He wouldn't have to scale the walls at least. Anastasia had managed to find a rope to let down for him. That would make sneaking back by the guards at the edge of the estate a little less exhausting if nothing else.

"Please," Anastasia called after him. "Hurry back."

Akos knew he couldn't turn around, or he would never leave at all. Instead, he gave a brisk nod, and then swung himself out over the edge of the windowsill. The descent was quick enough work. He'd had a lifetime of practice in the rigging of the various vessels he had sailed upon. Within minutes he was striding down the road toward the docks, the Varrie estate fading into the distance.

This trip should be enough, Akos mused. He'd come so close to amassing the wealth that Lord Varrie demanded of any suitor to his daughter. Combined with Anastasia's support, he would have no trouble convincing the old man to give him his daughter's hand. Then he could put his years of privateering behind him and find some other way to support her, most likely with a title and an estate of his own.

The idea left a bittersweet taste in his mouth. Leaving the life of a privateer behind him had always been a part of his end game. Akos did not want to die an old pirate on some forgotten sea. When he had first become the master of his own fate, he knew that he wanted to retire to live a life of leisure somewhere. That idea had taken on a more solid form when he had met Anastasia, but she'd merely given a face to the dream. The goal itself had never changed.

Still, the *Mist Stalker* had become his home, and her crew had become his family. Though most of them were hired hands, many of them had become his truest friends, weathering all his life's ups and downs with him. He couldn't imagine what he would do without them around on a day-to-day basis. It was something Akos knew he would have to learn to live with, much as they would. He didn't know how he would break the news to them.

Vibius and Vibia already knew. Akos kept no secrets from the wayfarers. They had been the first of his crew, the only thing that had legitimized him as a captain in his own right. He owed everything he was to them. They had become like the brother and sister he'd never known. Vibia approved of his plan. She had always wanted him to settle down and stop taking so many risks. Her idea had been to turn their ship into a merchant charter, or even a smuggling vessel if Akos still needed some danger in his life.

Vibius had mixed feelings about the idea. He hadn't said as much, but Akos knew him well enough to divine what he was thinking. The man was sincerely happy that he had finally scrabbled together enough marks to make a reality out of his dreams. Akos could tell that Vibius didn't want him to leave despite that happiness, but he was too selfless to ever say anything of the sort aloud.

After an hour or so of walking, Akos could tell he was coming up on the docks. The familiar smell of the sea soothed his thoughts somewhat. Regardless of any of his other troubles, he still had to make it through this last voyage. *One thing at a time*, Akos reminded himself.

By the time he reached his ship, he had managed to force all thoughts of an early retirement from his mind.

Unsurprisingly, the *Mist Stalker* was ready to travel. Akos smoothly ascended the ramp and gave the order to have it pulled up. His men were already at their stations and prepared to cast off. They were simply waiting for his orders. He jogged up the steps to his spot by the helm.

"All ready?" Akos shouted anyway.

"Aye, Captain," Leo replied from his place on the deck.

"Let's be off then."

And like that the crew sprung to life. They carried out their tasks like clockwork, moving with drilled precision. Akos had recruited a crew of veteran sailors, and Leodysus had trained them to work together. Akos heard that other captains had trouble keeping experienced sailors, but he'd never had that problem. He liked to think that it had something to do with his personal charisma and leadership skills, but he suspected it was more because of his success and the prize money they were paid.

The *Mist Stalker* crawled out of the harbor and set its bearing toward the nearest way that would take them by the void.

Chapter 4

Swords rang off each other, the sound singing throughout the deck as men shouted and cheered. The blades were dulled, and the blows were ever so slightly pulled, but still Calia winced as Valesa left a welt across the back of another sailor. The crewmen had been skeptical when she had requested to join their sparring sessions, but over the last week, the daily events had become something of a spectacle. After warming up, Valesa dueled them one after another, and she hadn't lost yet.

Calia knew the woman was putting on such a show as much to let the men know that she and her charge were not to be trifled with as she was for the actual practice. The captain had assured them that their safety was his top concern, but Valesa liked to assure herself. She'd even sparred with the massive Leodysus. That had been the most spectacular duel of them all, but after a massive effort, Valesa had been able to slip through his guard and deal what would have been a fatal blow in a real fight.

Calia watched from the aft castle, where she could see over the heads of the crowd. The man's yelp turned into a grumble as he tried his best to play off the injury. Valesa beckoned for a water skein, which one of the men happily tossed to her. Once she was done drinking, she poured some of the cool water over her face and resumed her place in the center of the circle.

Reminded of the heat, Calia also resumed waving her fan under her face. It wasn't doing much to help. She wore a loose, breathing dress, but the sun still beat down on the deck more intensely than it ever did in Geralis. In the few weeks they'd been at sea, Calia had already burned once. Since then she had limited her time above deck. She had to admit that she was more than a little jealous of Valesa's complexion.

Rather than burning, the woman's skin was taking on a dark-olive complexion that matched many of the sailors.

"Your maidservant is quite skilled," Vibius said from next to her.

"Indeed she is," Calia replied. "It was the reason Father picked her."

Calia had briefly spoken to Vibius about her research, enough to explain her premise. The man had been surprisingly receptive to the idea. Calia had even lent him several of her books on the subject, and to hear him talk, he was already through half of them. The wayfarer had promised that once he had finished going over the manuals, they would have a much more in-depth discussion.

"Still, it must be fairly embarrassing to have your whole crew defeated by one woman who is unused to fighting on a rolling deck," Vibius said, too loudly to be speaking only to Calia.

"You're a part of the crew as well," Akos replied. "Feel free to have a go at it."

"I'd hate to injure anyone," Vibius said with a wry smile. "But please do show us how it's done. Isn't the captain supposed to set the standard for his crew?"

Calia listened to their friendly ribbing with great curiosity. Despite having been on the vessel for weeks, she still did not know much about her host other than what her brother had told her. He seemed polite enough, if his manners were a little rough around the edges. The only time she'd had to observe him had been when he'd been on deck, commanding his crew.

It didn't tell her much about him as a person, but it did tell her that they listened to him. Whether it was personal loyalty, a strong sense of duty, or a love of money, the men hopped to obey his commands. The way they worked made her think that the crew truly loved their captain. She'd also learned that he and Vibius were fast friends. They even had dinner every night together along with Vibius's twin sister, Vibia.

"I set the standard," Akos shot back. "It's up to Leo to enforce it, and he seems to be doing a poor job."

"Then get in there and remind him of how it's done." Vibius gestured toward the circle.

Some of the men overheard their conversation, and within moments the crew was chanting his name. Calia was unsure of whether they had that much faith in their captain, or if they wanted to see him taken down a peg. Perhaps it was a little of both. Akos looked over his crew and gave Vibius a dirty look before holding his hands up to silence his men.

"Fine," Akos said finally.

The cheering resumed, and Akos made his way to the deck. Vibius clapped encouragingly, and even Calia joined in. The man was handed a training sword, and he gave it a few test swings as he made his way to his place.

"I hope you won't mind helping me warm up a little before you go full force," Akos said.

"The captain of this mighty fighting vessel is asking a humble maid for mercy?" Valesa asked with feigned surprise.

"Right then."

The pair bowed their heads slightly toward each other and then crossed blades. They began to circle slowly, making sure of their footing on the deck. Calia leaned over the railing to get a better look. Even the crew had gone silent as they waited for the pair to take each other's place in the circle and begin the match.

The moment they stepped into the proper place, Valesa launched into action. Calia didn't know whether she was trying to prove a point to the crew or to herself, but the woman was showing no mercy. The blade flashed through the air, striking as swiftly as a snake. Before it could touch flesh, however, it was intercepted. Akos had *just* managed to parry the blow when he launched his own counterstroke.

The two whirled and fought, their blades appearing to Calia as little more than silver streaks. They parted for a moment to better gauge their opponent, and then launched right back in. Calia had no training in dueling, but she thought that Valesa was getting the upper hand. She was gradually pushing him back toward the wall of men who surrounded them.

"Akos is much stronger," Vibius said beside her. "And his bladework is good. But his footwork is lacking. Valesa is going to win this duel within the next few strokes."

As if it were a premonition, Akos staggered slightly when he put a foot down wrong, and Valesa jabbed the practice blade into his side. Akos grunted, and the men began to shout for a rematch. Calia let go of the breath she hadn't realized she was holding. Leo had held out for only a few seconds longer than Akos. That made sense. After all, he was the captain, and the crew did most of the actual fighting for him.

"Two out of three?" Valesa offered.

Akos grinned wolfishly and resumed his starting place. Valesa matched his smile and joined him. They seemed to be enjoying themselves. Within moments they were circling again, though this time when their feet crossed the starting point and the match began, they were much more cautious. After a moment of doing nothing but look at each other, Akos launched a flurry of blows that put Valesa back on her heels.

He's pressing too hard, Vibius mused. *He's going to run out of stamina far too quickly.*

Once again, Calia watched as the wayfarer's words came true. Akos slowed his pace a hair, and Valesa was back on him. One stroke at a time she wormed her way through his guard and struck him across his shoulder.

"Once more?" Akos asked.

"Do you intend to keep at this all day?" Valesa asked.

"Humor me."

Valesa looked as though she would refuse for a moment, but instead she relented. She paused to take another swig from the water skein and cool off. While she was doing that, Akos took off his shirt, now drenched with sweat, and threw it to Leodysus. When Calia looked at his bare torso, she could barely refrain from gasping.

He was well muscled, though that hardly surprised her. Though he tended to wear loose clothes to help deal with the heat, she had stolen a few glances when the wind pressed his shirts tight against him. She would never admit that to anyone, though, not even Valesa. Calia could tell from those few glances that the man kept himself in excellent physical shape.

What surprised her so much were the long white stripes against his otherwise tanned back. There were a few other scars across his front, but nothing like the ones crossing his back. She lost count after two dozen when he turned around to face Valesa. He rolled his neck and arms, and then settled back into his dueling stance.

This bout was much more even and subdued. They still moved with lightning speed, but their blows were much more measured and careful. Calia realized that they must be tired. Even so, neither of them faltered. They traded blow after blow, the ring of steel on steel louder than any church bell she'd ever heard.

"Who is going to win this one?" Calia asked breathlessly.

"I…don't know," Vibius admitted without taking his eyes away from the fight.

This bout was the longest of the three. After what seemed an eternity, Akos finally gained an advantage. He'd forced Valesa back with a trio of quick lunges, and when he pressed immediately afterward, he forced out an awkward stutter in her step. He used that to knock her blade off balance and land a slashing blow across her ribs. Calia almost cried out in sympathy for her maidservant, but Valesa merely grunted. The force of the blow knocked her off balance, and she fell to the deck.

Within a half a heartbeat, Akos was next to her on a knee. He offered Valesa a hand to help her up. She gratefully took it. Akos bowed to her once she was standing.

"My deepest apologies," Akos said.

"Think nothing of it," Valesa said. "I gave you two just as good."

"Well, it seems that I'm going to have to practice that much harder. If a captain of a mighty fighting vessel can't defeat a humble maid, how much can he be worth?"

"You took the last bout," Valesa reminded him.

"The score still stands two to one in your favor, and I don't intend to press my luck any further. Thank you for the fight."

"Thank you."

Akos then turned to where Vibius and Calia were standing together against the railing of the aft castle.

"Satisfied?" Akos asked.

"Quite," Vibius called back. "It's always entertaining watching you acquire new bruises."

Calia could see that a pair of purple blotches were already forming on his shoulder and his gut where Valesa had struck him. A matching bruise was spreading across her ribs. Calia could almost feel them herself and was reminded once again why she had never had any interest in fencing.

"Perhaps tomorrow we'll see you pick up a few," Akos said with a grin as he retrieved his shirt.

"Doubtful," Vibius replied with a smile.

Akos rolled his eyes and turned to the crew.

"Stow the weapons and swab the deck," Akos shouted.

"You heard the captain," Leo bellowed even louder. "The show's over; it's time to get back to work."

The crew dispersed, laughing and talking as they went. Rather than return to his place on the aft castle, Akos went below decks toward the cabins. Calia watched as he went, catching another glimpse of the scars across his back. They were horrific. She'd never seen anything like it. Calia wanted to ask Vibius what caused them, but she knew it would be a rude question. A proper lady was not supposed to notice such things, and she didn't point them out.

"You seem to know quite a bit about fencing," Calia said instead.

"Before I realized my gift," Vibius replied as he turned to her, "I was the son of a noble. I never had much skill with swordplay, but I had a talent at understanding what was going on in other people's fights."

"You are a nobleman?"

"No, not anymore. I'm afraid my father disowned my sister and me when I joined the wayfarer's guild."

"Why would he do that?"

"He disapproved of our choices. I refused to stay in one place and be his perfect little heir. I had far too much wanderlust in me for that."

"What made you want to be a wayfarer?"

"I suppose I was called to it. Very few who are born with the gift can resist working in the field. Both my sister and I have a deep wanderlust as well, and a desire for adventure. I also suspect that at least a part of it was the same thing that brought you out. I had an intense desire to learn more."

INTO THE VOID

"Oh, I'm afraid I am here only to prove my worth so that the Royal University will accept me."

"I think there is more to it than that. What drives you to want that position so deeply that you would risk everything on this voyage?"

Calia tilted her head and frowned as she considered his question. She turned and walked toward the port railing of the ship and looked out over the water. Vibius followed her and waited patiently for her answer. She supposed he was right. She had always thirsted for knowledge. Specifically, knowledge of the ways. Perhaps it was because they were still such a mystery, despite having been used for a thousand years.

"You may be right," Calia replied after a while. "I do enjoy learning about the ways."

Vibius nodded and leaned on the railing. Calia looked out at the ocean. The crystal blue water lapped against the ship, churning into white wake as they cut through it. Clouds drifted through the sky as a strong breeze filled their sails. If it weren't for the heat, and maybe even in spite of it, it was the perfect day. Calia had to admit that Vibius made for good company as well.

"I wanted to ask," Vibius said after a short while, "if you, and Valesa of course, would join us for dinner tonight?"

To this point, Calia and Valesa had taken their meals in their own cabin, or out on the deck. She had assumed that it was either that or eat in the galley. Regardless of how polite the crew had been, Calia had no desire to eat in the same room as dozens of them. She had managed to get used to the constant smell of salt water, but the smell of sweat was something she hoped she never had to acclimate to.

"We would love to," Calia answered. "But are you sure that Captain Akos will agree after this afternoon?"

"The captain is a good sport," Vibius assured her. "I think she may have even gained his respect. He's always appreciates good fighters, even if they are beating him."

"Maybe I don't want to eat with him," Valesa said from behind them.

Vibius raised an eyebrow at her and gave an incredulous look. Calia's maidservant barked out a laugh. Calia wondered if she had any true misgivings still. For the first several days Valesa had refused to extend any trust to the members of the *Mist Stalker*'s crew. Her attitude had softened after she'd intermingled with them for a while. If Calia had to guess, she had also begun to enjoy some of the crew's company, Leodysus and Akos included.

"I suppose I'll join as well then," Valesa said.

"Good," Vibius said with a smile. "It's settled then. Meet us in the captain's cabin at eight."

• • •

"Did you enjoy the show this afternoon?" Akos asked as he and Vibia waited for their other guests.

Vibia sat next to him, cradling a glass of red wine. Unlike Akos, she had a deep appreciation for wine. He didn't understand the fascination, but she could tell him the approximate age of a bottle of wine and where it was grown with nothing but a few sips. She glanced up at him with the same golden eyes that she shared with her twin brother, and he saw amusement there.

"The show itself was entertaining to say the least," Vibia responded. "I have a question though. Why bother to do it at all?"

"What do you mean?"

"You don't have anything to prove to the crew. They would already follow you to the void and back without question. In fact, they're already doing it."

"Have you considered the idea that I had something to prove to myself?"

Vibia snorted and rolled her eyes, taking another long sip of her wine. She had known him long enough to know when he was making things up. Sometimes Akos felt as if she could read his mind.

If Akos were being honest with himself, he didn't know the truth of why he had chosen to accept Vibius's challenge. Vibia was right, he had nothing to prove to his crew, nor did he have anything to prove to himself. Backing away from a challenge had never been Akos's strong suit, but he'd ignored Vibius's ribbings and dares often enough before.

"Well, I had to defend the crew's honor," Akos replied half-heartedly.

Vibia pursed her lips incredulously and raised an eyebrow.

"I think you wanted to blow off a little steam and have some fun," Vibia responded. "And if you got to show off for the crew and our guests. What's the harm in that?"

Akos rolled his shoulder and winced when it pulled at the bruise. He hadn't felt the pain in the heat of the moment, but as the day wore on, it had set in. He hadn't taken a blow like that in quite some time. The bruise was as large as his hand, and it hurt every time he moved his arm. His gut was not quite so bad. He'd managed to roll with that blow to soften it. Still, when he breathed in, he could feel a slight twinge of pain.

"Yes," Akos replied dryly. "So very fun."

"Don't pretend you don't like a good scrap." Vibia countered.

Instead of arguing, Akos tilted his head to concede the point.

"Now that you've had some time with them," Akos said instead, "what do you think of our guests?"

Vibia considered the question for a moment. Unlike her brother, she tended to be a little more thoughtful in her replies. Vibius was a brilliant man, but he often spoke faster than he could think.

"Lady Hailko seems to be a very lovely woman," Vibia said. "And Vibius seems quite taken with her."

"I'd noticed that as well," Akos said.

"It's hard to blame him. It isn't often that we meet anyone capable of matching wits with him and interested in the same topics to boot. She may be somewhat mad, with her insistence on sailing to the void, but who aboard the *Mist Stalker* isn't?"

"Speak for yourself."

"You're the worst of all of us. Regardless, I think it may be time that he looked for a suitable match. He won't be an eligible young bachelor forever."

"And what about you? Shouldn't you start thinking about that before you become a lonely old spinster?"

Vibia smiled at the jest.

"You know I have no interest in romance."

"Neither did Vibius until about a week ago. You could meet a strapping young lording who will steal your heart. I believe the new Lord Hailko is still single."

This time Vibia made a face that was half feigned anger and half disgust. The day Akos had returned from the Hailko estate and told the crew of their predicament, she had listened with barely controlled anger. Even if she had come to accept the plan, she still held Hailko in low regard for placing them in this predicament.

"It seems as if your beating this afternoon caused some brain damage," Vibia said. "I'll see if I can get Valesa to knock everything back into place."

Akos held up his hands in mock surrender. Doing so caused him to wince from the pain in his shoulder. That drew another chuckle from Vibia, and Akos joined in.

A sharp knock at the door drew their attention. Akos rose and opened the door, allowing Vibius and their guests in. Once they were all in the cabin, Akos motioned for the cabin boy to fetch their food from the galley. The lad rushed off, and Akos rejoined the table.

"Vibia," Vibius said. "You'll never believe the theory that Calia was telling me."

Akos listened along to the conversation without understanding a thing that was said. Like most captains, he had a basic understanding of way theory. This conversation was well over his head, however. He was a little surprised that Vibia was keeping up and contributing to the conversation. Unlike her brother, she had no scientific interest in the ways. She'd always viewed them in a more poetic light than her brother. It had been the source of more than one disagreement that Akos had heard.

A quick glance over at Valesa revealed that she had all but tuned them out as well, focusing on her glass of wine. When their eyes met, Akos could tell that she most likely dealt with this on a regular basis and had grown accustomed to it. Akos could hold his own in most conversations, but he knew the twins were much smarter than he, and much better versed in this subject.

With the timely arrival of their food, Akos was saved from having to try to make conversation. Luckily for him, it seemed that Calia was so wrapped up in her discussion with someone on her intellectual level that she had all but ignored Akos and Valesa. He'd made it very clear that he had little interest in learning about the ways, or the void, in any manner that wasn't immediately practical and helpful. He'd been as polite about it as he could, but he didn't have time to stuff his mind with theoretical knowledge that would in no way help him sail his ship. The Antonius twins knew wayfaring inside and out; Akos would stick to things that he could have some control over.

Soon enough, dinner was done. It was excellent as always. Akos had learned early in his career that a well-fed crew generally had much higher morale than one forced to eat the same gruel day in and day out. In their business, morale was especially important. It was hard to get a hungry crew to engage in battle.

"My compliments to your cook," Calia said after she was finished.

"I'm sure that Remford will be grateful to hear it," Akos replied. "He's always dreamed of preparing food for a noble lord or lady. He's going to be devastated when our voyage is at its end, and we part ways."

"If he keeps preparing meals like this, I will be devastated as well."

"What were we speaking of before dinner arrived?" Vibius asked.

"I was going to explain my theories on the void, and why I believe I can protect us against them."

Akos had been prepared to tune the conversation back out while everyone nursed their wine and talked. Despite himself, he had to admit that he was at least a little curious about what her method entailed. Akos was sure that he had heard her talking to Vibius about her theories before, but he couldn't remember her ever mentioning the way that she would protect them from being swallowed by the void.

"How could I forget?" Vibius asked rhetorically. "Please do explain."

Calia set her wine down and a sparkle entered her eyes as she began her explanation. Akos could see why Vibius was so taken with her. He'd often seen his friend's eyes with that same light when speaking about his interests.

"Well," Calia started, "It is well enough known that the minds of wayfarers are different from the minds of normal men."

"Glad to know that we wayfarers are not normal men," Vibius said. His smile defused the idea that any offense might have been taken.

"No, wayfarers are not normal men," Calia said with a matching smile. "On average they tend to be more intelligent and more observant. That may be why you are so skilled at predicting the duels earlier."

"You predicted me to lose?" Akos asked.

"You did lose," Vibius replied.

"A true friend would have predicted my glorious victory."

"Unfortunately, I'm an honest friend and not a true one. Please continue, Calia."

"It is this increased sensitivity that many of us who study the ways attribute the gift to. It is widely believed that this is because of a sixth sense that allows wayfarers to 'feel' the ways. It is my theory that this enhanced sense is also what causes proximity madness when a ship sails too close to a realm without trying to enter it. The same effect that takes place around the void."

"Many people have tried to defeat proximity madness over the years," Vibius interjected. "They've tried everything from smelling salts to using only deaf, mute, and blind wayfarers to steer their vessels. Nothing has ever worked."

"But none of them have tried turning off the sixth sense."

"Is that even possible?" Akos asked.

"Very few people think so, but I believe I've found a way. The eleventh realm grows a plant known as the xheiat bush. Have you heard of it?"

Very few sailors who traveled the realms hadn't. Akos knew it served much the same purpose to the elves as alcohol did to humans. Elves' bodies were wired differently, and drinking did nothing for them. Instead, they chewed xheiat bush roots to experience the same kind of buzz.

Unfortunately, much like alcohol not affecting an elf, xheiat roots had a very different effect on the human body. The main difference was that it wasn't addictive to elves, and the effects tended to wear off an hour or so after chewing. For humans, it was incredibly addictive, and a large enough root could keep a man in a stupor for a full day. It was illegal to import into most human empires, but that hadn't stopped the rise of xheiat dens in some countries. Akos had met more than one man who was addicted to the stuff.

"Are you planning to turn Vibius into a xheiat addict?" Akos asked.

"I have to say," Vibius added, "I'd prefer to avoid that outcome as well."

"No, I wouldn't do anything like that." Calia began to turn red, but she pressed forward anyway. "New studies are emerging that show that xheiat is addictive only when consumed. When boiled into a tea, it is virtually harmless, but produces much of the same effects. There are several reports of wayfarers not feeling the effects of proximity madness when they consumed xheiat tea. I theorize that proximity madness affects even those who approach the realm we know as the void head-on. Then, the ships that enter are stuck because their wayfarers have gone mad and can no longer sense the ways to exit. If we eliminate the risk of madness, then we should be able to approach and exit without peril."

"And if your hunch is wrong?" Akos asked.

"It isn't a hunch." Calia seemed insulted. "It is…an educated guess."

"Still, you are risking all our lives on nothing more than a few reports and studies."

"Risks must be taken in the name of science."

Akos considered pressing the point but thought better of it. There would be nothing to gain from arguing further, even if he could somehow manage to keep up with Calia's mind. They had already set their course. It was a little too late to refuse this task. It helped that Akos and Vibius had already put a plan into place to avoid placing themselves in any real danger. There would still be some risk to it, but it would be much less perilous than what Calia was proposing.

"I suppose so," Akos replied after a moment.

"I'm quite sure of this, Captain Akos," Calia assured him. "I'm not asking you to do this for me. I've placed myself right alongside you to take the risk with you."

There was something there that Akos could appreciate. He'd always led from the front, and it seemed that Calia shared his attitude.

He could appreciate someone putting everything on the line for something they believed in.

"The theory sounds solid," Vibius said after a moment of reflection. "I must admit that I have my own reservations, but I have heard enough to assuage most of my fears."

Akos glanced across toward Vibia, but she gave him only a slight shrug. He couldn't tell whether she agreed with the assessment or not, but she knew the plan as well. And there was no indication that their guests had any inkling of that plan.

Akos had no intention of sailing into the void, and as far as he could tell, neither Valesa nor Calia were wayfarers. They would have no way of confirming whether they had tried to enter the void. It would get colder as they neared the void, but there were no other observable ways of determining their proximity unless one possessed the sixth sense. Vibius would take them close enough that they could say they had done it and then continue home. They would declare the experiment a failure, and then let some other poor sod down the road be the one to go through with an attempt.

"If Vibius is comfortable with the idea," Akos said, "I am as well."

"I'm glad to hear it," Calia said, obvious relief on her face. "I know you aren't necessarily here by choice, Captain, but just think. If we can be the first ever to pierce the void and return, we would go down in history. We'd be spoken of for generations to come. Not to mention the new business opportunities this would open up for sailors."

"You are correct there," Vibius said. "The discovery of an entirely new realm. It would be a momentous occasion. What kind of creature might live there? Would there be another sentient species? If not, can you imagine the race that might occur to claim all that unclaimed land?"

Calia and Vibius began to speculate on these things while Akos excused himself from the table. The wayfarer wasn't wrong about anything he had said, but it was idle speculation, the same that had been happening for centuries. Akos knew his friend well enough to know that all he was doing was selling the idea that he was on board with her plan. They may never know the answers to the questions he was asking. Akos certainly hoped they wouldn't at the very least.

Chapter 5

Calia leaned over the railing in anticipation. Today was the day. Akos told her that with the speed they had made, they would be reaching the ways soon. Vibius had confirmed it. He said that he could "feel the mist," though what that meant, Calia could only guess.

The wayfarer stood next to her, and he looked much less anxious than she felt. He'd become a near constant companion, despite Valesa's protestations. Calia wasn't sure why her maidservant was so mistrusting of Vibius. He had done nothing untoward or even the slightest bit rude. In fact, Calia was sure that if she had spent half as much time with any of the court dandies, or even her peers at the university, they would have already attempted something improper.

The wayfarer was a perfect gentleman. The man's manners were so impeccable that she was having a hard time discerning if he had any romantic feelings toward her at all. It was driving her mad. Perhaps that was why Valesa was so on guard about him. She probably thought her ward had developed feelings for some privateer wayfarer far below her station and was trying to protect her from herself. Calia was a grown woman though, and her feelings were her own to decide whether to pursue or not. If there was anything to pursue at all.

"This will be your first time seeing the mist, won't it?" Vibius asked.

Calia was startled from her thoughts and glanced up at the man. His eyes were fixed on the horizon in a thousand-yard stare, as if he could see something she couldn't. Calia had become used to seeing his striking golden eyes alive with a smile and thoughtfulness, and today was no different. They seemed to be even livelier, almost glowing.

"Yes, it will," Calia answered. "I must admit, I'm quite nervous."

"Don't be." Vibius turned to her and flashed a smile. "There's nothing to be afraid of."

He put his hand over hers on the railing and patted it. Then, Vibius let it linger. Calia didn't object. It was the first obvious sign of affection he had given her. A flutter went through her heart. Calia glanced around to see if anyone was watching. On the deck a slight distance away was Valesa, who gave her a knowing and disapproving look. In that moment Calia had to resist both the urge to blush, and the urge to stick out her tongue at the maidservant.

"I've always been told that the first transition from a realm into the mist is jarring," Vibius continued after a moment. "So be prepared for that. And it will be much cooler once we have left the realm."

"So I've read," Calia replied. "There are many theories on why that is."

"Which do you think it is?"

"I think it is the simplest of them. There is no sun in the mist. Our realm orbits the sun, but there has never been a verifiable or credible source that claimed to have seen a sun in the mist."

"The simplest answer is often correct. I would tend to agree with that as well. I prefer Old Haroln's version, however."

"Is this one of the famous ghost tales I've been told about?"

"Indeed it is. I assumed that with the amount of research you've done you would have studied all the old stories that sailors tell each other."

"I'm afraid that part of my research has been lacking. Would you care to explain the theory?"

"I'm afraid I can't."

Calia looked up at the man, but he shrugged in response.

"It's horrible luck to tell the stories before we're in the mist," Vibius explained. "Once' we're in, I'm sure Old Haroln will be more than happy to explain."

"Haroln is a sailor on this vessel?" Calia asked.

"Of course. That's how I know the story."

"Each ship that plies the ways has its own stories," Another voice from behind them almost made Calia jump.

Akos joined them at the railing, peering out much as Vibius had. Despite the heat, he was wearing a jacket. *We must be much closer than I'd thought*, Calia mused. She half expected Vibius to move his hand now that his captain was there, but he didn't so much as flinch. For his part, Akos didn't comment. With the way his gaze was fixed on the horizon, Calia wasn't sure he noticed.

"They are handed down from one generation of sailors to the next," Akos continued. "You'll not hear the same version from one ship to the next."

"Fascinating," Calia said. "How do sailors remember them all?"

"Most sailors start out young. You hear them so many times, they simply become a part of you. Vibius, unfortunately, does not get to hear as many. Once we enter the mist, he will be otherwise occupied."

"Well, I certainly look forward to hearing a few."

The group went silent, watching over the prow of the ship as it cut through the water. The sun was setting behind them, casting the ship's shadow farther and farther out in front of it. After a half hour, Akos finally moved.

"We're here," Akos said. "Leo, rig for the mist!"

"Aye, Captain!" Leo replied from the deck.

The first mate began shouting various commands, and the crew leaped to obey them. They began to strike down the sails, and the ship slowed to a crawl through the water. Calia leaned over the rails, but she couldn't see what the captain was talking about. There didn't seem to be any mist in front of them that she could observe. Just the steadily darkening horizon.

"Look behind us for a few seconds," Vibius said. "And then look back."

Calia followed his directions, wondering the entire time what she was going to accomplish. This had to be some sort of joke. The captain and his crew might be trying to fool their guests. Calia didn't think Vibius would participate in something like that, but she had to admit that the man had a rather dry sense of humor. The sky behind the ship was exactly what she'd expected, a mix of red, yellow, and purple with the sun just now starting to dip below the horizon.

When Calia turned back around she gasped.

The sky and the ocean seemed to have merged into a gray wall. It swirled in the breeze. Though they still plowed forward through the water, it never seemed to move closer. She tilted her head back and saw that the same mist extended upward as far as she could see. It was awe inspiring and terrifying at the same time. It was what she had spent her entire life studying, but she had never imagined that it would look so hauntingly beautiful.

"Why couldn't I see it before?" Calia asked.

"You were looking too hard," Vibius explained. "First timers can rarely see it until it's pointed out to them."

"It's breathtaking."

"I've always thought so too."

"Are you ready, Mr. Antonius?" Akos called from his place by the helm.

"I'm afraid that's my queue." Vibius sighed. "He calls me by my last name only when it's time for work."

Vibius gave her hand a squeeze, and she returned it. Then he turned and strode to his place. Akos stood shoulder to shoulder with Vibius next to the helmsman. The wayfarer stood a full head taller than either of them, and Calia could see that he had his eyes closed as he braced his arms behind his back.

"Aye, Captain," Vibius said, his voice hardly a whisper now.

"If you please, then," Akos replied.

For a moment, nothing happened. Then Vibius opened his eyes. When he did, his eyes were glowing with a golden light that matched their shade. For a moment, she thought they were simply catching the sun's light, but then she remembered that the sun was behind them. They were truly glowing light like twin lanterns in the dark. Calia watched as the air around the ship seemed to shimmer, like heat over the water, and then they were engulfed in the mist. Calia took a step back from the railing as the whole world seemed to lurch in place. It was a sensation she had no way of describing. It was as if everything had shifted sharply and suddenly but without moving a single inch. A quick glance at Valesa told her that she was not the only one who felt it.

"We are under way," Akos announced. "All crew not assigned to the watch or other duties have freedom to do as they please."

The crew who had gathered on the deck began to disperse. Some stayed behind to carry out their chores, while others moved to their posts to begin their watch. Valesa joined her by the railings, looking somewhat green.

"That was…unpleasant," Valesa managed after a moment.

"Quite," Calia agreed.

"Is it everything you ever dreamed of?"

"It is, and more."

The moment was overwhelming. Calia had planned a half dozen experiments for the moment they entered the space between realms. Now that the moment had come, she found herself rooted to the spot. This was part of the realization of a dream for her, and she was going to soak in as much of it as she could.

"Look at the way it swirls," Calia said, leaning over the railing to get a better look.

"I'm more concerned with the way it feels," Valesa said. "Aren't you freezing?"

Now that her maidservant had mentioned it, Calia was getting rather chilly. It didn't seem that the summer dress she was wearing was much of a match for the cold that accompanied the mist. Calia shivered as it cut straight through her dress and chilled her to the bone.

"Come," Calia said after a moment. "Let us fetch some warmer clothes. And then we can retrieve my instruments from the hold, and I can begin some experimentation."

• • •

Akos was grateful for the warmth of the interior of the ship. Despite his preparations, the cool breeze that accompanied the mist had gone right through him. It was a jarring shift from the usually warm temperatures of the realm of man, and no one ever truly got used to it. Akos had shifted between the realms and the mist dozens of times, and it still always caught him off guard.

Normally, he took meals in his cabin, but not when the ship was between realms. That was when the stories were told. He'd grown up on a ship much like this. He'd always been kept too busy to stop and listen, but Akos had always treasured the bits and pieces of stories that he had managed to catch. Now there would be crewmen gathered around in the galley, the crew cabins, and anywhere else they could warm their hands around a lamp and tell the tales that would see them safely to their destination.

The captain wasn't supposed to take part in such things, but Akos still loved to sit and listen. He'd taken care to recruit some of the best story tellers he could find. They were almost as important to a vessel as a good helmsman, or a competent gunnery commander. Many would say that they were more important than a good captain.

As Akos was making his way through the ship toward the galley, he caught sight of his guests making their way up from the hold. He'd seen them on deck, taking various measurements and making notes in a journal. He wasn't exactly sure what they were measuring. Akos was no expert, but he was more or less certain that almost everything that could be measured about the mist had been measured long ago.

"Good evening my ladies," Akos said as they stepped out into the hall with him.

"How can you tell it's evening?" Calia asked.

"An old sailor's trick. We have a special instrument. Would you like to see?"

"I would love to. I have never heard of any such instru—"

Calia cut herself off midsentence as Akos produced a pocket watch. She sighed as Akos chuckled, and Valesa's hand went to her mouth to prevent her own chuckle from escaping. After a moment, Calia smiled and joined in the laugh.

"Do all sailors have such dry senses of humor," Calia asked. "Or is it unique to your crew?"

"I'm afraid I got my sense of humor from Vibius," Akos said. "Were your measurements what you were hoping to see?"

"Yes, they were exactly what I expected. I didn't expect to find anything new, but there are certain measurements and experiments that are rites of passage for students of the ways."

"Well, if you'd like to accompany me to the galley you can experience a rite of passage for sailors."

INTO THE VOID

Both Calia and Valesa raised their eyebrows in mock suspicion. Akos raised his hands in surrender.

"No jokes this time."

"I suppose that we can accompany you then," Calia responded.

Akos led the way to the galley, where the men were already circled around Old Haroln as he spun a tale. The old dog was a masterful story teller, complete with hand motions and different voices for all his different characters. They only amounted to a slight change in the pitch of his voice, but it still went a great way toward setting the mood. Akos fetched plates for everyone while the women seated themselves where they could hear the story being told.

By the time Akos was sitting down, the story was finishing up. The men around the circle were whispering comments and criticism of the tale. It was a time-honored tradition that no story was told right. Someone had to make some correction, no matter how small.

"The sirens don't eat men," Ranric said. "They sacrifice them to the void. Everyone knows that's how they keep their youth."

"Nay lad," Old Haroln shook his head. "Much like young Valesa here, sirens are vicious creatures." Everyone turned to look at the maidservant, who smiled wolfishly and mocked a curtsy. "My old mate One-Armed Ollie saw one once. Said their teeth were like a shark's, perfect for ripping limbs off."

"Is that why they called him One-Armed Ollie?" Akos asked.

"No, he lost his arm to a deep-turtle that he'd been pestering. But he had seen a siren, I swear it to you."

Old Haroln almost certainly had once known a man named One-Armed Ollie, but Akos doubted the man had ever seen a siren. It was much more likely that he had told a tale where his friend had seen a siren. It was the way things went in these tales. Akos had listened to enough to pick out the scattered details that he had heard before. He often wondered if there was a true telling of the tales, or if there had ever been one before they had been bastardized and told so often that they changed.

"Does the captain have any requests?" Haroln said after the crew's grumblings had quieted down.

"I don't," Akos replied. "But perhaps one of our guests will."

Old Haroln turned his gaze onto the two women. He was much younger than he looked, but weather and hardships had given his skin the texture of old leather. And the moniker was appropriate. He was old enough to be Akos's grandfather, and many of the younger lads on the ship thought he was old enough to be their great grandfather. His brown eyes were still sharp enough though, and they twinkled when he was spinning a tale.

"Vibius was telling me about your theory of why the mist is so cold," Calia said after a moment's consideration. "He was saying that you tell it best."

"Well with flattery such as that," Haroln replied, "How is an old dog supposed to say no?"

The man leaned back in his chair for a moment and closed his eyes in thought. He took a long pull from the mug of rum that he was cradling. When he was finished wiping his chin, his eyes opened, full of life as he called to mind some story.

Akos had heard the tale so many times that he had the words all but memorized. But Haroln rarely told a story the same way twice. It was part of the beauty of his storytelling skills. No matter how many times you had heard the tale, you still had to listen close, lest you miss some new detail. It also gave the rest of the crew a chance to find new things to comment on afterward.

The tale was one of the oldest, and one of the first that any young man plying the ways learned. It was the tale of a man who descended into the void in search of a loved one, lost at sea. Akos had heard it many ways. In some tales it was a brother, pulled under when he fell overboard during a crossing. Other times it was his lover, killed by some cruel disease while on route to a new life with her beloved. Akos had even heard one version where the teller claimed to be the man, having clawed his way back from the void after dying at sea.

Old Haroln told it as the tale of a lover. The way his eyes darkened and sadness weighed on his words when he spoke of her death at the hands of an infection would have fooled anyone else into believing that he was the man in the tale. Akos happened to know that the only women Haroln had ever loved were whores, and they were all safe in their brothels. Still, part of the storyteller's craft was putting real emotion behind the words, and Haroln was a master. The man in this tale, however, was a wayfarer, and at the first opportunity he had steered his ship directly into the void.

"So stricken with grief was he," Haroln said with great melancholy, "That he ignored all warnings and reason. When his helmsman asked for a heading, he gave it. Aye, but he was a broken man, and no one realized that he was steering them into the void until it was far too late."

"At first, there was nothing," Haroln's voice had dropped to a mere whisper, forcing his audience to lean in to hear him properly. "Nothing but black and cold. The wayfarer screamed, realizing what he had done, but no sound escaped his lips. He tried to thrash about, but his limbs would not obey his mind. He drifted through the darkness, cold, alone, and afraid."

"Then, there was a voice. It was his lover," Haroln began to grow animated again. "She asked why he had come. But he could not respond. Instead she told him that it was not yet his time, and that he had to go. She said that she would try to find him again, once his time was up, and he joined her in the void beyond."

"But she warned him that the void was infinite. They might never find each other again. The man tried to protest, but he couldn't. And so, he was cast out of the void, drifting on a part of his ship back into the realm of man."

"The man claimed that as he was forced back into the world of the living, he could see everything that the ways entailed. He claimed to know why the ways were so cold. The wayfarer said that the mist was made up of the souls of those who had gone before, constantly searching for their loved ones, cursed to never find them. As their spirits lose hope and grow cold, so too does the mist."

There was absolute quiet as Haroln finished his story. No one dared break the silence. It was one of the best telling's of the tale that Akos had ever heard. It was a shame that Vibius missed it. That was one of his favorite tales. Akos would try to convey it to him, but he was sure that he would miss some of the nuance and details that Old Haroln had managed to put into the tale.

"What happened to the wayfarer?" Calia finally asked, entranced by the tale.

"Alas," Haroln sighed, "He did not think much of the life that his love had bought him. But he knew that his tale needed hearing. So, he told it to the crew that found him drifting. After that, he waited until the night had come, and snuck a pistol from one of the crewmen. He declared that he was going to get a head start on finding his lover and pulled the trigger."

"A fine telling," Akos said. "But you're wrong there."

"How so captain?"

"The man didn't shoot himself. He found a length of rope and hung himself from the mainmast."

"No," Calia said. "I've heard this before. Immediately after telling them he grabbed the captain's knife and cut his own throat."

Old Haroln gave Calia an approving look, and Akos had to admit that he was impressed as well. To most outsiders, it would seem as if they were needlessly criticizing the man. Even for sailors, it tended to take a while before they realized that this was part of the process of telling a tale. She was a quick study.

"Aye," Haroln nodded after a while. "Aye, now that I think about it you're right. My old mind must have forgotten that."

"Now that we have that tale settled," Akos said, "How about you spin us another?"

Chapter 6

Calia hadn't been able to sleep for two days. Now that they were this close, she could feel it. The void, or what they had called the void to this point, was within a few hours of their current position. She supposed they would have to come up with a new name for it after they came back, but Calia decided to worry about that thought later.

Not that there was any real way to tell through the cloying mist that swirled about the *Mist Stalker*. Vibius had mentioned it to her while he was preparing to go back out onto the deck and resume his wayfaring. It pained her that they hadn't had much opportunity to speak as of late. She'd come to enjoy their conversations. But when Vibius was on deck, he was concentrating to the point of only being able to give simple directions; when he was below, he was either shoveling food into his mouth or sleeping.

Akos told her that was a side effect of wayfaring that wasn't often talked about. It gave the wayfarers seemingly endless stomachs. After seeing how much food he could put away in one sitting, Calia was surprised to see that, if anything, the man had lost some weight. It was unnerving.

Still, that hadn't been the reason for Calia's inability to sleep. Uncharacteristic doubt gripped her. No one had ever knocked her self-confidence. Calia had held her own in scientific discussions with professors who had dedicated their long lives to the field of wayfaring. She'd forwarded several theories on the nature of the space between realms. To date, none of them had been disproved or even disagreed with on any of the major points. So why was this doubt gripping her so?

Because, Calia's subconscious muttered, *you've gambled a hundred or so lives on a cup of tea.* The logic was sound. The reports had not been scientifically verified or tested, but the sources were credible. Xheiat tea eliminated the risk of madness that was posed by passing too close to a realm. If the madness that afflicted those entering the void was the same thing, then it made sense that the tea would prevent that as well.

Unless, of course, it was not the same madness. Or unless it hit the wayfarer with such magnitude that it would not matter how powerful the tea was. Calia cast a nervous glance over toward Vibius. For the first several weeks of their journey through the mist, his face had been serene. Now, it was much more focused, and every so often he would snarl and grit his teeth as if he were in pain.

It was the madness, she was sure. Calia had no previous experience, but she could only imagine what the man was going through. Written accounts on the madness varied. Some said that it was like the sound of fingernails being drawn down a chalkboard in the back of the mind. Others claimed to feel insects crawling around behind their eyes, in the deepest parts of their ears, and underneath their skin.

The accounts that terrified her the most were those that told of voices. A small number of wayfarers described the madness as a voice, ominous and dark, murmuring in their ear. They said it was as if someone were standing over their shoulder, but when they looked, no one was ever there. Worse still, they claimed that the voice spoke the secrets of hell into their minds, things that no mortal man should ever know. Calia wondered if this was nothing but a story. Wayfarers were not known as the most credible sources for information on their craft. It was odd, but wayfarers often lied or told half-truths about their trade. Many were afraid of letting too much out, as if spilling the actual machinations might accidentally create more wayfarers. Trade among realms was lucrative, and the wayfarer's guild held it by the throat. Most retired before their hair was gray and lived the rest of their lives as princes.

"Is it me, or is it getting colder?" Valesa said beside her.

The suddenness of the comment almost made Calia jump out of her skin. She steadied herself and looked toward her servant. They were both as bundled as they could manage, but nothing served to keep out the chill. Valesa was nothing but a head poking out of an immense jacket, which was one of many layers. Judging by the size, she must have borrowed it from Leo. It was the only one that could fit over all the clothes that she was wearing. Calia knew that she looked just as ridiculous as her maidservant, pulling down her scarf so that she could speak without her voice being muffled.

"I wouldn't be able to tell you," Calia replied. "I lost feeling in my extremities an hour ago."

"Why don't we go below decks and warm up?"

"You may if you'd like, but I don't think I can."

"Afraid you might not come back above deck again?"

Calia shrugged, though she doubted Valesa could see the motion through all the clothes she was wearing. It was eerie how well her maidservant could read her. Calia knew that if she retreated below deck now, she would not return. She would likely call the whole expedition off. She told herself that it was worry for Valesa, Vibius, and the other hundred crew aboard the *Mist Stalker*, but a rather large part of it was concern for herself.

One can't be a coward if one is literally frozen in place, Calia reasoned.

"I would be wroth with myself if I missed the transition," Calia responded instead. "And I have to make sure that the tea is administered."

Calia knew that her words would ring as false to Valesa as they had to her, but she reasoned that saying them aloud might help her steel her nerves. Both of those things were true after all. What scientists would be able to live with themselves if they had an excellent opportunity to observe the greatest breakthrough of a generation, but missed it because they were cowering below deck?

There was no way that she would be able to continue after that point. Even with her magnificent discovery, she would never be able to live it down within the academic sphere. She could always lie, but she had never been a particularly good liar. Her father and brother could always read her like an open book, and Valesa could read her mind. Given time, someone would call her on her bluff, and she would be exposed as a fraud.

No, the only way she would be able to face her peers and claim this achievement as her own would be to stand firm and witness it herself. Calia comforted herself by thinking that she would at least be able to lie about how scared she had been in the moment. No one needed to know that detail.

"I know they aren't the brightest bunch." Valesa chuckled. "But they ought to be able to boil a pot of tea."

"You'd be surprised," Leo said from a short way away. "How do you think Illys lost his ear?"

Illys gave the first mate a rude gesture, and Calia couldn't help but laugh. Valesa laughed along with her, and it took several moments for her to gather herself. The tension that had been creeping into her soul vanished. The fear was still there, but she managed to push it back. How long it would stay there was anyone's guess, but at least she wouldn't be a quivering mess before they ever reached the transition point.

The big first mate looked as if it were any other day at sea. The big burly man wasn't even bothering to wear a shirt, which amazed Calia. Leo wasn't even shivering. Calia suppressed a shiver as realizing that fact made her feel even colder. Akos told her that it was because orc blood was hotter than a human's, but she didn't think that was backed up by any science.

"Are you not freezing, Leo?" Calia asked.

"See these tattoos?" Leo responded.

His entire torso was covered with swirling patterns. Calia once thought them to be nothing more than a random assortment of swirls. Closer examination revealed that there was a pattern to them. It was hard to pick out the dark ink against his dark skin, but she tried to follow some of the curves. Calia was forced to give up after she lost the line for the third or fourth time.

"What about them?" Valesa asked.

"They protect me against all sorts of things," Leo replied with a shining grin. "Heatstroke, chill, bullets, and blades. Makes no difference. I'm practically invincible."

"Is there any weakness to these magical tattoos?"

"Stupidity," Akos said from his spot by the helm.

Calia looked over to where the captain stood by the helm. His eyes had not left the prow of his ship, but a grin turned up the corner of his mouth. She had noticed that the man assumed his position at the same time as Vibius, and left it only to relieve himself and eat. Calia had to admit that it was reassuring to see his stoic visage unchanged by nearing the void. She could see the tension beginning to affect everyone else, but he never so much as flinched.

Instead of allowing the tension to build back up inside her, Calia filled her mind with thoughts of what she would name the new realm she was about to discover. As the first explorer to discover it, naming the land would be her right. She had considered naming it something to do with her given name, but that was a bit too egotistical for her. Hailkan had a nice ring to it. She could always name it Halisland, to honor her father. Calia mulled that one over in her mind. She liked that name better than any other she had thought of to that point.

The other realms were named after their inhabitants, with a single exception. The realm of man was the original home of men, before they had discovered wayfaring and spread throughout the five realms. The realms of orcs, elves, and trolls were the same. Only the dwarfs preferred a different name, and theirs wasn't a particularly difficult one. They called it Grathr among their own kind, which translated literally to "the realm" in their native tongue. Among other races they specified their own as Dwagrathr.

That thought made Calia wonder if there would be any inhabitants in Halisland. If so, she likely wouldn't be able to name it. They would have to call it whatever the original inhabitants called it. Not that it was likely that they would be able to understand them at first. If there were people living in the void, they had been cut off from the other realms since the beginning of time. The races of the five realms had developed a common language to facilitate trade among them. If there were any, the people of the void would likely speak their own tongue.

There was a slight stirring, and Calia glanced over to see that Vibius had leaned over and whispered something to Akos. The captain listened without speaking, his stony gaze never wavering from the horizon. After Vibius finished speaking, Akos looked over to her.

"It's time," Akos said. "We are an hour or so away."

Calia felt her heart pick up its pace as she nodded. She was going to say something back, but the words escaped her. Instead she turned back to Valesa. Even still, the words were catching in her throat, but Valesa knew what she needed.

"I'll go fetch the tea," Valesa said. "Would you like me to bring a cup back for you?"

"No," Calia managed with more confidence than she felt. "I'll be quite fine."

"Suit yourself. I might try some if it gets rid of these damned nerves."

Valesa made her way below deck toward the galley. If everything was going as planned, there should be a pot of xheiat tea boiling at this very moment. They would provide some to Vibius, with plenty of time for a second cup if the effects of the first were not adequate to quell the madness. Then they would pierce the void and prove that it was another realm like any other.

If not, then Calia would have led them to the very depths of hell. Or there simply would be nothing. Calia wasn't sure which of the two she would prefer.

• • •

Akos watched as the xheiat seeped into Vibius's system. It would have been funny, if the stakes weren't so high. Despite the years they had spent together, Akos had seen his friend drunk only a few times, and it was always a sight.

But considering the situation, it was hard to find much humor. And despite the tea having an obvious effect on the wayfarer, he wasn't acting his usual drunken self. Vibius was concentrating too hard on keeping them within the ways. Akos was grateful that he managed to keep at least some modicum of control. Horror stories abounded of ships that had lost their wayfarer while in the ways, and he couldn't remember ever hearing of an occasion where the wayfarer failed, and the ship and her crew survived.

Still, it wasn't as if Vibius was their only option. After he was sure that Vibius wasn't going to collapse from the tea, Akos excused himself and made his way below deck. He needed to get some of this tea, though it wouldn't be for himself. He'd seen how hard Vibius was fighting the madness before getting the tea; he could only imagine what Vibia was going through as they neared the void.

No one outside of the crew knew that Vibia served as the *Mist Stalker*'s second wayfarer. Very few ships employed multiple wayfarers. One charged a king's ransom for services; two would be a cost that no captain was willing to swallow. Fortunately, Vibius and Vibia did not charge a commission, as was standard for their trade. Instead, they owned a percentage of the ship, and took a percentage of the spoils the same way Akos did.

Having two wayfarers was the only thing that made what they did possible. Not only could they travel through the space between realms almost twice as fast as any other ship, with Vibius and Vibia switching off to keep fresh, but it also allowed Vibius to search the ways for other ships while Vibia kept them from slipping off into nothing. It wasn't an uncommon trait among wayfarers to be able to sense other ships as they neared them in the ways, but it was rare that they could reach out and locate them over a great distance. They were too busy keeping the vessel moving and keeping the cold mist of the space between from completely overwhelming them to track other vessels and bring their ship alongside.

It was one of the things that allowed them to be as successful as they had been over the years. And much safer than many other privateers as well. Akos had always been proud of the fact that he had suffered half the casualties of the next-best privateers while claiming half again as many prizes. Very few ships were prepared to fight in the ways. Even though his crew was filled with veteran sailors and fighters, he still preferred to leave as little to chance as possible.

Remford stood in the hallway, waiting for him with a steaming mug of xheiat tea. Akos took it with a nod of thanks. Few enough of his crew knew of the plan. Only those few who had to be involved were aware of it. Akos didn't want his men to act too unafraid of sailing into what was a certain disaster. Lucky for him, they were well drilled enough not to mutiny. Akos had built up a great deal of trust with them over the years, and he was trading on all of it now. Still, he'd worried that as they neared the void they might start to whisper. He wouldn't have blamed them either. Akos knew that it was suicide to sail for the void, as surely as any of the rest of them did. No amount of reassurances from Calia would ever make that ingrained sense go away. Even if she did make a strong case for the existence of a sixth realm, not many would risk their lives to prove it.

But these men had trusted him through all sorts of situations, and they weren't changing their minds now. Akos thanked whatever gods were listening for his crew. Few men would ever find such a loyal group in their lifetime.

Akos made his way to the cabins, where Vibia waited for him. Much like her brother, Vibia's face was twisted in concentration. She'd told him that the madness wasn't necessarily painful, just acutely unpleasant. She gave Akos what she must have meant to be a grateful smile as she took the tea. It was more of a grimace, but he knew what she meant.

"That should help with the madness," Akos said.

"I hope so," Vibia growled.

Within moments, the tea was gone, even though it was still steaming hot when he handed it over. A few seconds later, Vibia appeared noticeably less agonized. Akos considered getting a cup of tea to steady his nerves. It was working well enough for everyone else.

"Thank you," Vibia said, her smile much warmer now. "I thought that I might actually have to wrest control of the ship away from Vibius and turn us around."

"Has he changed his angle yet?" Akos asked.

"Not yet, but there is still time…or not?"

Akos tilted his head. Vibia sounded unsure of herself. That in and of itself was disturbing. Vibia was as sure of herself as anyone he had ever met.

"What does that mean?"

"It means that the ship has sped up drastically. I don't know what is going on. This tea might be making him forget what he's doing."

"And what is it that he's doing, exactly?" Valesa said from the door of the cabin.

Akos spun around. He had been so intent on Vibia that he hadn't heard the other woman enter. His face hardened into his mask. He wondered how much the maidservant knew or could guess.

Even knowing that Vibia was a wayfarer was already far more than Akos wanted her to know. If she had guessed their plan, it could be disastrous to his future.

"Heading toward the void," Akos said. "As we agreed."

"But that's not what he's supposed to be doing, is it?" Valesa said, stepping just inside the door. "He's supposed to change course at the last moment."

Akos didn't say anything, but he didn't look away from Valesa's eyes either. He saw contempt there, but also fear. She may love her charge and she may have been willing to risk her life for her in any other situation, but this clearly wasn't something she had thought she would have to deal with. A quick glance confirmed that her hands were trembling as well.

No use lying, Akos mused, *but I still might manage to win her over.*

"Yes, he is," Akos replied matter-of-factly. "You think any of us want to die, or worse, for your mistress's curiosity?"

"We won't perish," Valesa said, much more confidently than he was sure she felt. "Lady Hailko would not have brought us here unless her theory was sound."

"Is that why your hand is trembling?"

"Regardless of how I feel about this, you swore an oath and signed a contract. But I should have known that a pirate such as yourself wouldn't honor it either."

Akos resisted the urge to come up out of his chair and challenge her right there. It wouldn't have done any good, and he wasn't sure he could win. The fact that she was right only added sting to the words. He had planned this from the moment he had agreed to the expedition in the Hailko mansion.

"Can you wrest control of the ship from him?" Akos asked instead.

"No," Vibia replied. "He's got too firm of a grip. And it's too late anyway. We're too close. I couldn't change course fast enough."

"This won't change anything," Valesa declared. "I'm still going to spill your secret to the world."

"Do it," Akos said as he rose. He brushed past and spoke over his shoulder. "But I'd suggest taking a moment to pray to whatever gods you worship. We'll be meeting them shortly."

Akos didn't bother to see if the woman was following him. Instead he strode back out onto the deck. Despite the mix of emotions he felt deep in his soul, he made sure to keep the same stoic expression on his face that he always wore when acting as captain. He was sure that his men were just as terrified as he was, but he knew he could lend them some peace before they went to their ends. They had seen him through so much that he owed them that, at least.

As Akos took his spot next to Vibius, he had the sudden urge to shake the man. To yell in his ear, to scream. Anything that might snap him out of his stupor and force him to turn around. Akos locked his hands behind his back instead, facing out over the prow. Vibia had already told him that it would do no good. There was nothing to do now but accept his fate.

Akos allowed his gaze to wander among the crew as he waited for the inevitable. Most of them wore a look that was half terror and half anxiety. They'd marked their course, and they were ready to see it through, regardless of the outcome. It was admirable. Akos knew that he had never deserved such men under his command, but he was honored by every moment of it.

He turned his head enough to see Valesa returning to Calia's side. Valesa gave him a venomous glance but didn't open her mouth to speak. Akos could only imagine that she didn't want to ruin what she thought to be her charge's last moments. Akos supposed that he could respect that dedication as well.

Calia, for her part, looked to be one half horrified and the other excited. There was no doubt that she was ready to have all her theories vindicated. He wondered how long Halis would give them before he held her funeral. If he had the measure of the man right, it would not be very long, but he had been surprised by the strength of familial bonds before.

"We're…there," Vibius announced beside him.

Akos gave his wayfarer a long look. Vibius had been his best friend since before he had ever won his freedom. Akos owed everything he had ever gained, and everything he had managed to make out of his life, to him. Without Vibius, he most likely would have died before he had ever seen his midtwenties.

After a long sigh, Akos reached out his hand and squeezed his friend's shoulder. Then he issued the most difficult command he had ever given.

"Make the transition."

Chapter 7

There was nothing but darkness. Akos's heart began to beat faster and faster as he wondered what was going on. Would he be like the unfortunate wayfarer in the stories? If he opened his mouth to scream, would any noise come out? Akos wanted to scream just to find out.

"Is everyone all right?" he yelled instead.

A chorus of ayes from his crew and a meek yes from Calia answered him. Akos sighed in relief. At least that part of the stories had been nothing but imagination. He patted his chest with timid hands. He didn't feel incorporeal, so he guessed that he wasn't dead either.

"Will someone light a damned lantern?" Akos said.

His request was greeted by the sound of men scrambling about. Finally, one struck a match and Akos could see his face. He had to admit that it was one of the most beautiful things he had ever seen, despite the face belonging to Old Haroln. The man lifted the match to a nearby lantern, and the deck was awash with light.

Akos took a moment to take in the surroundings. It looked as though everyone was there and no worse for wear. He gave a quick glance to ensure that his guests were still upright as well. Calia looked as if she might faint, and all Valesa's attention was being directed toward her charge. *The only downside to living*, Akos mused, *is that now I must deal with that problem.*

Still, compared to the other problems he *could* have now, an upset noblewoman seemed almost trifling. He could likely cut her a deal once this whole thing was over. Almost everyone had a price. Akos turned his attention to more pressing matters.

"Vibius, do you feel anything?" Akos asked.

"I feel…" Vibius grinned at the lantern light. "Amazing. Thank you for asking."

The lanky wayfarer proceeded to plop himself down on the deck and attempt to whistle while rocking back and forth. Akos raised an eyebrow. It could be the effects of the xheiat tea, or it could be that the madness had taken him when they transitioned.

"What's my name?" Akos asked.

"Why, you're none other than the famous Captain Akos Freedman!" Vibius cheerily replied. A flash of concern crossed his face. "Had you forgotten that?"

That seems like the xheiat, Akos thought with a scowl. Vibius knew he hated his full name. Then, he had to suppress a chuckle of relief. They had managed to transition into the void and without any apparent misfortune. He would have to apologize to Calia for doubting her. If Valesa didn't tell her his plan right away, and he got the chance.

"Someone go below deck and ensure the rest of the crew is all right," Akos ordered. "The rest of you get some more lanterns lit."

Men scurried about, carrying out their orders. Akos wondered if they were as surprised as he was that they had managed to make it through unscathed. He would never have placed money on this expedition being a success. There was the issue of the impenetrable gloom that surrounded them, but that seemed like a much easier thing to deal with than what he had been expecting.

"Captain!" a voice from the crow's nest shouted.

Akos looked up to see what the man was shouting about. He followed the pointing finger and saw that there was nothing supernatural about the darkness around him. A moon peeked through the cloud cover for a moment, and then another cloud took its place. The gleaming silver face of the moon helped to further set his mind at ease. None of the stories he'd ever heard had mentioned hell having a moon. It was looking increasingly like Calia's theory had been right all along and that they had stumbled their way into a sixth realm.

The implications were earthshaking. Members of every nation of every realm would scramble to claim any bit of it that they could. If the realm were uninhabited, it would trigger the greatest mass exodus and what could be the largest war in history. Depending on the richness of the lands, this could become a battleground for interrealm interests for the next century. It would also be a privateer's paradise.

That all depended on the realm being unoccupied. Theorists had always speculated that the realm would have to be devoid of intelligent inhabitants, or they would have found a way out by now. Akos wasn't so sure. It was essentially a fluke that they had managed to find it. Now that they knew the method in and out, he wasn't so sure that anyone in this realm could replicate it.

Xheiat bushes grew only in the depths of temperate forests. Only the elves and a few kingdoms in the human realms had ever managed it. Several things would have to go right for wayfarers to have ever made it out of this realm. They would need the capability of growing xheiat bushes, they would have to have discovered the bushes' effects on wayfarers, and they'd have had to have someone brave enough to test it. And that was if the realm had wayfarers at all.

Akos wondered if he should turn his ship right back around and have Vibia take them back into the ways. Calia had proved what she set out to prove. She would be vindicated, revered even, in the eyes of her peers. Her name would be known until the end of civilization.

As if she heard his thoughts, Calia appeared at his side. Akos glanced down at her, and then past her to Valesa. Calia looked exuberant rather than angry, so Akos guessed that she hadn't been told of his plans yet.

"So, you planned to turn us at the last moment and declare the expedition a failure?" Calia said without a hint of anger.

So much for that thought, Akos said.

"I did," Akos said. "I thought you would get us all killed."

"Well," Calia said, beaming from ear to ear now, "like my doubters at the university, it seems you've been proven wrong. All's forgiven, Captain. Who knows? I might have done the same thing in your shoes."

Akos's eyes widened. He didn't know exactly what he had been expecting, but it wasn't that reaction. A glance at Valesa informed him that Calia might have forgiven him, but she hadn't. Her eyes glared daggers, and he glanced away. If all he had to suffer for his plot was Valesa's displeasure, Akos thought he could manage.

"I wonder if there is any land nearby," Calia said. "About how long do you think until sunrise?"

"Judging by the moon, I'd say we have a few hours at least. But I don't know. This realm could be unlike anything we've ever known."

"I know," Calia said with pure excitement in her voice. "I would hate it if it were locked into an eternal night. I know we have provisions to worry about, but I would love to search for any nearby land before departing for Geralis."

Akos supposed that he owed her that at least. Maybe if they managed to find a small patch of land, she might manage to forget to mention his plan to her brother. Much like Valesa, Akos doubted that he would be as forgiving as his younger sister. At best, he would likely forgo the bonus he had offered; at worst, he would tear up Akos's letter of marque and have him branded a pirate.

"We can make a quick cruise to see if there is any land nearby," Akos said after a moment. "But I'd like to wait until morning, or until this cloud cover clears away."

"Excellent," Calia said. "In the meantime, I've a great many tests to conduct. Do you think you could spare some of the crew to help?"

"Take as many as you like."

Calia wondered off toward her equipment, gathering any crewmen who strayed too close. Akos wondered whether they would be able to find any land, or if they would sail around for a few days before heading home. It would be very disappointing if they had managed to find a new realm with nothing in it but water. He'd leave the heavy lifting of that matter up to future explorers.

Akos made a quick mental note to check the armory before they went anywhere. If there were people here, it was unlikely that they spoke the trade language of the realms. There was no telling how advanced they would be or how hostile they might be either. It would be best to avoid contact with anyone, but if they did encounter anything hostile, he wanted to be ready.

"Captain?" Vibius said from his seat on the deck.

"Yes, Vibius?" Akos replied.

"I don't think Old Haroln was right. I think the void is actually just another realm."

Akos laughed at that. He laughed out all the tension and worry. Several crewmen joined him, too happy to be alive to do much more than laugh. When he finally finished, Akos looked down to see the wayfarer looking up at him with a raised eyebrow.

"I think you might be right," Akos said.

• • •

"Well, there isn't eternal darkness," Valesa said as the sun crept over the horizon.

Calia glanced up from her place on the deck. She'd been too busy performing her various experiments to notice much of anything. The sun stabbed at her eyes, and she shaded them. The sun burned its way through the cloud cover that kept the moon hidden for most of the night.

Dozens of experiments had yielded fascinating results. There was so much that she and her peers were going to be able to pore over when she returned. Most of it was nothing of consequence. She had been able only to test the water around them, but so far she had found that it was not acidic; it was of about the same salinity as the water in the realm of man, and it could theoretically sustain life. To this point she had not observed any sign of fauna, but it was a big ocean; in most other realms animals tended to avoid the mists.

As soon as the sun was out, Akos gave the order to get under way. Sails were unfurled to catch the wind, and they began to move through the dark-blue waters around them. Calia glanced back toward Valesa, who was glaring at the captain. She didn't stop until he had half-led, half-dragged Vibius below deck.

"You shouldn't hold a grudge," Calia said. "He was just trying to do what he thought best for his crew."

"Still," Valesa said angrily, "he lied to us, and he was going to put all your research in jeopardy. Doesn't that make you the least bit angry?"

That gave Calia a moment of pause. She supposed that it should make her angry. If Akos's plan had proceeded as Valesa explained it, she would have never had this chance. They would have sailed right past the void, declaring it a failed expedition. And she would have been none the wiser.

But Calia couldn't find it in her heart to stay angry at him. She'd had her own doubts after all, and she had proven to herself that the existence of a sixth realm was inevitable. He had nothing to go on other than his own experience, and that told him that the void was a deathtrap. As she'd told the captain, she likely would have done the same thing in his shoes.

Even the fact that Vibius had agreed to his plot didn't change her opinion of either of them. They'd both been doing only what they thought was necessary to keep them all alive. And the plan had been made and set long before they'd gotten to know each other and before they'd gotten to know the validity of her claims. It wasn't the least bit surprising that they'd choose to do what they did. It was the rational thing to do, and Calia had always prided herself on being a rational person.

"Not in the least," Calia said honestly. "He did what he had to do. All is well that ends well, and all that. It's hard to feel anything but joy at being proven right."

Valesa gave her a wry smile, like a mother watching her daughter play.

"I suppose I'll just have to distrust him for both of us," Valesa said. "But I'd definitely recommend informing your brother of what actually happened here."

"I'll take that under advisement," Calia said. "Now, I'm going to take a nap. If we manage to find land, I want to have the energy to explore it."

Calia felt like she had closed her eyes for only a few seconds when she was being shaken awake by Valesa. After she managed to rub some of the sleep out of her eyes, she dressed and joined her maidservant on the deck. She emerged into the rising sun.

"That didn't take long," Calia said.

"You slept for a whole day," Valesa murmured to her.

It took Calia a moment to realize that her maidservant wasn't trying to joke with her. She realized that the sun was lower than she remembered it. Her stomach rumbled, as if on cue, letting her know that it had been quite some time since she'd last eaten.

"Why didn't you wake me sooner?" Calia said.

"There was nothing to show you," Valesa replied. "And you hadn't slept in several days."

Calia opened her mouth to argue, but she was right. It had been several nights since she had managed to get any sleep, as nervous as she had been when they were approaching the void. *Halisland*, Calia reminded herself. At least, if there was no one there.

That thought reminded her of why she had been awoken and brought above deck. Calia peered out but saw nothing from her vantage point. She frowned.

"Not to complain," Calia said, "but why did you bring me out here?"

"The crow's nest said there was land." Valesa shrugged.

Calia couldn't see much, and she had to wonder whether they were playing another elaborate prank on her. Then Akos dropped to the deck from the ropes near her. Akos looked back out over the horizon.

"There is land," Akos confirmed. "A very large island, or perhaps a continent. I couldn't see the end of it."

The captain offered her a looking glass, and Calia fumbled with it as she tried to look through it. Eventually, she managed to focus it on the waves. She felt Akos's hand helping to direct her gaze.

"Focus on the horizon," Akos said.

As she did, Calia saw the outline of land begin to take shape. There was not much detail from this distance, but she could see it. Calia's heart soared. This was exactly what she had been hoping for. Halisland wasn't a barren ocean scape after all. Calia didn't worry much for wealth, but she knew that this discovery would make her family wealthy beyond the dreams of most kings. What she cared about was vindication, and this would do the trick in the eyes of those who hadn't wanted to count her among their peers.

"We'll head there," Akos said. "Once we make sure it's safe, we can land a small party to look around. We can't spend too much time there, though. We don't have enough supplies to hang around."

Calia almost dropped the looking glass in her excitement. She gave it back to Akos with as much grace as she could manage. This was beyond her wildest dreams.

She would be one of the first to set foot upon this new land. She could study the flora and fauna. She could name the island, possibly the *continent*, they had found. Calia thought that she wanted nothing more than to be vindicated in her studies, but now that the opportunities were laid out before her, she wanted more.

"Thank you, Captain," Calia said. "Now if you'll excuse me, I could use something to eat."

Chapter 8

The coast looked much the same as any other Akos had ever seen. A sandy beach lined with driftwood leading up to the edge of a jungle. Even with the looking glass he could not see any signs of movement within the trees. Akos wondered whether that was a bad sign. The foliage was thick; there was a small chance that he just couldn't see anything moving. There was also the chance that there wasn't anything there that could move. Akos wasn't sure which of those options he would prefer.

As they closed distance on the beach, Akos could see some creatures moving along the beach. They looked like crabs but with a few too many limbs and odd colorations. Rather than the red shells he was used to, these had mottled gray and green shells.

"I don't see anything big moving," Akos said as he handed the looking glass to Vibius.

The wayfarer had recovered from his xheiat-induced stupor within a few hours of their transition. They had awoken the man mere moments ago. There were still bags under his eyes. Transitioning between the mist and a realm usually took a lot out of the man, but Akos had never seen him affected quite like this.

"Those rocks have claws," Vibius muttered to himself.

Ignoring the wayfarer, Akos motioned for Leo to come over. The burly first mate joined him at the railing.

"We'll get as close as we dare," Akos said. "Then we'll launch a longboat. Make sure the men you pick are armed and ready for anything. We still don't know what might be in this realm."

"Aye, Captain," Leo replied. "Will I be leading the shore party?"

"No, I need you to stay and watch over the ship. I'll be leading the shore party."

Akos turned to see both Leo and Vibius glaring at him. Akos ignored their silent protestation and strode toward their guests. They might want him to take fewer risks, but after the stress this voyage had already put him through, Akos wasn't about to sit around and wait for someone else to make a report. If this land was dangerous, he wouldn't put a single person in harm's way unless he was also taking the risk.

"I can't wait to set foot on this new land," Calia was telling Valesa as Akos approached.

"I'll be happy with setting foot on any land," Valesa replied. "I'm getting tired of being cooped up in this ship."

"When will we depart, Captain?" Calia was now looking at him.

"First a small crew will be sent ashore to make sure that it's safe enough," Akos said. "If I determine that it's clear, I'll give the signal, and you may join us on shore. I'd prefer to spend no more than a day here, however. We are nearing the halfway point of our provisions, and I'll not risk resupplying anything from here unless necessary."

Calia nodded absentmindedly, returning her gaze to the approaching land. Akos was glad that she hadn't argued the point. She could always charter another ship to return and study the island all she wanted after they returned. Akos wasn't about to risk any more than he had to, especially not with his goal so close.

And Akos hadn't lied about running low on supplies. They had enough to last another week, at the most, before they had no choice but to return. Akos wasn't going to risk getting caught here by a storm or sustaining any preventable damage to his ship. The last thing they wanted was to get marooned with no supplies, tools, or even basic knowledge of what they could and couldn't eat here. Akos didn't even know if the water here was drinkable, and he didn't want any of his crew to risk it either.

Akos made his way back to his cabin to prepare for the landing. He didn't think he needed to be armed to the teeth, but he also didn't want to be unprepared. If there were some large, territorial creature residing on the edge of the jungle, it might take offense to them landing on it. If that something were to charge out of the forest at them, he wanted to be able to at least shoot at it.

There was no need for him to carry a long gun, though. Akos knew that he had some of the best marksmen found on any vessel. If they weren't enough to stop something, that something wasn't going to be stopped. Akos settled for his heavy cutlass and a pair of pistols. He also slipped a boarding ax into his belt in case they wanted to go deeper into the jungle, and they needed to clear some brush.

Once he was equipped, Akos made his way back out onto the deck, where the sailors Leo had picked were already forming up. Akos took a short moment to judge the distance between the shore and his ship before giving the command to drop anchor. This was close enough. He didn't want to run into any hidden sandbars or reefs that might damage the *Mist Stalker*. The much lighter and shallower draft of the longboat would allow them to pass over any such obstacles.

There were about two dozen men ready and waiting for his command to load into the longboat. Akos mentally noted who was going and checked to make sure they were appropriately armed for the occasion. Most of them carried the same gear that he did, a sturdy cutlass and a pair or so of pistols. A few among them carried rifled muskets, and a few others carried heavy blunderbusses. Akos nodded his approval and gave the signal to lower the longboat into the water.

Within a few moments, the shore party had piled into the longboat. Unlike most other captains, Akos grabbed one of the oars that was arrayed around the edge of the boat. Carag sat by the rudder, and once they had used the oars to push out and away from the *Mist Stalker*, he began to call out a cadence. Akos dipped his oar in time with the cadence, and the longboat was soon striking toward the coast.

The familiar feel of an oar in his hands gave Akos a little bit more peace of mind than he might have otherwise felt. For a few minutes, he managed to lose himself in the mindless act of rowing. It cleared his mind. Akos knew that he would need all his wits about him when he reached the shore, but for now he didn't have to worry about anything but pulling the oar through the deep blue water in time with the others.

In what felt like no time at all, their longboat reached the shore. Akos hopped over the side once they were close enough and helped pull the vessel ashore. Once they'd stowed the longboat where it wouldn't wash back out to sea, Akos took a better look at the surroundings. The beach was long and curved, bending off to the left farther than the eye could see. To the right, it ended a few hundred yards away where a cliff began to rise out of the water.

The jungle before them seemed to be empty of any life. Now that he was closer, Akos could see a little bit into the thick foliage that rose up a few hundred yards from the coast. Akos pursed his lips as he realized that he still couldn't see any movement. The sweat trickling down his neck and back from the exertion began to turn cold in the gentle breeze coming off the ocean, and he had to suppress a shiver. Something didn't feel quite right, but there was nothing that he could put his finger on.

"Fan out," Akos ordered. "And move toward the trees."

The crew obeyed his orders without hesitation, and Akos had to wonder whether he was the only one to feel a vague sense of unease. His crew didn't seem to be glancing around as nervously as he was. Akos risked a glance back over his shoulder to make sure that the *Mist Stalker* was still where he'd left it and chided himself for his foolishness when he laid his eyes on it.

They were within fifty yards of the forest when the first sign of life stirred within it. Birds exploded from the upper canopy of trees, nearly stopping Akos's heart. Once again, he mentally scolded himself for his nervousness. He was no child scared of shadows and the monster in the shadows.

The birds circled around them for a moment, as if to get a better look at them, and then descended upon the beach. Akos watched as several of them picked up the odd crabs he had seen. They had half buried themselves in the sand, and Akos could see how Vibius might confuse them for rocks. However, their natural camouflage had not fooled the birds, who pecked away at their hard shells until they cracked or carried them away in their talons for later.

The birds looked enough like a normal seagull to fool the casual observer, though they were twice as large. But Akos noted that their beaks looked much sharper than the average seagull. And their feet were tipped with large talons. Akos judged that it wouldn't be pleasant if they decided to attack one of his crew, but he didn't think it would be particularly deadly either.

"Let's cut a little way into the trees," Akos shouted. "But watch your feet. I'd hate for one of you to step on a spider the size of a dog."

He saw several of his crewmen cringe at the thought. Akos had never traveled through the realm of the trolls, but the tales said that they kept spider wolves as pets. While he'd never seen the creatures with his own eyes, several of his crew had traded there. They all confirmed that the creatures were exactly as terrifying as they sounded.

Careful to watch in front of him, as well as around his feet, Akos made his way into the jungle. The brush was thick near the outskirts, but Akos drew his ax and made short work of the brush blocking his path. Once he'd made it a short way into the jungle, the ground-level vegetation grew less dense. Soon enough they were in a kind of clearing, interspersed with the thick trunks of various trees.

"Anyone see anything?" Akos shouted out.

Akos's question was met with a chorus of negative responses. He counted the responses in his head until he was sure that everyone had answered. Despite his eyes telling him that everything was all right, Akos still couldn't shake the vague feeling of dread creeping down his spine. Still, there was nothing that he had seen that convinced him that this place was dangerous.

"Let's get back to the beach," Akos ordered.

As he turned around, Akos thought he saw something deeper into the jungle. He paused to take a better look at it, but there was nothing there. He watched for a moment longer, his heart pounding in his throat, but it calmed after a few moments. There was nothing there. It must have been a trick of the shadows cast by the canopy above him shifting in the breeze.

Akos returned to the beach to find that his men were readying the flagpole that would give the all clear to the *Mist Stalker*. They waited until he gave the order, but they already had the green flag prepared. As soon as Akos gave them the OK, they affixed the flag to the pole and raised it in the air. A man waved it until an identical flag was waved from the ship, and Akos could see that they were lowering another longboat into the water.

Now there was nothing to do but wait and try to shake the vague sense of unease sending shivers down his spine.

• • •

The sand sank in beneath Calia's feet, and she took in a deep breath. This was the first time she had ever stepped foot outside of Macallia, much less tread in another realm. The ocean air smelled much the same as it did on the beaches near Geralis but much cleaner. That most likely had to do with the lack of a bustling port town nearby.

She wandered over toward one of the crabs that Vibius had pointed out to her while they were waiting for the all clear sign. They were somewhat larger than Calia had expected. They were about a foot around, with legs stretching out at least that far on either side of their bodies. They were a mottled green and gray, some natural camouflage. As she approached, the crab used its large claws to scoop out a shallow spot in the dirt before settling down into it.

"Fascinating," Calia mumbled to herself.

While she had been attempting to secure her professorship, Calia had continually taken courses at the Royal University to keep up her standing. She had accrued enough time in several different areas of study that she could request a diploma for any one of them at any moment and have it granted. She'd never bothered. The science of wayfaring was her only true passion, but she'd studied biology and several other natural sciences.

"Halislandian stone crabs," Calia muttered more to herself than anyone else.

"What was that?" Valesa asked.

"Naming this new species."

"You're not going to name it after yourself?"

"I already named the entire realm after myself. I think that's enough."

"Very humble of you," Vibius added as he strode up. "Captain Akos has identified a hill a short walk into the jungle. Would you like to go and get a better look around the island?"

"That would be wonderful," Calia said.

He offered her his arm, and she took it with a grateful smile. It would be nice to get to spend some time with Vibius again, though Calia thought she might be a little too distracted to enjoy it. There were so many things to see and not much time to do it in. Akos had already made it clear that he wanted to be gone before nightfall, and it was already creeping toward midday.

Footing was poor in the jungle, and Calia soon wished she had worn a lighter dress. The crew kept a wary eye on the foliage around them, but apart from a few birds, the jungle seemed devoid of any life. It was strange, to say the least. Calia had always noticed in her studies that jungle environments tended to have a rich and thriving ecosystem. She'd brought along a small notebook and jotted down the lack of land animals.

The going was slow. Calia stopped every few minutes to make another comment about something in her journal. She noted the features of the trees, the vines that were creeping up them, and the dense underbrush that the crew was cutting away from their path. Things were like what she was familiar with in the realm of man, but she thought there were slight differences. Calia cursed herself for forgetting to bring along a manual on foliage and fauna of the realm of man to use as a comparison guide. She'd have to compare from memory when she returned to her home.

Vibius was very patient with her, stopping every time she paused to take notes. He tried to keep up the small talk, but she was too busy observing the new realm. He didn't seem to mind particularly. If he was getting frustrated, it wasn't showing in his tone or demeanor. After what seemed like several hours, Calia found that they were standing on a small hill.

"I didn't even realize we were walking uphill," Calia said.

"The slope is gentle from that side," Akos said.

The captain and several crewmen stood waiting by a copse of trees at the edge of a cliff. Calia strode up to see that they were several hundred feet above the ground floor of the forest. The sudden realization made her take an involuntary step back away from the edge.

"If you look just right," Akos continued, "you can see the *Mist Stalker* from here."

Calia peered out over the landscape toward the sea and saw that he was right. It seemed like the black-hulled ship was an ant on the horizon. It was hard to believe that they'd walked that far, but when she checked the position of the sun, she saw that it had been several hours. They would have to depart soon if they wished to make it back to the vessel by nightfall.

"What you won't see," Akos said absentmindedly, "is any sign of life other than those gulls and the crabs."

After a few moments of gazing down at the foliage below, Calia realized that he was right. There was no movement below other than the gentle shifting of the canopy in the breeze. Calia had thought that the animals might have been scared away by their approach, but it seemed that there simply weren't any.

"That certainly is odd," Calia said.

"Do you think they ran away?" Vibius asked.

"We can see for miles from here." Akos shook his head. "If they were running, we'd probably be able to see at least one sign of it. But I've had the men looking around while we waited for you. They didn't even find any tracks."

Calia imagined that sailors didn't make the best trackers. Even so, they should have been able to find something. If there was much life in this jungle, something would have left tracks that even she could follow. She frowned as she thought through the implications of the lack of land animals.

"Perhaps there are no natural land animals on this island?" Calia wondered aloud.

"It's a possibility," Vibius acknowledged. "But what if there are, or at least were? What might have caused their extinction?"

"There are any number of events that might cause the extinction of a species."

"Every species on an island that couldn't fly away or scuttle into the sea?" Akos asked.

"That…does seem less likely."

"I take it that you have a theory, Captain?" Vibius asked with a raised eyebrow.

"A couple," Akos said. "Either the land species of this island were hunted into extinction, or they are so good at hiding that we cannot see them. The second theory scares me much more than the first."

"Why is that?" Calia asked.

"If they were hunted into extinction, then whatever did the hunting would have either died out or moved on without prey to feed on. But if they are that good at hiding, then there must be something on this island worth hiding from."

Calia cast another glance over the canopy. The jungle seemed a bit more sinister now. Before, she had seen only the positives of finding a new land, but Akos's words reminded her that exploration came with a natural risk. Now she understood why the sailors had been so well armed, despite no visible threats.

"I'd like to head back to the ship now," Akos said. "If that is all right with you, milady?"

"Of course, Captain," Calia said.

The walk back to the beach was much quicker than the walk up the cliff. Not only were they going downhill, but Calia no longer stopped to take as many notes. Still, by the time they reached the edge of the trees, the shadows within the jungle were deepening. Calia had to resist the urge to jump every time the breeze made the shadows of the canopy dance. By the time they reached the edge of the trees, she realized that she had a tight grip on Vibius's arm. Calia managed not to blush, but a quick glance up at the man indicated that he didn't mind.

"Stop," Akos whispered harshly as they neared the edge of the trees.

Calia froze. Valesa was in front of her within an instant, eyes scanning about for any sign of a threat. Calia's heart dropped when she saw that both of their hands had gone to the hilts of their swords. Akos motioned for them all to stay back and crept toward the tree line. Calia wondered what he had seen to make him so wary suddenly, and all kinds of monsters filled her imagination.

Akos came back and motioned for them to come closer. He put a finger to his lips to silence them, and he spoke in a low, soft whisper.

"There is another ship," Akos said. "A galley."

"Hostile?" Vibius whispered back.

Akos shrugged. "It was flying a white flag. That could mean parley, it could mean nothing. There was a longboat rowing to shore as well."

"What's the plan?"

"I'm going out to see what they want. Hopefully we can figure out a way to communicate. Gerrin, keep everyone here and out of sight unless you see me wave you out."

A grizzled-looking sailor with a long scar cutting across his cheek nodded. Akos clapped the man on the shoulder and turned to Vibius.

"If things go poorly, keep everyone safe," Akos said.

"I'm sure your boundless charm will carry the day," Vibius replied dryly. "But if things go poorly, I'll still need a ship to get away on."

"I'm sure you'll figure something out. Now if you'll excuse me, I'm going to say hello."

Chapter 9

The sun sat low against the sky as the dinghy made its way to shore. Akos stood with his boots planted in the soft sand. This would be a horrible place to try to fight. The ground was uneven and would impede their movement. Any close combat would be a grueling affair. It would be better to try to set up near the jungle, at the edge of the beach. That would force the incoming force to wade through the sand to come to grips with them, all while weathering his men's gunfire.

Akos shook the thoughts from his mind. He was going to do everything he could to ensure that this encounter did not turn violent in the first place. There were no outward signs that this force was hostile. They hadn't tried to attack the *Mist Stalker*. That was a good sign. The white flag they flew on their lone mast was a universal sign for peace in the five realms. But Akos couldn't be certain that it meant the same here. The people of this realm could be alien to everything he had ever known.

The dinghy was now close enough that he could get a good look at the occupants. Akos was shocked to find that they were human, with a few dwarfs and orcs mixed in. It seemed that not everything was as alien as he assumed it would be. His mind raced as he wondered how they had all managed to end up in the same realm, one that nobody had ever been able to access.

Nobody who has ever returned anyway, Akos corrected himself. A sudden thought occurred to him. The first part of Calia's theory had proven correct. Their souls had not been sucked out of their bodies, nor had they been imprisoned in hell as Akos had feared. Perhaps the second part of the theory was correct as well. If the wayfarers who tried or were forced to transition into the void all went mad, then their crews would have been marooned here.

But what if those crews had managed to make a home for themselves here? There could be dozens of colonies. They would be lost to the world, but they might have formed some kind of society here. One made up of all the different races, by the looks of it. That would have been uncommon in the rest of the realms. The various races tended to prefer their own realms, though some individuals and groups traveled extensively. Akos himself had spent time in every realm, save the realm of trolls. Here they would have likely had no choice but to work together to survive.

Akos pushed the thoughts of the history of the void to the side. There were much more pressing issues at hand. Whether these men, or their ancestors, were originally from another realm had no bearing on whether they were a threat. It might make it easier to communicate with them, though. Especially if any of them had been shipwrecked since the creation of the universal trade language. Still, just in case things took a violent turn, Akos turned his eye on the men to see what kind of weapons they carried.

They were in uniform, indicating that there was at least some government or society that had formed here. Their shirts were a pale yellow, coming out from beneath steel breastplates. The armor looked to be of a much older design, more useful against blades than bullets. He couldn't see their weapons from here, but he had to assume that they were carrying some form of arming sword. Either that, or they had spears stowed away out of sight.

Despite his desire to maintain peace, Akos did a quick count in his head. There were around two dozen men in their shore party. He'd brought along at least that many, and more had come with Vibius. The newcomers had the advantage in armor, though his men would have a drastic advantage in firepower.

As far as their ships were concerned, there was no comparison. The galley had a great ram mounted to the front, but Akos didn't see so much as a single chase gun on its deck. If things came to blows, Leo and the *Mist Stalker* would pound the thing to splinters before it ever got close enough to use the ram, or the contingent of marines he was sure waited inside. The fight on the ground would be much closer than that, but Akos was sure that he could fight his way out of this if he needed to. That thought boosted Akos's confidence in the coming parley. Whether the newcomers would recognize it or not, he had the upper hand.

Once they drew near the shore, it wasn't hard to spot their leader. He was the only one among the dinghy that was unarmored. When the oarsmen jumped out of the boat to pull it onto shore, he remained in the vessel. There was an air of nobility about him. He stepped onto the beach as if he owned it, his back ramrod straight and his hands clasped behind his back.

That might be because he does own it, Akos reminded himself. If this place was settled, it was unlikely that they had somehow managed to land on an unclaimed piece of land. Almost as unlikely as it would be for this ship to find them and reach them so quickly. Akos mulled that over in his mind. He couldn't imagine it to be anything other than pure luck. There was no other way that anyone would have been able to get a ship out to this deserted stretch of beach with such little warning.

Soon enough the man was striding toward him, with the soldiers falling into line behind him. Akos had the man pegged as a noble, or whatever that equated to in this realm, within seconds. It was readily apparent in the way that he walked.

The man stopped about ten paces from where Akos stood, his men halting a few steps behind him. Akos knew that his own men were standing behind him in much the same way without having to turn around. He'd told them to keep their hands away from their weapons unless provoked. They were well drilled enough to follow orders, but the air was still thick with tension.

As he drew closer, Akos could see that he was pale. Clearly not a man who spent a great deal of time outside. His nose was short but sharply pointed. His eyes were the same color as freshly turned dirt, with matching hair pulled back into a ponytail behind his head. A smug grin tugged at the corners of his lips, and it wasn't until they'd been judging each other for several seconds that the man took his hands from behind his back.

Akos had to resist the urge to reach for his blade at the sudden movement. He managed to control himself, if only just, and the stranger's hands were empty when he swept them aside for a half bow.

"Welcome," the stranger said.

Akos blinked. The accent was thick, something you might hear in a bad actor's voice during the portrayal of some ancient play. But it wasn't so thick that it was unintelligible. Akos realized that Calia's marooned sailors theory was most likely correct. He returned the quick bow.

"Thank you."

"I am Lord Anson," the stranger said.

"Captain Akos."

"You are from outside of the realm, yes?" Anson made it sound like a question, but Akos could see from his eyes that there was no doubt.

"Yes, we are."

"Another ship fallen prey to the void. I must say, it has been some time since we last had any newcomers. I take it your wayfarer ventured too close?"

"Actually, no. We sailed straight in."

"Are you suicidal, or just foolish?"

"Neither, we were hired for a scientific expedition. Our patron wanted to prove that there was another realm hiding within the void."

"Well, it seems that your point is proven. Unfortunate that you'll never get the chance to share that news."

Akos didn't particularly like the confidence with which Anson made that statement, but he shook it off. It was more likely that this lord was trying to commiserate with him, and he was hearing threats where there were none. After all, this man or his ancestors could have lived here for entire generations. Several generations if his accent was anything to go by.

"Actually, we were about to make our way back to the realm of man," Akos said.

"You were?"

It was hard to resist the nervous temptation to shift his weight from foot to foot. Akos could not place a finger on it, but there was something off-putting about the pale man. There was no surprise on his face. If anything, there was excitement. Akos could understand. This could be the first news the void had received from the outside world in a century.

"Yes," Akos replied.

There didn't seem to be any reason to lie. There was nothing that Anson could do to keep them here if Akos decided that they were going to leave. Leo would have the cannon crews ready as soon as he saw another vessel. The second he heard a gunshot from shore, he would know to open fire. If there were local governments, they would need to be ready to open to the traffic that would soon be coming their way.

"Your wayfarer did not go mad?" Anson said.

"No, we have discovered a way to stave off the madness long enough to get into the void. Or, rather, what is it that you call this realm?"

"Well, I suppose we call it home. But if you are looking for a proper name, this place is known as the realm of behemoths."

Akos raised an eyebrow at that. If this realm followed the same naming conventions as the other realms, then that would mean that the original inhabitants of the realm were behemoths. He didn't know exactly what a behemoth might look like; as far as he knew, that was a generic term for a large creature.

"Behemoths?" Akos asked.

"Fascinating things," Anson replied. "They were the original rulers of this land. Now, I rule them."

"I see."

Akos was beginning to wonder whether the prolonged isolation from the rest of the realms had driven the inhabitants insane. So far he hadn't seen hide nor hair of any other land-dwelling creatures. Perhaps allowing this parley to happen hadn't been the best idea after all.

"And what is a behemoth?"

"You'll see soon enough," Lord Anson replied.

As if to punctuate his sentence, a bloodcurdling scream erupted from the jungle behind him. This time Akos placed his hand on the hilt of his blade, though he did not draw it. He turned his head to get a better view of the trees, though he did not take his eyes away from

Lord Anson or his soldiers. None of them so much as flinched. From the look on Anson's face, this wasn't a surprise to him.

Akos knew that the scream had to have come from Calia. It had come from a female voice, and he didn't think Valesa was the type to scream in terror. He could see several figures emerging from the jungle, all of them his sailors. Vibius was hauling Calia bodily out of the trees, while Valesa stood between them and whatever had elicited the scream. Pale faced, the rest of the men were retreating from the jungle with weapons drawn.

Akos wondered what could make such veteran men so scared. Then he saw the first behemoth and understood.

The creatures resembled the great apes that were found in the jungles of Illyris, but without any of the hair. They even had the same style of walk, rumbling forward on what appeared to be their knuckles. Their skin, mottled and swirling gray, was taut over cords of muscle. Each one had a pair of eyes on either side of its head, and a mouth that split its large head in half. He guessed that if one stood up on its hind legs, it would be around twice the height of a man.

They were not standing, however. Nor were they so much as snarling. Instead, they trudged forward, keeping a measured distance between themselves and Akos's men. One looked toward him, and the way its four eyes gleamed in the sun reminded him of the creature he thought he saw in the forest. If he had to guess, Akos would say that it weighed at least half a ton, all of it pure muscle.

"Ugly things, aren't they?" Lord Anson mused. "Still, they have their uses."

Akos turned from the behemoths. Every hair on his back went up, warning him not to put the creatures to his back, but he ignored his instincts and faced Anson. The man's face was split in a grin, and his head was cocked as he looked over the group. For a moment, Akos saw a great deal of resemblance between the man and the beasts he commanded.

"You expect me to believe that those things answer to you?" Akos demanded half-heartedly.

"Watch your tone, cur." One of the soldiers stepped forward. "You speak to a god."

Anson held out a hand, stopping the soldier in his tracks. Akos eyed the men. It was clear that the other soldiers believed what the man had said. Akos wondered if Anson believed it too.

"To answer your question," Anson said, "yes. They'll do handstands if I will it."

Akos could not help the look of incredulity that he was sure crossed his face. Anson merely laughed. He gestured at one of the creatures, and Akos turned his head to watch. His eyes grew wide as the creature took a precarious stance before balancing on its head with its legs stuck straight up in the air. These were either the best trained creatures that he had ever laid eyes on, or something else was going on that he could not comprehend.

"Captain Akos." Anson's voice snapped his head back around. "I invite you and your crew back to my city to enjoy my hospitality. I do hope you'll accept."

"I do," Akos said, his mouth going dry.

There was nothing that he could do for now. He didn't know what it would take to kill one of these behemoths. Judging from their looks, it wouldn't be easy. They looked as if they would soak up bullets, and there was no telling how tough their hides were.

Akos didn't want to try to find out how hard it would be to kill one of the things while having to fight the human soldiers at the same time. If Anson had as much control over them as he seemed to, it would be almost impossible to fight them both. The odds had been in his favor before, but Akos knew how to tell when the tides had changed.

Their best bet now was to go with the lord and hope that he didn't have any ill intentions. Akos sighed internally as Anson beckoned toward their ships. He was getting very tired of nobles inviting him to their homes.

• • •

Calia couldn't help but glance back over her shoulder as Lord Anson's galley rowed home. The behemoths had been allowed onto the ship. They lounged by the railing, looking as nonthreatening as it was possible for a ten-foot-tall monster to look. Still, every time she closed her eyes, she could see the massive creatures melting into view against the trees. Their mottled camouflage worked perfectly in the shade of the jungle, and she hadn't been able to see them until they were nearly on top of her.

The eyes had been the most disturbing thing. They reminded her of a doll she had owned growing up. Perfectly round, black, and unfeeling. Calia was no theologian, but she was convinced that the creatures didn't have souls.

Even though the threat was past, part of her still wanted to curl up and cry. She'd been left shaking the entire time their longboat had rowed toward the galley. Only the soothing presences of Valesa and Vibius on either side of her had stopped her from bursting into tears. Calia refused to be reduced to a blubbering mess in front of either of them.

The steady presence of Valesa next to her calmed her somewhat. She, along with the rest of the *Mist Stalker*'s crew, had given up their weapons. The sailors had done so without quarrel at Akos's command, but Calia doubted that there had ever been much choice. Anson had not made any open threats, but no one had doubted the true meaning of him inviting them to put their weapons in the care of his crew.

That did not mean that Valesa was unarmed. She had at least one pair of knives somewhere. Calia had never known her to go anywhere with less than two. She doubted that the blades would do anything useful against the behemoths though. Calia fought the urge to glance back at them. It would not do to show any fear in front of their…host.

Anson had spoken at length only with Akos, though he had asked the man to give him the proper introductions. Despite Akos introducing her as Lady Hailko, sister of a great lord of the Empire of Macallia, Anson had looked her over as if she were no more than a piece of meat. It made her itch all over. It was by no stretch the first time that she'd experienced that, and she'd managed to remember her courtly training, as difficult as it had been. Anytime she'd caught someone looking at her like that before, she'd had the option to leave the person's presence. Calia knew that would not be an option this time.

Though she hadn't been in many situations like this, Calia knew from spending enough time around other nobles that this was a show of force. Anson was trying to impress upon them how much power and control he had over the situation. Her brother had always told her that the best way to deal with a show of force was to act unimpressed. *It makes the other party wonder what you have up your sleeve*, Halis had always told her.

Not that Calia knew what she could be hiding up her sleeves. Their entire arsenal was under the watchful eye of the yellow-clad soldiers. Calia had watched Lord Anson look over a pistol after his men had taken it from Akos. He clearly did not know what, exactly, it did, but he seemed to understand that it was a weapon. It was a subtle thing, but Calia noticed that when Anson asked for their weapons, Akos had freely given him his sword, but made no moves toward his pistols. He hadn't given them up until Anson motioned for him to hand them over as well.

The captain was far cleverer than she'd realized. Calia had assumed the man to be intelligent, at least in the field of ship handling. And she knew that he was competent in the fields of command and swordsmanship. Now she was realizing that he was far more intelligent than he let on. If she had to guess, it was a deliberate act, allowing others to underestimate him.

Calia scolded herself for not realizing that sooner. There weren't many clues, but there was one big one that seemed obvious now that she had begun to make the connections. Vibius was one of the most intelligent men she had ever met, and Akos had his respect. If he had been a simple man, that wouldn't have been the case. She wondered if he would continue to play the simple captain now, or if he would change his tact.

"Are you all right?" Vibius asked her.

"I'm fine," Calia said.

It was only a half lie. Physically, she was unharmed. Emotionally, she was a wreck. Calia knew that it was plain to see. Still, she knew that the best thing she could do in this situation was button up and keep her emotions in check until they were out of danger.

"Good," Vibius said. He leaned in closer, and when he spoke again it was a whisper. "How many people know of your trick to enter the void?"

"Ah…" Calia was surprised by his sudden question. She counted in her mind. "Just your officers, Valesa, and myself."

"Let's try to keep it that way. We don't want them to know too much about us."

Vibius leaned back out, commenting on the moon in the sky. Calia was surprised by the sudden shift in conversation, until she realized that one of Anson's men had wandered closer to them. She responded to his comment, though she wasn't sure what he'd said. If Calia were being perfectly honest with herself, she wasn't sure what *she'd* said. Her head was still spinning. It would be difficult to adjust to their new situation. Calia knew that she had to get used to it, though.

All their lives could depend on it.

Chapter 10

The steady beat of the drum was a familiar sound to Akos. He'd practically been born on a galley after all. The drummer beat a slow and steady rhythm that the oarsmen could follow with ease. The single sail that the ship sported had been lowered as well, allowing the wind to help the men out. They pulled into a natural harbor framed on either side by juts of jungle. Against the opposite side was a town, with a mountain looming dark and ominous behind it.

Even with the men rowing through the night and the friendly breeze, it had taken until dawn for the ship to pull back into the nearby port. Akos was amazed that they had seen no sign of it sooner. His sense of unease had only grown as he realized that there was no real traffic coming to or from the town. A few fishing boats languished in the bay, but there was nothing else there. If this were a true port city, as Anson claimed, Akos would have expected to see some signs of trade coming and going.

The docks at least had people on them, but Akos watched as they got up and left as the galley approached. There was no fuss, nor did he hear a call go up. The men and women merely collected their fishing poles and other belongings and left the docks. Soon enough, the only figures Akos could see moving throughout the town were wearing the same yellow uniforms as those on the ship.

The town didn't seem to be very industrious. Faint wisps of smoke rose from the chimneys, and the only sound was that of the gulls that cried out as they swooped around the docks. Akos wondered if they were expecting a raid, or if this was the usual state of the city.

They would know soon enough. This was the only place to dock that he had seen. Akos rubbed some of the remaining sleep from his eyes. The sun had been up for only a few hours, and he hadn't been able to sleep well. Anson had offered him the use of his cabin, but Akos had deferred that to Calia and Valesa. He and Vibius had slept with the rest of his sailors aboard the galley, in the cramped crew quarters. The hammocks had tried their best to rock him to sleep, but his mind was too active to allow him to rest.

Akos glanced back at their host. Despite not having slept the last night, Anson hadn't so much as yawned since Akos had awoken. It could have been simple excitement, but the man was so odd that Akos couldn't help but think that there was some other reason.

If the man noticed Akos's scrutiny, he gave no sign of it. Anson strolled around the deck as if he didn't have a care in the world. Every so often he would pause to look at something, or to speak to one of the yellow-clad soldiers who had wandered up onto the deck. But within moments, he would resume his circuit, pacing slow circles around the deck. Soon enough, his circuit brought him back toward where Akos and the others had gathered to look at the town.

"Not much to look at, I'm afraid," Anson said. His accent had become easier to understand as the night went on, and he seemed to have no problems understanding any of Akos's crew. "Ferundan was built to be a shipping hub, but of late it hasn't been much more than a garrison."

"What prompted that change?" Akos asked.

"My neighbors are less interested in trading and more interested in taking what isn't theirs."

Without waiting for a reply, the man was moving on again. Akos shook his head. He'd met eccentric nobles before, but none who were quite like this. Akos wondered if it was only Anson, or if all the men and women of the void were this odd.

Akos recalled the soldier telling him that he spoke to a god and realized that it was probably all the inhabitants of this place. Akos wasn't sure how the man had trained his behemoths so well, but he was sure it was nothing more than a simple trick. He'd once known a sailor with a small monkey that he'd trained to pick pockets. Anything was possible if the beasts were intelligent enough. At least, that was what he forced himself to think. The alternative was almost too chilling to consider.

Despite his hollow self-reassurances, it seemed a stretch that the behemoths would be interested in working with humanity, rather than hunting them into extinction. The creatures were even more terrifying up close. Looking at their skin, Akos wasn't even sure that a sword would be able to cut through their hide. They looked as if they were made of steel, and their haunting pitch-black eyes seemed to follow him everywhere.

Akos chided himself for being foolish. The creatures had to have a weakness. He was allowing his fear to get the better of him. If they were invincible to any weapons, the humans here in their realm would never have survived to build cities. They certainly wouldn't be lounging on the deck of a galley at the command of one of the human lords. A bullet or a blade would likely work as well on them as on any other creature.

Not that I have either at the moment, Akos thought ruefully. It must have been too obvious that their firearms were in fact weapons. Anson had demanded them as well, despite the obvious fact that he didn't know exactly what they did. If he had the capacity to build a town, and he knew what a gun was, he would have gunsmiths. Akos had seen no sign of any guns, even rudimentary ones. There weren't even any cannons or bombards on the galley.

If Akos was right, the man was smart enough to figure out how to use them quick enough. They wouldn't have long before Anson had managed to divine their use, though the secret of how to craft black powder might elude him for a while. Akos could only hope that was the case, anyway.

The galley drifted into its mooring, the oarsmen pulling in and stowing their sweeps. Anson finally stopped his pacing long enough to observe his men securing the ramp. He made his way back over to his "guests" and gestured for them to follow him.

"I was in such a rush to meet my visitors that I forgot to pack any food," Anson said. "It's only a short ride to my manor, and I'd like to invite you and your officers to break fast there."

"Of course," Akos replied.

The man smiled and led them down the ramp. Akos had to admit that the dock was almost the most unsettling thing he had encountered so far. It was all the familiar smells and form without any of the activity or sounds he was used to. There were no longshoremen or teamsters hustling to haul their loads, no yelling foremen trying to direct the chaos, no sailors chanting old tunes as they swabbed their decks. Just empty wharves, with the odd gull screeching and swooping for fish in the water.

Anson led them to a pair of carriages that were waiting near the docks. Each had several mounted guards surrounding it. Akos realized that Anson might not have known exactly what he would find on the beach, but he had been well prepared. It might not have been as long since the last ship as Anson had implied, or perhaps he was an incredibly thoughtful person. Either way, Akos's flimsy hopes of escaping during the carriage ride to Anson's manor dissipated like the crowd at the docks.

The horsemen were much better armored than their galley counterparts. They wore almost full plate and held lances in their hands. Akos knew that without their firearms, his crew would have no chance against those men on land. Unless they could force the fight in very favorable positions, this foe would be too well armored and armed to deal with.

Not that it's looking like we're going to get a chance to fight our way out of here anyway, Akos thought. He cast a glance over his shoulder to see what was going on with his vessel. It had been moored between several of the galleys that sat along the wharves. His crew were arranged on the deck, watching as their captain strode away with their captor. Armed guards were posted around them, watching them like hawks. Anson kept referring to Akos's crew as his guests, but Akos had no doubt that they were his prisoners.

Akos felt a pang of guilt as he met eyes with Leo. The man had no anger or fear on his face, and he even winked at his captain. Still, Akos felt almost as if he were betraying them by leaving them behind. There was nothing to be done, however. The best way that he could help his crew was by going along with what Lord Anson said until they could find out what he wanted from them.

Within moments they were moving along the road, the carriages bumping against the cobbled streets. The streets were as bare as the docks, but Akos thought he could see curious eyes glancing out from windows and door frames. At the very least, he could tell that the city wasn't abandoned. He could now see lights within the buildings, and signage that told of each building's purpose. They passed many of the things that one would expect to in a town of any size. One sign showed a hammer and anvil, another the grinding bowl of an apothecary, and on another was a pair of crossed cleavers denoting a butcher.

"It's not much," Anson said, almost as if to himself, "but it's home."

Akos glanced across at the man and saw that he was staring out the window. They had reached the edge of town, and the buildings were growing scarcer as they went. Akos turned so that he could see out of the window where Anson was looking.

The mountain that he had seen from the bay was much closer now, with what Akos had thought to be a sheer cliff facing them. Now that they were closer, he could see that it was a wall. The wall was at least a hundred feet tall and carved of the same dark stone that made up the mountain behind it. Akos struggled to pick out the crenellations against the sky behind it. The stone was too dark to tell for sure, but it appeared to be covered in arrow slits. It looked as if it had been crafted with more than mere looks in mind.

Several towers rose up along its length, and the wall ran until it dead-ended into the actual cliff face. Akos was unimpressed. It sat close enough to the water that it would be an easy target for any warship that made it into the harbor. The wall looked well-constructed, but it had clearly been built in a different time. In this realm it could be the pinnacle of defensive emplacements. In the realm of man, it would be little more than an antiquated draw for tourists in the best of times, and target practice for a ship's gunnery crews in the worst.

Seeing the way that the towers and the wall were constructed further persuaded Akos that this realm had never used gunpowder. Nor did it seem that conflict was that common. At least, around cities. There had been no fortifications on the harbor itself, and the castle looked as if it was there more to awe visitors than to serve any practical purpose.

INTO THE VOID

Akos glanced around the base of the massive wall, taking in all the sights that he could. The town had faded into farmland as the city had died away, but there was a second town that seemed to be built against the wall. Much to his surprise, Akos could see people moving about this town. He half-expected them to scurry away like the other townsfolk, but these continued to toil away as the carriage rumbled past them.

The carriage was slowing down as it reached the gatehouse carved into the bottom of the wall, and Akos peered out at the working groups. Several of them were tilling a field with nothing but hand tools. It looked to be backbreaking work. Akos noticed there were several armed men with crossbows standing around the field, watching over the men and women as they worked.

Akos's heartbeat quickened as he realized that the men were also carrying whips. Not a single person working in the fields looked up at the carriage's approach. Akos felt rage building inside his chest as he realized that these people were slaves being forced to carry out this labor for Anson.

One of the slaves looked up to watch them pass, pausing for a moment. She was a slight girl, weathered and dark from long hours in the sun. Their eyes met for the briefest moment, and Akos recognized a familiar hatred there, mixed with a sense of profound helplessness. The girl received a lash across the back from one of the nearby guards for her laxity.

Akos barely noticed when the carriage pulled to a stop in front of the mansion itself. He forced himself to breathe and keep his mask on. It didn't seem like a good idea to attack a man who had them in the center of his power with his bare hands.

"I'll have my men show you to your accommodations while I go to have the chefs prepare us something to eat," Anson said as he stepped out of the carriage.

Without another word, the man started walking up the steps. Akos hadn't even disembarked the carriage before the man was disappearing within the halls of his home. Several armed guards were waiting around the entrance, and many of them approached the carriages. Anywhere else, those guards would have been there to take their coats and ensure their safety. Akos knew that these men were jailers, here to show them to their cells.

Akos made sure that the others had dismounted as well before he turned back toward the guards. He looked up at the tower. It was constructed in much the same way as the wall around it, though far shorter. It had the same utilitarian appearance, with the few windows outnumbered by arrow slits. It looked as if it would have a commanding overview of the courtyard below it if someone managed to break through the curtain wall. The architecture was imposing, but not expert. He could see several areas where the stones were uneven or even missing altogether.

The guards wasted no time shuffling them up the stairs and into the keep. Akos blinked as his eyes adjusted to the dimmer light inside the keep. When his vision cleared, he gasped despite himself.

The atrium was carved of white marble with thin red veins flowing through it. The floors were polished until they shone in the light of the chandelier that was burning above and the torches set in sconces along the wall. Columns of the same white stone rose to a ceiling twenty feet above, seamlessly joining with it. It was a shock compared to the dull, utilitarian visage that the castle presented to the outside world.

Against the far wall, flanked by a pair of grand staircases, was a painting. It was almost the same height as the wall and filled up the entire space between the stairs. If Akos hadn't known better, he would have thought the work belonged to one of the masters of the realm of man. The brushstrokes were perfect, the lighting exquisite. Akos didn't care much for paintings, but this one was something else. He had to resist the urge to walk up to it and study it as if he were an art student trying to glean inspiration from a classic.

The scene it displayed had a tinge of familiarity, though its subject matter was entirely alien. It was a battle, but instead of armored lancers or infantry clashing together, behemoths clawed at each other. It looked random at first glance, as if the behemoths had all gone mad and started to claw at each other, but Akos recognized it for what it was. These were two distinct armies fighting each other. He was sure if he studied it enough he would be able to see the subtle differences between the forces, but for now he didn't know where or how to look to see those differences.

In the background behind the behemoths were other, larger things. They looked to be the size of houses, though they held the same general characteristics as the behemoths. Where they clashed, their massive limbs dug furrows into the ground. Akos's blood ran cold as he realized that this painting was implying that there were creatures even larger than the behemoths they had already encountered in this realm, and they were under the same control as their smaller counterparts.

At the rear of the armies were the only human figures. A pair of men, one to each side, sat locked in an eternal staring match. The man on the right had hawklike features, with a heavy brow and a sharp pointed nose. He scowled in concentration as he stared across the battlefield.

The other man was Anson. The features were dead-on, far too close to merely be a relative. He even wore the same smug smile that Akos had seen on the beach. Akos puzzled what that might mean even as he was escorted past the painting. Underneath the painting was a placard with the name of the work emblazoned on it.

Ascension of a God.

Chapter 11

The rooms they were given weren't exactly luxurious, but they weren't lacking anything either. It was almost exactly like Calia's room at Hailko mansion, but without any of the charm and lived-in feeling. The beds were comfortable enough. That might be important, since Calia had no idea how long they were going to be there.

At least they hadn't locked her up away from Valesa. Her maidservant sat on the bed, staring at the wall as if trying to remember something. Calia didn't want to disturb her when she was so deep in thought. Just the steady and stoic presence of Valesa was a massive relief from all the stress that had been building inside of her.

It might have already brought her to tears if it wasn't all so surreal. Taken captive by a man who claimed to be a god and who could control the actions of monsters with his mind? When Calia thought about it, she almost had to laugh.

Calia's chuckle faded away as soon as it began. This was no story told in the belly of a ship; this was really happening to her. And, it occurred to her, she had no idea of what Anson had planned for them.

His plans had to be more than adding them to the population of slaves she had seen outside. If that was the only goal, Calia couldn't imagine why the man would invite them to his castle to eat first. She was sure that the self-styled god had some other plan for them, but Calia couldn't puzzle out what it might be.

"Why couldn't he have put us together with the others?" Calia mused aloud.

"To keep us from cobbling together an escape plan," Valesa said.

The comment was so sudden that it made Calia jump. Her maidservant had risen from the edge of the bed and made her way over to the small arrow slit that served as their only window. Calia was sure

INTO THE VOID

she'd seen actual windows in the tower, but they must have been higher up. Valesa peered down, frowning as she did so. Calia didn't know exactly how high up they were, but they had climbed a good number of stairs to reach the room.

"Not that there is any good way out of this castle," Valesa continued. "This whole section has only one exit. And there were two armed guards there. I'd be surprised if we weren't at least fifty feet up, so there's no chance we could survive a fall, and that's even if we could somehow open this window up enough to squeeze through."

Calia's heart was sinking with every word. For some reason, despite everything they were dealing with, she had still expected to be able to come up with something. At least, she had expected Valesa to come up with something. Calia wasn't familiar with all her bodyguard's training, but she knew it was extensive and supposed to cover things such as this.

"What are you saying?" Calia managed after a moment.

"We'll have to see what this Lord Anson wants," Valesa replied. "Perhaps he just wants to negotiate a trade deal from a place of power. Maybe he wants to sacrifice us to some dark power to maintain his 'godhood.' Maybe he wants to add us to his harem."

"You think so?"

"Considering the fact that he hasn't spoken directly to either of us the entire time we've known him, I'd say there's a fair chance that he doesn't have a high opinion of women. As far as the other two go, I don't know what his motivations are. There is a chance that isolation has driven him mad, or he could be a shrewd lord looking to increase his power. We won't know for sure until he tells us."

"You think he'll outright tell us what he wants?"

"Probably not. But if we pay attention, we might be able to figure it out. But then, it is possible. After all, what purpose would hiding his intentions serve?"

"So, all we can do is wait?"

"I suppose we could pray as well."

Calia had never taken Valesa for a particularly pious woman, but at this moment she couldn't fault her for wanting to call upon divine aid. It seemed like the only thing that could get them out of their current situation. Calia supposed that all she could do was hope that Anson was like any other lord she'd known, jockeying for political power. The man had mentioned having enemies, which implied that there were other lords, which in turn implied that there was some sort of international politics.

"Extraordinary, isn't it?" Calia asked aloud.

"What is?" Valesa replied.

"That a society that has to have been founded by marooned sailors could advance so far without any contact with the other realms."

"It is impressive. Especially if they had to contend with those behemoth creatures."

Calia shivered. "Don't even bring those up. They were the most terrifying thing I've ever seen."

"They certainly had an air of danger about them. But I bet if you cut them they bleed the same as anything else."

"You'd have to get close enough first."

"That might be a challenge. But you know me, I always have a few tricks up my sleeve."

That was true enough. Calia had never seen Valesa stumped in any situation. Except this one. If anyone could kill one of the monsters, Valesa was the one Calia would put her money on. She would just as soon not have to watch her try, though.

"Tell me honestly," Calia said. "Do you think we'll ever see home again?"

"I do," Valesa said. It was remarkable that there was no hesitation in her answer. "I'm sure the crew of the *Mist Stalker* have no wish to remain here either. They'll be plotting their own way out, and at least Vibius will make sure we're included in that."

"You don't think Captain Akos would plan to include us?"

"I think he would if it helped him, but if he had to go out of his way…" Valesa shrugged. "I'm not so confident. He's close enough with Vibius that if he insists, then Akos will plan for us."

"You're being too harsh on the captain."

"Don't forget that he's a pirate, and he's already tried to betray your trust to save his own hide once."

Calia wanted to argue, but Valesa made a compelling point. Akos had already attempted to mislead them. She had the impression that he was an honorable man, but each man held his own definition of honor. He might hold the safety of his crew above all else, and they weren't members of his crew. If he had to choose between men who he'd sworn to protect and two women he barely knew, whom would he choose?

"You may be right," Calia said.

"Whether I'm right or not, it's better that we plan on being on our own," Valesa said.

Valesa grew quiet after that, and Calia allowed her time to think. She needed to think as well. Within moments of their falling quiet, however, their thoughts were interrupted. A firm knock on the door was immediately followed by a guard throwing it open. Valesa was standing before Calia even knew what was happening, but the guard didn't have any weapon in his hand.

"Lord Anson would like you to join him at his table," the guard said.

Calia rose and followed him back down the stairs, noticing that the other officers of the ship were being gathered as well. Despite their current circumstance, Calia was glad to see Vibius. Much like Valesa, his mere presence calmed her. She moved to stand with him, and he smiled as she approached.

"I hope Lord Anson prepared enough food," Vibius said nonchalantly. "I'm starving."

It was all Calia could do to nod and smile. She didn't know how the others were managing to remain calm enough to joke at a time like this. Calia felt as if she was only ever a moment from a breakdown. It could be experience or training, but she couldn't imagine what kind of experience would prepare someone for something like this. This situation was about as alien as she could imagine.

Thankfully, the calm of the others was infectious. Calia had managed to keep from breaking down because of those around her so far. But what Valesa said was settling into her mind. For all intents and purposes, they were on their own. Calia refused to be a burden to those around her. She stiffened her resolve, vowing that she would not allow herself to break. *And perhaps if I tell myself that often enough, I'll manage to do it*, Calia mused. There was power in keeping up appearances after all.

Vibius offered her his arm, and she hooked her own through it. They made their way through the halls of the castle as if nothing were wrong in the world. The only indication that this was anything other than a dinner party was the fact that armed guards were escorting them to the dining room rather than simple servants.

Soon enough they were being seated. There didn't seem to be any order to it, though a spot at the head of the table seemed to be reserved for Lord Anson. Calia seated herself between Vibius and Valesa. Vibia and Akos seated themselves across from them. Even though Akos had identified Leodysus as his second in command, Anson had not invited him to the castle.

Calia looked over to the other pair to see how they were handling the situation. Akos had a blank look of bland indifference written across his face. It didn't look as if he was impressed by a single thing in all the realms, though Calia guessed that it was an act. She knew, through Vibius, that he was skilled in keeping his true emotions away from his face as a part of his experience of being a ship's captain. Vibia, on the other hand, looked a little more like Calia expected she herself did. The woman was disheveled, but it was obvious that she was trying to keep herself together as well as she could.

Calia offered her what she hoped was an encouraging smile when their eyes met. Vibia returned the smile, though it was weak. Calia could only imagine that her own smile was nowhere near as reassuring as she'd meant it to be. She glanced at Valesa, but she was the same way as Akos. Her face showed no emotion other than mild displeasure, as though she had been pulled away from some minor task.

"My deepest apologies for the delay," Lord Anson said as he briskly walked into the hall. "It's incredibly rude of me to make my guests wait."

"Think nothing of it," Akos answered for them.

"Well, let's not waste any time. I'm starving."

Anson raised a finger, and the servants began pouring forth from the doorway. Despite her misgivings, Calia had to admit that the food smelled delicious. It was standard fair, roasted chicken with various vegetables. There were fresh fruits mixed in, which was a pleasant surprise. They also brought out what looked like glasses of wine for all their guests, and one for Lord Anson as well.

"Before we begin," Anson said, "I'd like to toast to new friendships and new possibilities."

Calia raised the glass to her lips, but she felt both Vibius and Valesa's knees nudge her under the table. She glanced at her bodyguard first, who sent a pointed glance toward their host. Calia wondered what was going on, glass poised on her lip, when she realized that they were all waiting for Anson to take a sip. She had to keep from wrenching the glass away from her lips as she realized that they were worried that their host might be trying to poison them.

But Anson wasted no time in taking a deep draw from his own glass. After a moment, Akos followed suit and then the rest of them took their own sips. Calia thought that it was a little sweeter than the wine that her father and brother preferred, though she was by no means an expert. She set her glass back down as the servants gave her a plate with some of everything they had brought out portioned onto it.

Vibius tore into his food with gusto. Calia thought she saw Akos roll his eyes and give a slight grin, but the gesture was gone as soon as it appeared. It seemed that he was still feeling the effects of wayfaring. Calia took her time, allowing the chicken to cool before taking a bite.

The food was good enough. Calia wondered whether all their fears and suspicions were for nothing. It could be that Anson wanted nothing more than to treat them to a nice meal and keep them safe. But there was no doubt that he would want something more. Calia was no fool. She was beginning to believe that it might be something less dastardly than they had all been assuming. He might only want to negotiate a favorable trade deal before letting them depart.

Anson talked as he picked at his food, asking them all sorts of questions about the realm of man. It was quite clear that this realm had received no news for some time. Calia could see that many of the nation names were going right over his head. She also noticed that whenever she or Vibia answered a question he would hear them, but not acknowledge them. Instead, he would move on to some other topic.

It seemed that Valesa was right in assuming that he didn't have a favorable view of women. That wasn't particularly surprising. The realm of man hadn't been especially egalitarian until recent times.

"I've asked you all about current events," Anson said after talking for a while. "But I have failed to ask about you. Please, tell me a few things about yourselves."

Anson motioned toward their side of the table first, indicating that it was Vibius's turn to speak. The man took a few moments to swallow his mouthful of food before answering.

"Well, I am Vibius Antonius, wayfarer of the *Mist Stalker*."

"Where are you from?" Anson continued.

"Gellerit, originally, though I was young when I left home to be a wayfarer. If it's not impolite to ask, Lord Anson, were you born here or were you marooned?"

"Please, call me Anson. I'm afraid I was lost here, though it was so long ago that I forget the name of the place I came from, and from what I've been hearing, it might not exist anymore anyway."

Anson, somewhat to Calia's surprise, gestured to her next.

"Well, my name is Calia Hailko. This is my maidservant, Valesa Laris. We are both from mainland Macallia."

"Is there a great distinction between the mainland and the islands of Macallia?" Anson asked. Calia didn't think he'd responded to anything she'd said yet. It threw her off guard.

"Only among the house of lords. The isles are a newer addition, and their lords have a junior standing compared to their mainland counterparts."

"Interesting. Captain, would you care to tell us something about yourself?"

"There isn't much to tell. My name is Akos, and my home is the *Mist Stalker*."

"Surely you hail from some land before that?"

"If you're asking where I was born, I have no idea. I grew up in the free city of Illyris, however."

"That might be the first nation you've spoken of that I recognize."

Akos raised an eyebrow but continued anyway.

"It is an ancient nation, wasting away as it revels in its past glory."

"I see you hold no love for your former nation."

Akos didn't respond but took another sip of his wine instead. Anson seemed satisfied for the moment and didn't press the issue. Calia wondered what the man was getting at. If he wanted to broach the subject of a deal with them he'd had many opportunities to have done so by now.

"Lord Anson," Calia said, "if you don't mind my asking, why have you brought us here?"

Anson glared at her, and for a moment she thought he might not reply at all. Then he grinned.

"I have to admit," Anson said, "my reasons are purely selfish. I wanted to get the chance to speak with you before my rivals. You may have already noticed, but in case you didn't, my neighbors and I do not have the best relations. Each isle in this realm has its own god, much like me, and for one reason or another we all hate each other."

"Well, now that we've spoken," Akos said, "I assume we are free to return to our vessel and our realm?"

Anson's grin didn't waver, but Calia saw his eyes harden as they flicked toward Akos. The captain gazed back levelly, his eyes challenging. Calia realized that he was forcing Anson to reveal his true plans for them.

"I'm afraid we haven't had the kind of conversation I was hoping to have before you left," Anson said.

"Well, what would you like to speak about?" Akos asked. "I'm afraid we are running low on supplies. I'm anxious to get back to the realm of man before we've depleted them."

"You're certainly very forward. I take it they didn't teach manners in Illyris."

"It never came up."

Calia watched as a pall of tension thickened around the table. Her eyes flicked back and forth between the two men, wondering which of them would flinch first. Calia noticed that Valesa was looking around the room, marking where the servants and guards were standing.

Suddenly Calia felt very nervous. It was clear that Valesa was planning on having to fight her way out of the dining room. Calia knew that she would be worthless in a fight, and she didn't even remember the way to the front door of the keep. Even if they managed to escape from here, they would have to get past that enormous wall, and then go at least five miles to a town they would then have to navigate through. With only the five of them against the hundreds or even thousands of soldiers at Anson's back. The odds of that kind of escape didn't seem to be in their favor.

"Well then, I suppose it's right down to business," Anson said, leaning forward and lacing his fingers in front of his face. "But I feel there is no need to burden everyone with this conversation. I'm sure you're all very tired. Everyone, please go rest while Akos and I continue this talk."

• • •

Anson didn't say anything else as his guards and servants ushered the others out of the room. Akos waited with far more patience than he felt while the man refilled his wine glass. The man sat back in his chair, swirling the glass of wine and studying Akos. Akos studied him right back. He was sure now that there was something more than mere curiosity and trade on Anson's mind.

"You know," Akos said, "Lady Hailko is my employer and sister to a very powerful lord in Macallia. It would be more fruitful to speak to her about any hopes or plans you have."

"You may drop the act," Anson replied. "We both know I don't want something so benign as a trade deal. My designs for the realm of man are much larger."

Akos cocked an eyebrow but didn't say anything. Even if the man had no interest in peaceful trade, it still would have been more fruitful for him to speak with someone who had standing in the realm. He couldn't imagine what a privateer might have to offer that a lord of a powerful empire couldn't.

"Tell me, Akos, how long have you been around the sea?" Anson continued after another healthy pull from his wine glass.

"My entire life," Akos answered truthfully. "I've been a ship's boy since before I can remember."

"And how old are you now? I assume that you are very young to be a captain, but my impression of age is somewhat…filtered through my unique lens."

"I am twenty-eight. I'm not that young for a captain, but I am much more experienced in the role than most others my age."

"I am one thousand, five hundred and sixty-one years old."

Akos waited for the man to grin or give some indication that he was making a joke, but no such sign came. It seemed now that the others had left, the man was deadly serious. Not even the smug grin that Akos had come to expect in his short time knowing Anson was present.

Anson motioned to one of the servants who was waiting in the corner. The man stepped forward with a platter, unveiling the contents as he neared his lord. There was a single fruit sitting on the tray. It had a shape somewhere between an apple and a pear, and skin that appeared to be made from gold leaf. It was about the size of Akos's fist, and Anson looked at it after he'd taken it off the platter and dismissed the servant. He seemed to be lost in thought for a moment, contemplating the fruit as if Akos weren't in the room with him.

"I'll admit," Anson said as if addressing the fruit, "I didn't come to this realm as a god. I was almost seventy years old when I was marooned here. Our wayfarer became confused during our crossing and succumbed to the madness, dropping us here. I was a mere journeyman painter then."

"If the work in the atrium is yours," Akos said, "I'd say you are more than a mere journeyman."

Anson smiled, but did not look up. "It is true, I was very good at it. But I wasn't quite a master, and my health was failing. I needed to find something that could steady my hand and help me to make my mark on history before I passed into nothing. I'd heard that the elves had the secret to prolonging life, and, desperate for my masterpiece, I chartered a galley to take me there. When we wound up here, there was no Ferundan, but there was a small collection of men who had banded together, struggling to survive. Among these men was the former god of this island, Ferund."

Anson took a bite of the fruit, and it cracked like an apple. Akos wondered how it tasted. The flesh inside was the same golden color as the skin that surrounded it. Anson continued to eat it until there was nothing left but a core. Akos wondered if the man was playing some elaborate prank on him, or if he believed the story he was telling.

"Suffice to say, there was not room for both of us when I ascended," Anson said. "I didn't hate him, however. I was chosen for godhood, and he stood in the way. I could no more hate him than I could hate a log that had fallen in my path.

"As I grew in power, I realized that I was destined to be greater than merely god of this island. I am destined to be god of all men. That's why I was chosen so long ago. The other gods think they are the true rulers of their own lands, but in truth they are mere stewards. I have seen the truth. One day, this realm will bow to me, and then all realms will bow to me. I will take my rightful place as god over all creation."

"But…even a god needs help from time to time. Your vessel is the first outsider we've had enter the realm in three hundred years. Despite my best efforts, our science has stagnated since then. With your help, however, I could leap past my peers and take my rightful place as their ruler."

Akos could see where this was going now. Anson might not know the exact use of gunpowder, but it was clear he knew that the technology represented by Akos's ship was leaps and bounds above his own. He was right. Even if he could learn only the secrets of shipbuilding and weapon crafting that Akos could teach, he would have an enormous advantage over his rivals.

"And what would I get for helping you?" Akos asked. "Would I live like a king?"

"More than a king," Anson said. "You'd live as a demigod."

"Money?"

"What use would a demigod have for money? The world would leap to obey your every whim."

"Power?"

"Of course. You'd be second only to me."

"Women?"

Anson smiled and shook his head, as if bemused by the demands of a child.

"Once you've been around as long as I have, you will see that women are nothing more than a distraction. But so long as you desire them, you will have any and as many as you want."

"Oh? I get to live to fifteen hundred as well?"

"If you serve me faithfully. You'll find that I reward those who are loyal to me."

"And those who aren't?"

"I may not hate the log that sits in my path, but I do remove it."

"Fair enough. What exactly is it that you wish me to do?"

"For a start, you can build me a navy, and help me to understand your weapons. Assuming, of course, that you know how to do so."

"I do. What will happen to my crew while I do this for you?"

"I hope you'll understand, but I'll need them to stay here. I can't have them going back to the realm of man and spoiling the surprise. They'll be treated well. Yourself, your officers, and your employers will stay here as my honored guests, of course. Only until I can be sure of your loyalty, I assure you, and then they will be free to choose whatever they wish. Though I do hope you'll help them to see what an opportunity I am presenting them with. Particularly the wayfarer."

Akos leaned back in his chair and considered Anson's offer. If everything the man claimed was true, it was a very generous offer. The chance at a near eternal life with almost absolute power was tempting. Akos had never wanted anything but the simple life of a privateer and a happy retirement with Anastasia, but he would be lying to himself if he didn't admit that this offer was intriguing.

"I'll do it," Akos said.

"Wonderful." Anson smiled. "We'll begin tomorrow with a tour of my shipyard, so you can get an idea of what changes will need to be made. Is there anything I can get you to make your stay more comfortable?"

"In fact, there is."

Chapter 12

"Well that was…odd," Calia said. Valesa had returned to her post by the window and was staring out of it, lost in thought. Neither she nor Calia had said a word since being ushered back to their room by the armed guards. Calia guessed that neither of them knew what to say. This entire experience was alien to her, and she had to imagine that any training Valesa might have in this area was dwarfed by the situation. Preparation could go only so far after all.

"Yes, it was," Valesa agreed. "I wonder what Anson thought was too sensitive for our ears."

"I would imagine that he was offering him some sort of deal," Calia replied.

Valesa looked at her and raised an eyebrow. Calia shrugged in response.

"It's logical. We've both observed that Anson doesn't seem to care for women, so he wouldn't approach you or me, or even Vibia, for any kind of deal. And Vibius answers to Akos."

"I follow the logic," Valesa said. "I'm just surprised to hear it from you. I suppose I shouldn't be; you've always been a quick study."

Calia wondered if she should take some sort of insult out of that but decided that Valesa had meant it as a compliment. Calia had never been an expert judge of character, but she would have to learn quickly if she wanted to be of any use in this situation. She would likely have to learn a new set of skills in a short time if she wanted to have any real impact. But as Valesa said, she'd always been a fast learner.

Calia jumped once again when there was a sharp knock on their door. Valesa crossed to stand in front of her before the door opened to reveal the same guards as earlier. They stepped into the room without waiting for an invitation, and Valesa crossed her arms as she glared at them.

"Can we help you?" Valesa asked coldly.

"No, but Lady Hailko can," one of the guards said.

"With what exactly?"

"Captain Akos has...requested her company."

The other guard started to bark out a laugh, but the first one jabbed him in the ribs with an elbow. Calia wondered what Akos might want with her. She couldn't imagine that she had any skills or knowledge that he might need. And if Anson was trying to keep them from plotting, she couldn't imagine he would allow them to meet so simply. Then she noted the second guard's wicked smile, and her heart sank as she realized what he had in mind.

"If you'll come with us," the first guard continued, speaking to her.

"The hell she will," Valesa said, standing her ground.

Calia put a hand on her maidservant's shoulder. When Valesa glanced back at her, Calia shook her head enough for the maidservant to see. She could see the defiance in her bodyguard's eyes. Calia wasn't sure what she was doing either, but she gently pushed Valesa aside and stepped forward to accompany the guards. A glance back revealed to her a fuming and dumbfounded Valesa before the door closed.

Even though she would never claim to be an expert judge of character, Calia thought she would have realized if Akos were that type of man before now. Still, she'd made her snap decision not based on her own judgment. Calia refused to believe that someone as kind and gentlemanly as Vibius would be willing to follow and befriend someone who could do the things that these guards thought were going to happen.

Even as she told herself that, Calia's heart was pounding in her chest as they made their way up the stairs. If she was wrong, then she had no idea what might happen to her. For all she knew, it wasn't even Akos making the request. It could be a ploy by Anson to split them further apart. Calia scolded herself for not even considering that before jumping to join the guards.

They reached what had to be the top of the tower after several minutes of climbing stairs. Calia's legs were beginning to burn, her breath getting short, and her heart racing from the exertion. At least, that was the reason, she told herself, to explain the sudden weakness of her knees. If Calia ignored the cold ball of fear in her stomach long enough, it might go away. At least that was the plan, but it didn't seem to be working so far. The grinning guard stepped forward to bang on the door, while the first man stood back a little way with her. Calia noticed, with some indignation, that the guards waited for Akos to open his own door.

When he did, Calia began to regret her decision immediately. Akos was wearing nothing but his trousers. His unreadable mask of a face gave away nothing, but the way he was looking right through her made Calia's skin crawl. She tried to pull back, but the first guard was an immovable wall behind her, and she realized that she had nowhere to go but forward. Akos stepped back away from the door, motioning her in. Calia took a deep breath and stepped into the lion's den.

The door slammed ominously behind her, and Calia's heart almost froze with the sound. She turned to see that Akos was still glaring at her, though his expression had changed. Calia at least felt as if he were looking at her now, rather than through her, though she wasn't sure that was an improvement. He walked past her farther into his room, and Calia noticed that his scars were even more grisly up close.

The pounding of Calias's own heart drowned out any other sound. Her mouth was dry. The fear in her gut had only grown, and now it was threatening to make her lose control of her legs. She felt faint. She opened her mouth to say something, anything, that might help her get rid of some of this terror.

Akos held a finger to his lips. Calia's mouth snapped shut. Curiosity warred with fear as Akos turned his back to her and bent over a table. After a moment, curiosity managed to break through and enabled her to move again. Calia stepped around to where she could see what he was doing.

Akos was struggling with a quill and a piece of paper on the table, jotting something down. Before she knew what she was doing, Calia was standing at his shoulder, trying to read what he was writing. His handwriting was not as clear and concise as she was used to, but it was still legible.

Don't speak. Akos wrote. *They might be listening.*

Calia looked up to find that he was looking at her with an eyebrow raised. She opened her mouth to ask a question, but he jabbed the piece of paper with the quill with a look of mild annoyance written across his face. Calia snapped her mouth shut and held out her hand for the quill. Akos gave it to her, and she dipped it in the ink before writing a response.

Are you sure? Calia asked.

No, but I'm not going to risk it, Akos responded after a moment.

Why did you bring me here?

I need your help.

Calia looked up to see that Akos was looking around the room, as if trying to spot anyone listening in. The fear had all but disappeared, replaced by relief. Her faith in Vibius's judgment was well placed after all. Akos motioned for her to write something after a moment, and Calia realized she was sitting dumbfounded with the quill in her hand.

What do you need me to do?

Hold on to this cord.

Now Calia was very curious. She looked up, and Akos crossed over to the only window in the entire room. Unlike all the others, it was a full-size window. It seemed that the original architect had drawn the line with arrow slits at a hundred feet in the air. Next to that, Akos had fashioned a rope out of his bedsheets.

She frowned as she wondered what he planned to do with it. The rope was at most ten feet long. The drop had to be at least one hundred feet, if not more. There was no way he would be able to climb all the way down. She joined him by the window as he tied the makeshift rope around his waist.

After he was done, Akos picked up the loose end and handed it to her. Calia looked at it as if it were a snake and gingerly took it from him. As soon as she had it, Akos swung his legs out the window and set his feet on a slight ledge before turning around. Before she could speak, he was facing the window from the outside, looking up for handholds on the tower's face. Calia scrambled to take a better hold of the cord.

"What are you doing?" Calia gasped.

"I'm going to see if they are actually listening," Akos whispered back.

"Why am I holding this?"

"There's nothing close enough to tie off to. Now hold still and stay quiet until I give the all clear."

Without another word, Akos was clambering up the tower face. Calia could do nothing but grasp on to the ever-shortening bedsheet rope. She wondered what she would do if he were to fall. It wasn't as if she would be able to pull him back into the room on her own. She was a scholar, not an athlete, and Akos was made of solid muscle. The best she could do was slow his fall and hope he grabbed something before he pulled her out of the window with him.

Only a few tense moments passed, but it felt like an eternity. Calia half-expected one or more of the guards to kick down the door at any moment. But no guards came. Within a few agonizing minutes, Akos dropped back down and through the window. Calia peeled her white-knuckled fingers away from their grip on the bedsheet as Akos untied himself.

"There's no listening room," Akos said, his voice a whisper. "But watch your words regardless. I'll bet the two bastards at the door are listening in."

"Are you mad?" Calia hissed. "What if you had fallen?"

"I've been scaling the lines since before I could walk, and I've a good deal of experience scaling walls as well. This tower is old and in ill repair, no trouble at all."

"What was the rope for then?"

Akos shrugged. "Peace of mind?"

Calia didn't know what to say, so she ignored Akos and went to sit down. A pair of chairs faced the fireplace, and she took one of them. She put her hands out to warm them against the fire. She hadn't noticed it before, but the room was chilly. It was probably because of the elevation and the fact that Akos's window was nothing more than an open hole in the wall.

Rather than join her immediately, Akos went back over to the table. Calia watched as he scooped up the paper that they had written their messages on and tossed it into the fire, using the nearby poker to ensure that it burned to ashes. Once he was done, he sat across from her, peering into the fire as if it held the answer to a question that was burning away at his mind.

"What am I doing here, Captain?" Calia asked after a moment.

It was clear that Akos was doing something that he didn't want their captor to find out about. Calia could not imagine that he would have risked his life scaling the castle walls to see if there were any unwanted listeners. She didn't see how she could be of any use in this situation. She had no skills or knowledge that might help them get out of this kind of a situation. Calia thought he would have been much better off calling for Valesa. *Though, if they'd come for her the way they came for me*, Calia mused, *Valesa probably would have tried to kill him before he closed the door.*

"Please," Akos said. "I think we're past formalities now. Akos is fine. You're here because I needed a way to communicate with the others."

"What do you mean?" Calia asked. "Valesa is the only one they've put me with."

"After you leave here, I'm going to tell the guards to take you to Vibius's room."

"You don't think they will be suspicious of that?"

"Seeing how easily they agreed to bring you to me, I think they're used to their guests having…unusual tastes. Anson doesn't think much of women, and I'll bet that attitude has rubbed off on his staff."

"What did Anson wish to speak to you about after dinner?"

"He proposed a deal. If I build him a navy, he'll make me his right-hand man. Gold, women, immortality. Everything a man could desire."

"That's quite a deal."

It really was. Calia couldn't think of any reason why someone might turn something like that down. Even if it did mean working underneath someone like Anson. Most people would have agreed to the deal based on any one of those things.

"Did you accept?" Calia asked.

"I did," Akos said. "But only because I knew that we would all be slaves within the night if I didn't. Anson intends to conquer this realm and all the others."

"With you by his side."

"Well, yes," Akos admitted. "But I could never bring anyone else into slavery."

Several things clicked into place in Calia's mind. The last name Freedman was a common enough name in Macallia, but Akos wasn't Macallian by birth. In Illyris it was the name given to slaves who had, by some means or another, bought their freedom. The scars on his back were most likely from flogging. Now that Calia thought about it, she had never heard anyone on the ship speak of Akos before he took command of his own vessel. She'd always assumed it had never come up, but she realized now that they had purposefully avoided it.

"Oh," was all Calia could manage.

"I have no intention of keeping my promise to build his navy," Akos continued. "Unlike most other would-be warlords I've met, I don't doubt Anson's ability. I'll play along for now, though, until there is a chance to escape. Until then, I need to be able to communicate with everyone, and this seemed like the only option that wouldn't draw undue attention. It won't be without risks, however. If you don't wish to participate, I'll find a different method."

Calia considered it for a moment. Part of her mind screamed at her to refuse. That way if Akos was caught, she could pretend to be ignorant of the plot and at least save herself. She might not be able to have much of a life here, but it would be better than being dead.

Even as the thought crossed her mind, Calia discarded it. She had no desire to remain in this realm forever. It was less than an hour ago that she had resolved to do whatever she could to help Valesa plot their escape. Now Akos was presenting her with the perfect opportunity to do something that was well within her abilities. And Valesa was right when she said that Akos would most likely plan his escape to include them, even if it was for Vibius's sake.

She couldn't let everyone else take all the risks for her. Calia didn't think she'd be able to live with herself if she didn't at least try to help.

"I'll do it," Calia said.

"Perfect." Akos smiled. "I'm afraid I don't have any messages yet, other than be ready. I don't know how long it will take to get a plan together and earn enough trust to enact it, but I don't intend to stay here any longer than I have to. Even so, it could be months before I gain enough trust and autonomy to do anything."

"Is there anything else I can do to help?"

"Information is the key. We'll need as much of it as we can get. Try to learn everything you can about this island, the people here, and those behemoths. But, don't be too obvious about it."

"I'll do what I can."

"Thank you. I do have one other request."

"What do you need?"

"Please find a way to tell Valesa about what happened here. I'd like to keep all my appendages."

Calia struggled to restrain her laughter. She had to put her hand over her mouth until the urge passed. She wondered what her bodyguard was doing right now. *Most likely plotting the most painful way to kill Akos*, Calia thought. She could only hope that the woman hadn't done anything rash while she was gone.

"I'll take that under advisement," Calia replied.

Akos smiled for a moment, but it was gone as quickly as it came. His eyes went to the door and then to a clock that was ticking the time away in the corner. Calia wondered if he was as nervous as she was. If he was, his face gave none of it away. It was calming. She doubted that he could be as fearless as he acted, but Calia found that she was glad that he was on her side.

"I must say, Captain…Akos," Calia corrected herself, "you've surprised me."

"How so?" Akos asked.

"Well, I have to admit that I didn't have too high an opinion of you when we first met."

"I get that a lot."

"But, you've proven yourself to me. Valesa might take a little…a lot more convincing, but know I trust you."

Akos said nothing, but a wan smile pulled at the corner of his lips. He glanced back at the clock before rising to his feet.

"That's long enough," Akos said after a moment. "I don't want them getting too suspicious. I'm afraid I'll have to ask a few more things of you."

"What do you need?" Calia asked.

"I need you to make yourself look disheveled. As though your clothes were removed by force and then you threw them back on."

Once again, all Calia could manage was a surprised, "Oh."

Akos offered an apologetic smile.

"I need for Anson and his men to think that I am...ungentlemanly. Otherwise they might get suspicious of our method of communicating."

"Of course," Calia replied.

After a moment's hesitation, Calia set to work. It was harder than she'd thought it would be. She'd rarely ever had to go out without plenty of warning in her life. She didn't think she'd ever gone anywhere looking disheveled since she was a child. It took some effort to figure out what to do. Even though it pained her, she popped some of the buttons off her dress and tore some of the lace.

"How is that?" Calia said after she was satisfied.

"Good enough," Akos said. "Now, as the guards escort you down, try to look disgusted."

"All right, I think I can manage that. Anything else?"

"Yes, you need to be flushed."

"How will I manage that?"

"I have just the trick, and it will help fool the guards as well. Sorry about this."

Before Calia could ask what Akos meant, he dropped his trousers around his ankles. She looked at him dumbly for a moment before she felt her face turn beat red and spun around. No sooner had she turned toward the door than she felt Akos's hand on her back, guiding her toward the door. He flung it open and shoved her out, hard enough that one of the guards had to catch her to keep her from falling. She turned her head to see Akos addressing the other guard.

"Take her to my wayfarer," Akos commanded. It was somewhat shocking to see how fast his demeanor had changed from apologetic to vicious. "I'm in a sharing mood."

The door slammed shut and the guard turned to her as the other one helped her find her footing again. Rather than meet the guard's eyes, she looked down at the ground. Calia remembered that she needed to try to look embarrassed and ashamed. It didn't seem to matter too much. The guards hardly looked at her before they started to half-walk, half-carry her back down the stairs.

It wasn't long before they reached Vibius's room. Climbing down the stairs was much easier than climbing up them, and it gave her an easy excuse to stare at her feet and not have to look at either of the guards. Calia wasn't convinced that her meager acting abilities would be enough to fool anyone, but neither guard so much as said a word to her. She wondered if they were used to things like this, or if they had been trained not to care.

Just as before, the guard knocked on the door, and soon enough Vibius opened it. There was visible confusion on his face when he saw her, and Calia wondered if the look he had on his face was anger when he saw the state she was in. It was gone within a moment as Vibius looked back up toward the guards.

"The captain says it's your turn with her," the guard said with a grunt.

Vibius said nothing, but the blank look on his face turned to a smile, and he nodded. The guards released their grip on her, and Calia stumbled into Vibius's chambers. The door closed behind her with a heavy thud. Calia sagged with relief for a moment, before straightening up and looking around.

Vibius's room was much the same as hers, though it had only one bed. It wasn't large, and the only window was an arrow slit that faced out toward the courtyard. There was a small hearth and a pair of chairs facing it. Calia went over to one of the chairs and sat down heavily.

She hadn't noticed it while she was descending the stairs, but Calia's heart was pounding. This time she didn't even have the convenient excuse of physical exertion. Even that little bit of acting had terrified her. Calia was amazed that neither of the guards had seen through her or Akos's act and taken her to be questioned immediately. Perhaps they saw only what they expected to see. If they took their cues from their "god," they likely hadn't even taken a good look at her. It was the only explanation she could think of that made any sense.

Vibius crossed the room as well and sat down next to her. As she looked at him, Calia wondered how they were going to communicate. Unlike in Akos's room, there was no writing desk, nor did there seem to be any paper or ink. She glanced around as she wondered whether there was anyone listening in. Vibius caught her eye as he stoked the fire and seemed to read her mind.

"No one is listening," Vibius assured her. "Below this room is Vibia's room, above us is your room. The walls are not thick enough to conceal a listening room."

"Is everyone aboard the *Mist Stalker* an expert on these things?" Calia asked.

"No, but both Akos and I have some experience with this sort of situation."

"Where in all the realms did you get experience in this sort of situation?"

"Well, maybe not exactly this sort. I know the ways that nobles like to spy on each other, though, and I've taught him."

"Well at least someone knows what they're doing."

"I wouldn't go quite that far. I assume he had you called to his room to use you as a go-between?"

Now Calia was surprised. "How could you possibly know that?"

"We've used this ruse once before, a long time ago. The first time we met, in fact, thirteen years ago."

Calia wondered if Vibius had known Akos when he was a slave. Just the thought was an odd one. If she had never seen his back, or if he'd chosen a different name once he'd become a privateer, she never would have guessed that he was a former slave. He carried himself like a gentleman and a captain.

"I think I know the answer to this question," Calia said, "But I must ask anyway. Was Akos a slave at some point?"

Vibius sighed and leaned forward. He stared into the fire, and Calia could see the hesitation in his eyes. She realized it wasn't his secret to tell, and she shouldn't have asked. Her curiosity had gotten the better of her, like it always did. She considered dismissing the question, but there was no point in doing so now. Vibius would either answer, or he wouldn't.

"He doesn't particularly like anyone talking about it," Vibius said. "But Akos is trusting you with this, so I don't see why he would hide it from you. Yes, he was a slave for the first fifteen or so years of his life. I have always been disgusted by the very idea of slavery, but there weren't many ships that would take on a self-trained wayfarer and his sister, and we needed the money. So, I ended up in Illyris working aboard the galley of a particularly wealthy noble who liked to take pleasure cruises through the void. Akos was an oar slave aboard the vessel, but we became friends, and soon enough we conspired to free him and his brethren."

"And the noble never suspected anything?"

"No, not until it was too late. He was the type of man who would have gotten suspicious if he'd seen us speaking aboard the ship. But he had no hesitation in dragging one of his slaves to his wayfarer's room for...ahem...other purposes."

"Oh."

"I assume that Akos has judged Anson to be the same sort of man. I assume he didn't have any message for you this time. It's a little too early for him to have come up with anything useful."

Calia shook her head and leaned deeper into her chair. All this information was coming at her too fast, and she was struggling to make sense of it. It was little wonder now that Akos had so readily agreed to take her to the void, even if he had never intended to sail in. After rising from a slave to one of the most successful privateers in Macallian history, he would probably do anything necessary to keep from losing everything he had made for himself. Calia felt a pang of guilt that her brother had used the threat of revoking his letter of marque to get him to do what she wanted.

"I hope he didn't scare you too much," Vibius said sympathetically.

"I must admit," Calia said, "it was a bit of a shock when they knocked on my door and told me the captain wanted to see me."

"If I had to guess, Akos planned for your shock and used it to his advantage to better fool the guards. I'm surprised I didn't hear Valesa putting up more of a fight, though."

"I went with them willingly."

Vibius raised one eyebrow and cocked his head.

"I didn't think that any man you trusted so much could be the sort to take advantage that way," Calia said.

"That's quite a bit of faith you put in my judgment," Vibius said.

Calia shrugged. She couldn't explain it rationally. She'd acted more on instinct than anything else.

"I will say," Vibius said after a moment, "I'd been hoping to speak to you alone again. This wasn't quite the circumstance I had in mind, though."

Calia couldn't help but laugh at that. She covered her mouth and tried to quiet it down, but she couldn't stop herself. She could feel the tension that had been building in her drain out, and Vibius chuckled along with her. Calia could only hope that the soft crackle of the fire and the thick door had kept the guards from hearing their outburst. Slowly their laughter faded back into silence.

"Do you think you'd better get back to Valesa and ease her nerves?" Vibius asked after a long quiet moment.

Calia considered it. Valesa was probably pacing a rut into the floor trying to think of a way to rescue her. She shouldn't keep her waiting any longer than she had to. But…being around Vibius was making her feel like there was less to worry about. Calia knew it was silly; she was probably far safer with Valesa than with anyone else, but she couldn't help it.

What Akos was asking her to do was a risk. But if it paid off, it would help her as much as anyone else. But it was a risk she was taking on behalf of them all. Calia deserved to enjoy what little part of it she could. She stiffened her resolve and reached out across the chairs, taking Vibius's hand into her own.

"I think she'll keep a short while longer."

Chapter 13

The dockyards weren't much. Akos had seen dozens of dockyards throughout his life. Perhaps it was because of the reliance of the various kingdoms in the realm of man on naval power, but even the least of them were better than Ferundun's yard. Akos reminded himself that the facility had been created for galleys and small cargo vessels. Still, if he were planning to build a navy, there wouldn't any worse way to start it. Even starting from nothing would be better than utilizing this facility.

The horse beneath Akos shifted, and he had to resist the urge to clutch at its neck. The rolling deck of a ship in the harshest storm was nothing to him, but he had never picked up how to ride a horse. Vibius had tried to teach him once, but it hadn't taken very well. The horse Anson gave him had a bad attitude and kept trying to reach back and bite him. Akos knew that he was supposed to be thinking of how to improve the docks, but he was spending more time trying to stay in the saddle than he was planning improvements.

"What do you think?" Lorantes asked.

Akos turned his head to look at his handler, and the horse beneath him took it as an opportunity to try to throw him off. Akos had to grasp at the saddle horn to keep from being thrown. It gave him a little more time think of an answer. The honest answer was that the yard was a derelict pit that wasn't worth the lumber it was made with. Akos didn't think Lorantes would appreciate that assessment.

"It could use some improvement," Akos said. "But the foundation is there."

"I realize that compared to what you must be used to it isn't much," Lorantes said.

Akos had to resist the urge to agree. From what he understood, Lorantes was the head of Anson's navy. If it could really be called that. It didn't participate in naval battles; its sole purpose was to ferry troops around. The realm of behemoths seemed to be locked in the old method of land battles at sea, rather than the naval combat that Akos was used to. He wondered if it had anything to do with the fact that the gods of the islands felt the need to get their behemoths into combat as quickly as possible.

The thought of the beasts sent a slight shiver down Akos's spine, but he managed not to glance back at the behemoth that had followed them down to the docks. The creature had loped alongside them as they'd ridden out to tour the yard. Akos wondered exactly how fast they could move. It hadn't seemed to have any trouble keeping up with the horses, but they hadn't been pushing their mounts to the limit either.

Akos wondered whether Lorantes or the behemoth was his true handler. He knew that Lorantes was assigned to him in theory to bring him up to speed on the state of the navy. Akos knew that the man was there as much to keep a watchful eye on him as he was to facilitate Akos's new task. But something told him that the behemoth was the one that Anson trusted to keep him from misbehaving.

"Compared to most of the other isles," Lorantes said, "Lord Anson puts some effort into the upkeep of his vessels."

"How many does he keep in service?" Akos asked.

"We have ten war galleys and another ten configured as troop transports."

"We'll need to keep those spread out to intercept any incoming vessels to keep them from seeing what we're doing here. Then we'll need to expand the dockyards by quite a bit."

"Are the current docks insufficient?"

There was an edge of indignation in Lorantes's voice. Akos knew that the navy had always been his pet project, and the man seemed very proud of it. Akos wondered if he was going to try to stifle his work out of jealousy. Akos hoped so. He didn't know how long it would take to plan a feasible escape, but if he had an easy excuse for dragging his feet it might come in handy. Akos had no real intention of handing Anson a working navy.

"At best, I think we can build two modern warships in this space. That will do for a start, but I would assume Anson would like more than a pair of vessels."

"That would be a safe assumption," Lorantes admitted. "Lord Anson is not one to do things by half measures."

"Then we shall have to expand the docks. I also assume that you have work crews who can be moved to work on that?"

"You assume correctly once again. Lord Anson has ordered that you have any resources you need. He seems quite taken in by your strange vessel and the strange weapons it carries."

"The vessel is called a sloop, and it will be the mainstay of the navy we'll build here. But he has good reason for his fascination. With a pair of sloops, I could turn the entire galley fleet into splinters and flotsam."

Lorantes looked unconvinced, and Akos had to admit that he might be exaggerating a little. But only a very little. In fair weather his ships would outpace a galley over all but the shortest of distances. And so long as the galleys didn't reach them, the *Mist Stalker* would have no problems pounding them into nothing. It would be even easier than a cannon battle with the type of ship that Akos and his crew were used to. Compared to more modern vessels, galleys had shallower drafts and sat higher above the water. They would be little more than target practice for his gunnery crews.

"It's nothing to be ashamed of," Akos said. "Technology has advanced quite a bit since the last time a ship came this way to share their secrets."

The man stiffened at the comment, and Akos could tell he'd struck a nerve. He'd been wearing his captain's mask since before he'd left his room this morning, but he still had to resist the urge to smile. If he could make an enemy of Lorantes, it would give him plenty of opportunity to drag his feet. The longer he could draw this process out without yielding any significant results, the better. Though, he did have to be careful not to test Anson's patience to the breaking point. The urge to smile disappeared as he realized that he was dancing on a plank that he didn't know the width of. The thought sobered him significantly.

"Would you care to see your office?" Lorantes asked.

"Anything to get off this damned horse," Akos responded as the creature shifted beneath him.

The pair made their way down the gentle hill toward the dock with Lorantes in the lead. Akos was struggling to keep up without being tossed from the saddle. He had a feeling that Lorantes was going a little faster than was necessary just to give him trouble. It was good to know that he was a petty man; it could help Akos plan how to antagonize him. They arrived soon enough, however, and he was thankful that they could hand their horses over to a waiting groom before heading inside. A quick glance over his shoulder noted that the behemoth was lounging a short distance away, its pitch-black eyes following everything he did. Akos suppressed a shudder and stepped into the building.

The offices were nothing special. In fact, there wasn't even anything in them. Only one had a desk, and it looked to be Lorantes's. The man walked over to the chair behind it and fell heavily into it. Akos studied his handler. Lorantes was of middling age, his black hair graying at the edges and the lines in his face deepening. He had a soft face, and a gut that was only a few good meals away from needing a new belt. It was clear that he was not a physical threat, but with the monster outside waiting for them, he didn't need to be.

Despite his initial thoughts of the man, Akos knew he couldn't let his guard down. He was playing a part to get Anson to drop his suspicions, and it was more than likely that Lorantes was doing the same. Whatever else Akos thought about Lord Anson, it was clear that the man was no fool. Akos doubted that he would assign a bumbling idiot to watch over him for signs of betrayal.

Akos would have to make sure that he was careful in plotting his crew's escape. It might take some time to earn enough trust and leeway to do what would need to be done. But the inklings of a plan were already beginning to form in his mind. He strode over to a window that faced the yard, crossing his arms behind his back as he looked out over it thoughtfully.

"I think I was mistaken," Akos said after a long moment. "These docks are insufficient."

There was a grunt as Lorantes struggled out of his chair to join Akos at the window. He gazed out over the yards with anger shining in his eyes, trying to see whatever Akos was seeing. Akos continued to sweep his gaze over the yard. *I'm not entirely lying*, Akos said to himself. The docks would be insufficient if Anson wanted a modern navy and the capability to sustain it. At least, if he wanted it done anytime soon. It just so happened that changing facilities would help Akos with his own plans as well.

"Now that we are here, I can see that this is much too small," Akos continued. "And there isn't enough room to grow in the way we require. Are there any other shipyards on the isle that we could use?"

"The only other yards are smaller than this," Lorantes said grumpily.

"Then it seems we will have to make our own. Do you have a map of the isle?"

Lorantes nodded before returning to his desk and rummaging around inside. He pulled an old roll of parchment out and spread it across the table. Akos spread the parchment out with his hands and studied it while the man looked for something to weigh down the corners.

At a glance, it looked like the only natural harbor on the island was this one, in Ferundun Bay. The map was old and didn't have much detail, but the most important terrain features were all there. It seemed that much of the island was covered in jungle. There was a small spine of mountains that started near Ferundun and ran through the center of the isle.

Akos was surprised to see that there weren't many other settlements marked besides Ferundun. The island was even more sparsely populated than he thought. That could be good or bad, depending on factors that he didn't know. It might help them to escape if they didn't have to worry about running into populated areas often, but there could be more sinister reasons why those areas were unpopulated.

The thought of being hunted through the jungle by a behemoth was terrifying. Akos would have to find out whether there were any in the wild, or if they were all under Anson's control. He didn't know how he would go about that without raising suspicion, but he would have to find a way.

"I've personally scouted a few places to make bigger yards," Lorantes said. "But it was never high enough on Lord Anson's priority list for him to waste resources on."

"Where?" Akos asked.

"The best that I've found was here," Lorantes motioned at the map. "It's close enough to the mines and manufactories, and it has plenty of nearby lumber."

Akos studied the point on the map that the man had indicated. It was on the southwestern part of the island. If his guess was right, it was only a few days' ride west of where his crew had put ashore. With only the map to go by, Akos thought that the man might be right. There were no shallows or reefs marked on the map, and he spotted the resources that the man referred to.

"Do you have a realm map?" Akos asked.

"Why do you need to see that to decide where to put a shipyard?" Lorantes asked.

"If this realm behaves like the others, then most storms come from the center and head outward. I assume that since we didn't sail for long before hitting this island, it's toward the edge of the realm. But I'm not going to invest resources into a yard that will get knocked over by the first major storm that comes our way."

Lorantes pondered that for a moment, stroking his graying mustache before reaching into his desk and producing another map. Akos looked over it for a long moment, before realizing that he didn't even know what the name of the isle was. In all the excitement of the last few days, it hadn't seemed very important.

"Where are we?" Akos asked.

Lorantes indicated the island with a finger, and Akos looked at it. The name Logathia was inked next to the island. Akos studied the map for a long moment. The isle sat in the southwestern quarter of the realm, which meant that most storms would come in from the northeast. It seemed that Lorantes's choice was a good one after all.

Akos flipped back to the other map, as if continuing to consider the geography of the isle. He was trying to memorize the geography of the entire realm. It wasn't particularly hard. There was a large center landmass, the largest continent in the realm, surrounded by smaller isles.

It was arrayed almost like a wagon wheel, with a central hub and spokes running out in several directions. Once he was sure he had the maps memorized, as well as he could in one sitting, anyway, Akos rose.

"How soon can we take a tour of this site?" Akos asked.

Lorantes paused to consider it for a moment. He stroked the salt-and-pepper goatee that covered his chin as he thought. It seemed that even if he was petty and indignant, Lorantes wanted to see the navy grow and improve.

"We can leave tomorrow morning, most likely," Lorantes said. "We'll need to gather men and supplies for the ride, and it's almost midday."

"How far is it from Ferundun?"

"Several days' ride."

"Then we shouldn't waste any more time here. Let's get back to the castle and begin making our preparations."

Lorantes scowled at him, clearly unused to being ordered about by anyone other than Anson. Akos ignored his dirty looks and exited the room without another word. Whether the man liked it or not, Anson had put Akos in charge of this project, and he would obey Akos's orders. The fact that it could get under Lorantes's skin and cause him to resist Akos's orders was nothing more than a potential perk. If they set up their project several days away from Lord Anson's castle, Lorantes might think he'd be able to get away with it as well.

Being able to plot his escape without Anson staring over his shoulder would be nice, but it had its drawbacks as well. It would make it that much more difficult to communicate with the rest of his crew. He was sure that if he requested it, Anson would send any of the women he asked for along with him, but he might get suspicious if Akos continued to send them back and forth. It was one thing to send them up and down a flight of stairs, but it would be an entirely different prospect to send them between cities.

Akos would have to come up with some other way to get messages to Vibius and Leodysus. Not to mention getting them all together when it was time to put whatever plan he dreamed up into action. Akos sighed as he mounted his horse. He'd known it would not be easy to escape from Anson's clutches. His best bet was to play along for now and try to win some freedom for his crew before acting. Not that Anson was likely to let that happen until he was certain of Akos's loyalty.

Problems for another day, Akos thought to himself. It looked as if he would have plenty of time to figure out the solutions to the flaws in his escape plan. First, he needed to focus on deciding what that plan would be. There were several ideas forming in his mind, but they would all need fleshing out and examining before he tried to set any of them in action.

Before any of that, however, it seemed that Akos would have to get used to this damned horse. It looked as though they would soon be spending a lot of time together. Akos reached down to pat the creature's neck, but when he touched it, the horse tried to reach back and bite him. *Definitely a good omen for things to come*, Akos mused.

Chapter 14

Calia was finding that the most difficult thing about her captivity was the sheer boredom. She knew it could be much worse. Anson could be forcing them to work or torturing them or doing any other manner of thing. But in this situation, Calia was worried that she might get cabin fever.

It was even worse than it had been when they sailed aboard the *Mist Stalker*. At least there she had been allowed to converse freely with anyone she chose. In Anson's castle, Calia knew that every word had to be guarded lest she reveal too much to one of the ever-present guards. She had decided along with Vibius that letting the guards, and through them Anson, know too much about the other realms was more likely than not a bad thing. If the worst did happen, and they somehow forced Akos to build them enough of a navy to invade, Calia would at least want her homeland to have a fighting chance.

At least we aren't locked in our rooms anymore, Calia thought. She had to count the small blessings. Ever since Akos had left to scout out a location for a new shipyard, Anson had allowed the captive crew to roam certain parts of the castle. They were even allowed to congregate and speak with each other. Calia had not understood why he would risk that at first, but then she realized that he was afraid of Akos and Vibius plotting together, but not the rest of them.

She'd tried to think of a way to use that to her advantage, but she'd come up empty. With the ever-present guards, there was no way that Calia could talk to anyone about anything that might help them to escape. She could only sit around and read while she waited for something to happen. It was infuriating.

At least the books were interesting. Calia was leafing through a book that detailed the history of the first castaways who had been unfortunate enough to enter the realm. As was expected, their wayfarer had gone completely mad, and they had seen no choice but to try to make the best of the situation. They'd begun to scout out the islands, making landfall where they thought they could form a city.

The place that they'd landed was now known as Dead Man's Coast.

The behemoths at the time were nothing more than beasts, the history said. It wasn't until the rise of the gods that they were tamed. Even so, it seemed that they could be killed. Several dozen ships lost themselves in the early days of exploring the ways, and some had managed to survive long enough to pool their resources and at least carve out an existence among the isles.

It was a fascinating tale. Calia had to wonder how much of it was true. Certainly, Anson seemed to exert some control over the monsters. But that could all be taming and clever training. It would be much easier to control a populace if they thought you were a god, rather than a warlord with trained monsters at your disposal. Though, having seen the monsters, Calia thought that was an effective control as well.

Calia wanted nothing more than to speak of her readings with someone. Anyone would do at this point. Normally she spoke to Valesa, though lately she would have preferred Vibius. Calia knew that she couldn't process something she'd read until she had spoken it aloud. In any other circumstance she would have found the nearest interested person and talked the person's ear off about the subject, but these weren't normal circumstances.

Calia was worried about Anson getting wind of one of these conversations and deciding that she was trying to gather information for some reason other than pure curiosity. She didn't want to do anything that might jeopardize their chances of escaping. Calia worried about being discovered, even though she hadn't done anything to raise suspicion since the first night that Akos had called for her.

It had been half a week since the captain's departure, and her anxiety grew every day. It seemed that his ruse hadn't so much as raised a single eyebrow, however. Calia thought that she would face much more scrutiny than she had. She wasn't sure whether to feel relieved or indignant. It was clear that Anson and the guards of this place did not think women were capable of much. Calia knew that worked to their advantage, but it still annoyed her.

There were some perks to it, however. Anson was very intent on keeping Vibius happy. He was very aware that the wayfarer was the only key to ever fulfilling his dreams of a multirealm empire. Vibius had informed her that he'd made the same deal with Anson as Akos had in the days before. In exchange for wealth, women, power, and the possibility of an eternal life, Vibius had promised to be his wayfarer. Little did Anson know that Vibius had as little intention of keeping his promise as Akos did.

And their arrangement benefited her because it allowed for Vibius to call for her without raising suspicion. *Well,* Calia corrected herself, *without arising* Anson's *suspicion.* Valesa, she was sure, had her own suspicions. Calia had managed to find a way to explain to her what transpired the night Akos called for her and the plan when she was sure she wouldn't be overheard. She'd still been furious with Akos, but at least she'd understood the need to keep up appearances. And more importantly, Valesa had agreed not to kill the captain on sight.

Vibius had called for her every night since then, however. Calia was sure that Valesa suspected that they were doing a little more than chatting the time away. But they really were chatting. At least part of the time. It wasn't any of Valesa's business anyway. Whatever the woman suspected, she had kept it to herself, and Calia was grateful. She didn't think she could handle a conversation about it yet. It wasn't exactly a traditional courtship, but at least now she knew that the wayfarer was interested in her. And these were not traditional circumstances.

"An interesting choice." Anson's sudden words almost made Calia drop the book from her hands.

"It's certainly informative," Calia managed once she'd recovered her nerves.

"Mmm. Do you happen to know if Vibius is here? I had something to ask him."

"Um, yes, he's over there."

Anson smiled and nodded in thanks, and then he was gone. Calia had allowed her mind to wander, and all but forgotten where she was.

She knew she couldn't do that anymore. This place was too dangerous. Whether they thought much of women or not, the men in the castle would notice eventually if she continued to act so skittish.

Calia watched as Lord Anson made his way over to Vibius, wondering what he wanted to speak about. Not for the first time, Calia wondered how Vibius could smile and act as a friend and servant to a man she knew deep down he despised. Through their conversations, Calia had learned that he hated slavery and its perpetuators almost as much as she imagined Akos did. How he could hide that much vitriol was beyond her.

Calia did her best to pretend to focus on the book, an idle hand turning the pages as she strained her ears to listen to Vibius's conversation. It was no use, however; she was too far away. Calia brushed it aside and was about to continue reading when Anson departed, and Vibius rose and strode over to her.

"We've been invited along on a hunt," Vibius said. "All of us who are here in the castle, that is."

"A hunt?" Calia asked.

"Yes, though he was somewhat vague on what we would be hunting. I've learned it will require a ship and about a week's worth of sailing each way. I've accepted, but I'll understand if you or Valesa don't want to come along."

"Actually, I'd love the opportunity to get out of the castle for a while."

"Splendid. He said we would leave tomorrow morning."

"Well then, I'd best go prepare."

Calia rose and excused herself before returning to her room. The entire way she wondered why Anson would invite them along on a hunt. It was probably a show of power, or perhaps he wanted the wayfarer to feel like he was part of the upper crust of his society. *There's no reason it can't be both*, Calia reminded herself.

Still, she hadn't been lying when she'd said that she was happy for the opportunity. Calia was so bored that she would have jumped at the chance to get out of the castle regardless of what that entailed. She'd never joined her father or brother when they'd gone hunting, despite their best efforts to include her.

This would also give her the opportunity to see more of the realm. That had been the entire reason for coming here in the first place. Though it had been only a week since Calia had crossed into this realm, it felt as if it was an eternity ago. So much had happened so fast that Calia wondered if she had truly lived it, or if it was all a nightmare.

If it wasn't a nightmare, she would need to learn everything she could about this realm before returning to her own. Calia almost laughed as she realized how all this would sound to her peers at the university. One thing was certain; this was going to blow all their research papers away.

∴

Dozens of men milled about, making camp at the edge of the trees. If it had been his own crew, Akos would have been right alongside them, helping however he could. Unfortunately, they were all Anson's men, and Akos had no desire to help them in any way. If he were being completely honest with himself, he could do a while without Lorantes's incessant chatter as well.

So, he stood at the ridge that overlooked the ground Lorantes had proposed. It was three days' ride from Anson's castle through dense forest. Fortunately, there was a trail to follow. Lorantes seemed to have been planning this for a while, just waiting for Anson to give him the go-ahead. The man was passionate about building a navy. Or perhaps he wanted something to lord over his peers and use to curry more of his god's favor.

Either way, Akos was glad for at least that much preparation. It would have been miserable to try to make their own trail through the jungle. It would have taken at least twice as long, and he was already nervous leaving his crew so far away in the care of madmen.

Leodysus would be able to take care of himself, and so would the rest of the crew. Akos knew that they were fighters, every man, or they would not have lasted long on his vessel. Vibius on the other hand, was very much not a fighter. He was a calm, patient man. But it was rare that anyone threatened violence to a wayfarer. Vibius was tough, but he was no fighter.

Not that Anson was likely to risk harming him. The man knew that Vibius represented his only chance of reestablishing contact with the outside world. If his dreams of realm-spanning domination were to come to fruition, he would need Vibius, at least until he could find other wayfarers. Akos knew that the last thing he could do was allow either of the wayfarers to remain here. Anson didn't know about Vibia, but if he somehow discovered her gift, she would be as good as a slave. A well-taken-care-of slave, perhaps, but neither she nor Vibius would ever be free to make their own decisions again.

Akos turned his mind from the people he'd left behind and brought it back to the present. This was all but a perfect place for a dock. Lorantes must have scoured the entire coast looking for this. There was plenty of room for a large drydock, enough wharves for an entire fleet, and all the materials would be easy to bring in. They would have to carve a trail down from the manufactories to this area, and there would be a lot of construction, but once they'd laid down the infrastructure, it would be the optimal place.

And its distance from the castle meant that Akos could formulate his schemes without direct oversight from Anson. Lorantes might be easy enough to fool, but Anson was a different beast. Akos wanted to lie to Lord Anson as little as he could get away with. There was something in those smug eyes that told Akos that Anson was reading him like an open book.

Akos knew his preparations would have to be thorough. Not only were they outnumbered by hundreds, maybe even thousands, to one by Anson's soldiers, but they also had to contend with the behemoths. Akos still had no idea what their true capabilities were, but he didn't want to find out the hard way. Just being around the monsters sent a chill down his spine. He already knew more than he ever wanted to about the creatures.

When he'd asked why the soldiers were leading extra horses along, Akos had been met with laughter and promises that he'd find out. On their second night along the path, he'd found out. One of the horses was cut loose and sent running through the jungle. The behemoths tore off after it, like racing dogs when their kennels opened. Akos watched the dark jungle as he heard the horse screaming and watched as the behemoths wandered back into camp some time later. Their overwide mouths were dripping gore, and their clawed fists were coated halfway to the elbow.

Akos was not a squeamish man. He was familiar with death. He'd caused it, both by his own hand and through his crew. He'd witnessed it up close and personal, driving his blade through his enemies and holding crewmen and friends while they breathed their last breath. But something about these monsters set his mind on edge. If Akos had to guess, it was the way their mouths lolled open in hideous, bloodstained caricatures of a smile.

One of them was lounging not far from where Akos stood. He did his best not to acknowledge its presence. If he so much as glanced toward it, he would spend the rest of the day nervously glancing to see if it had moved. It was better to pretend that he was not afraid of it in the least. If he had a weapon, he might believe himself. But he knew that right now he was at the complete mercy of Anson's pet war beasts.

"What do you think?" Lorantes asked as he joined Akos at the ridge.

"This is a good place," Akos said. "How long did it take you to find it?"

"I've been scouting for years."

And Anson ignores you until I come along, Akos thought. *That must sting your pride.*

Aloud Akos said, "You did well. This place will do. We'll head back in the morning and get the labor teams together. The first thing they'll need to do is clear back the woods to make their temporary living spaces."

"Temporary? Do you think they'll be leaving?"

"No, but I would imagine a town will spring up around the docks after some time. Then the residences will become more permanent."

"I doubt anything will 'spring up,' as you say. Lord Anson will decide whether or not there is a new settlement here."

Akos nodded as though he understood, careful to keep the anger off his face. The very idea that someone could tell people where they could or couldn't live annoyed him. Even the most authoritarian regimes of the realm of man allowed their commoners some freedoms.

There are no common men here, Akos reminded himself. *Only slaves. Some just have gilded collars.* If Akos needed any more reason to resist Anson's offer, he had it.

"Tell me, Lorantes," Akos said. "Lord Anson introduced you as Sir Lorantes. What rank do you hold?"

"Well, I am a count," Lorantes said, surprised by the sudden change in conversation. "Lord Anson raised me from the ranks of his navy to the county of Lorantes. My true name is Culvin Narst."

"Impressive. Is that common here?"

"No, it is quite rare for Lord Anson to raise commoners to his nobility, but it isn't unheard of. He recognized my abilities and my loyalty."

"Is a count very high in his nobility?"

Lorantes bristled. "No, it is the lowest rank. Above it are dukes and princes."

"Princes? I was led to believe that Anson didn't have any need for such worldly desires."

"I don't understand."

"Where I am from, a prince is a son of a king. Are these princes not Lord Anson's sons?"

"Lord Anson is no mere king. He is a god."

Something in his face must have given away his true emotions. Lorantes waved his hand in a dismissive gesture and continued.

"I doubted as well, in my youth. But as I grew into maturity, I began to understand. His face has not aged so much as a day from the first day I saw him as a boy to now. Over fifty years, and he hasn't so much as a gray hair. And the way he commands the behemoths...trust me when I say that you too will come to know that he is a god."

Akos turned to the man but said nothing. After a while, he turned back to the coast, watching as the sun began to set. It seemed that the sun set in the west in this realm, much like it did in the realm of man. It turned the water before him crimson and the clouds in the horizon all the different shades of red and purple.

"Well, tomorrow we should head back and begin our preparations," Akos said. "I think I can smell the cooking fires starting."

"I do believe you're right," Lorantes said. "I think I'll break open that cask of wine I brought."

"I'm sure your men will appreciate it."

"I don't know why they would; it's all for me. If they want their own they'll have brought it."

Akos raised an eyebrow, and Lorantes offered a wry smile. Akos couldn't tell if he was telling the truth. He supposed that he would find out shortly. Akos took one last look over his shoulder at the future sight of his shipyard and then turned back toward the camp.

It was time to begin his preparations, both the ones that Lorantes would see and the ones he wouldn't. He'd already begun to settle on a scheme. Now all that was left to Akos was to find the proper tools and people to put in place to make it a success.

Chapter 15

"I must admit," Vibius said as he stood on the deck of Anson's personal galley, "It is odd being on a ship that I'm not working on."

"Surely you had to take a ship as a passenger at some point in your life," Valesa replied.

"I have, but it has been a very long time. I have been a wayfarer since I was a boy, and wayfarers rarely go anywhere they aren't being paid to go."

The group stood near the prow of the galley, where the din of the drums was less deafening. Despite the wooden deck between them and the oarsmen, the drums were loud. The steady beat only changed at planned intervals, when the ship was switching out the rowers or when they were trying to sleep. The sails were down and full of wind, but Anson did not allow his oarsmen to let up their pace.

The drums had begun to worm their way into Calia's consciousness. She heard them even when she was asleep, even though the oarsmen did not row at night. For over a week they had been pounding for every waking moment. If one listened closely enough, Calia was sure that they would hear the beat of the drums of the two barges that followed along behind them. Calia didn't know how anyone could put up with it for much longer than that. Fortunately, Anson had assured them that they were nearing the island where he liked to hunt.

Despite their nightly dinners, Calia still couldn't recall Anson telling them what they would be hunting. There wasn't much doubt in her mind that it would be men. She'd come to the morbid realization some nights before. If Anson were anything as old as he claimed to be, and she was beginning to believe that he was, what else could still hold his interest? And why would he need a half dozen behemoths to hunt with?

The very idea made her sick to her stomach. The fact that she had so agreed to the journey blind, without considering everything beforehand, made her even sicker. It was unlike her to *not* overthink things.

Still, there was nothing that could be done about it now. It wasn't as if Anson would turn the galley around and sail a week and a half back to Ferundun on her account. She would have to see this through to whatever grisly end it entailed. Calia consoled herself with the thought that Anson might insist that they stay behind on the ship or in camp while he took Vibius out to hunt.

The only good thing about this expedition was that she was learning quite a bit about the society of the realm. Calia hadn't been bold enough to ask for herself, but Vibius mentioned that she wished to write a tome on the realm and Anson's isle for the realm of man to understand it better. Lord Anson thought it was a marvelous idea and agreed to allow her to interview his officers so long as she wrote him briefings on the nations of the realm of man. On the surface, Anson claimed that he wanted to know the nations better for trade purposes, but Calia knew that what he truly wanted was to know his enemies before he attacked.

It seemed that the entire society of this realm was based around the raising and upkeep of the behemoths. They, unsurprisingly, required a great deal of meat to live. Large amounts of Logathia's jungles had been cleared over the years to provide enough ranchland to keep them from feeding on humans. Calia shuddered at the thought of a behemoth's massive jaws tearing apart a human body.

Their purpose, Calia imagined, was much the same as the knights of old in her own realm. The behemoths represented the pinnacle of military power and in a realm that consisted of dozens of warlords vying with each other for power. Their upkeep was understandably a top priority. The common soldier was important as well. But they seemed to exist more to keep the population in line than to fight against the kings of the other isles.

They prefer to be called "gods," Calia reminded herself. No matter how many times she repeated the thought, the title wouldn't stick. She wasn't a particularly religious person, but she refused to believe that these were anything but men who had discovered a way to extend their natural lives to unnatural lengths. To her, the gods were the beings that created the realms and the ways, not the men who craved dominion over those realms.

You'd better at least learn to pretend, Calia told herself. *I very much doubt that any of them will be very forgiving if you raise that point to them.*

Each of the *gods* used his common soldiers to keep their large population of slaves in line. These slaves seemed to do all the physical labor that was required to keep a kingdom running. Above them in the social sphere were the common workers, who, by Calia's judgment at least, were slaves with more skills. They represented the craftsmen and merchants of the realm. Though, Calia wasn't sure if merchant was the right term for them. There was no form of currency here. Anson had complete control over all resources on his island. The more appropriate title was distributors, or quartermasters. There didn't seem to be any international trade at all.

That explains the technological stagnation, Calia thought to herself. International, and even interrealm, trade was known to most who studied such things to be one of the main drivers of innovation. Especially to nations such as the highly mercantile Empire of Macallia; if there was a better and cheaper way to do something, it was adopted as quickly as possible. Here it seemed that any technological advancements that were stumbled on were closely guarded, and the only thing the isles shared with each other was bloodshed.

What little advancement that had been made since the last ship had blundered into the void was because of the noble class that the gods kept around themselves. Though they were not nobles in any sense of the term as she knew it. They were not autonomous lords free to govern their fiefs as they saw fit within the structure of the king's law as they would have been in the ages past of the realm of man. Neither were they the modern nobility that she had come from, inheritors of ancient titles that granted them certain extra rights in exchange for certain extra responsibilities.

Instead, they seemed to be nothing more than proxies for Anson. They were allowed to do only the things that he had ordered.

They were more like overseers, making sure that Anson's orders were carried out in a way that their god approved of. Even the ranks involved seemed to make little practical difference. A prince had no more power or import than a count other than the perceived favor of Lord Anson, and the additional luxuries he was given.

Calia would have been impressed with the whole thing if it weren't so disturbing. Anson seemed to have created a society of slaves that enforced itself. Sure, he stood over it with the ever-present threat of the behemoths. But the lords did most of the enforcing for him, despite having very little freedom themselves. And the people held him up as a god, further cementing the order he had created.

All these things combined to help Calia realize that Anson was not someone to be trifled with. Whether he had knowingly created this system, or somehow lucked into it, he was taking full advantage of it. The man wasn't stupid, and he had more experience than anyone else could ever hope to match.

Although he called himself a god, he was still a man. He would make mistakes. He would have his blind spots. Vibius and Akos seemed to have found one. Anson seemed to think that all men were as greedy and ambitious as he was. Perhaps that was true in this realm, but it wasn't true for everyone. *Hopefully*, Calia thought, *that's enough to get us out of this wretched realm.*

"Lady Hailko?" Vibius's voice brought her back to the present.

"Oh, yes?"

"Are you all right?"

"She gets like that when she's thinking," Valesa said. "Goes to a whole other world."

"I'm fine," Calia said.

"I was asking if you'd ever sailed before our expedition."

Calia was thankful for the small talk. If they'd let her go much longer, she'd have convinced herself that their escape plans would never work and that they were all doomed. Instead. she focused on chatting with the others and the beautiful day around them. Calia could worry about everything else later.

• • •

"Welcome to the Isle of Sanctuary," Anson said as the rowboats hit shore.

Calia accepted Vibius's hand as she stepped out of the boat and onto the sand. The soldiers who had landed before them were already busy setting up camp some distance from shore. It seemed that Sanctuary was much more temperate than Logathia. Calia wondered if it was the cool breeze that was causing a shiver to go down her spine as she looked around, or if her nerves were finally getting the better of her.

The beach was deserted, except for their group. *It wasn't as if I was expecting a welcoming party*, Calia reminded herself. Still, Anson had informed them that this was the biggest isle in the realm, more akin to a continent than any of the other isles. Calia had expected to see at least some sign of life here, in the original place that humanity had managed to carve out a place to live in the realm of behemoths.

The group made their way toward the camp, flanked on either side by several behemoths. Calia had managed to avoid ever having to go near them on the ship, but now it seemed that they were the honor guard. Fortunately, the creatures seemed to be focused outward, though with a pair of eyes on either side of their skulls, it was hard to tell.

Several of Anson's higher-up nobles were waiting there at the camp. These men were considered princes, though it seemed to Calia that they filled the same role as Valesa did to her. Calia very much doubted that any of them shared the same bond as she did with Valesa, though she was sure that they would all very much like to. Closeness to Lord Anson seemed to be the main differentiator in the circle of nobility. Though she'd never seen any official ranking or heard Anson speak of one, they all seemed to know their place within the informal structure they'd created.

"My lord," one of the princes said with a deep bow. "We've taken the liberty of scouting ahead."

"Have you now?" Lord Anson replied. "What did you find?"

"We already found a pack gathering itself. If we move now, we might catch them unawares."

"Well there is enough time left in the day. But I'll leave it up to my guest. It's been a long voyage, and he might want to rest for a while before launching right into the hunt."

The crowd turned to Vibius, who smiled and spread his hands.

"If you say there is enough time, then I see no reason to delay," Vibius replied. "We can rest later."

"Excellent," Lord Anson replied. "I think you'll find this quite the spectacle. Banin, fetch the horses."

Calia thought the prince would fall over trying to bow and turn to do as he was told at the same time. The other princes made small talk as they waited, but soon enough Banin was back with several dozen horses. Calia was familiar enough with a horse that she wouldn't embarrass herself, but it had been some time since she'd ridden last. She hoped it would come back to her fast enough that she'd avoid looking foolish.

Anson didn't seem to want to waste much time. He was mounted and trotting away from the camp with his behemoths in tow before Calia was even in the saddle. She and Valesa were among a large group of soldiers and nobles trying to catch up to the lord. Their rather large party made its way inland, picking its way down various trails they found in the underbrush.

Despite the chill, the plains were a nice change from the jungles of Logathia. Geralis was a temperate port, and the area around it was rolling farmland. Sanctuary looked like what she imagined that same farmland had looked like before anyone had come around to cultivate it. The underbrush was thick, but not impassable, and there were scattered copses of trees.

They rode for some miles, with Banin at the head of the column leading them. Calia wondered how long they expected this pack to stay in one place. Almost an hour had passed before they slowed to a stop. Anson gestured for Vibius to join him at the head of the column, and Calia instinctively followed. Her natural curiosity had overridden her trepidation about their expedition.

"Banin tells me that the pack is gathered over the next hill," Anson said in a hushed tone. "Normally I would go on to hunt alone while my princes watch, but I feel like making an exception today. You and your friends are welcome to join me."

"Thank you, I will," Vibius replied.

Before anyone had a chance to ask Calia or Valesa, Anson nodded and turned to begin riding up the hill. Vibius spurred his horse after them. Calia was about to follow when she felt a hand touch her arm. She turned to see that Valesa was watching her with a worried look in her eye.

"Are you sure about this?" Valesa asked.

"We've come this far," Calia replied. "Might as well see why. We need to know what he is capable of."

The worry didn't disappear from Valesa's eyes, but she nodded, and the pair rode off after Vibius. Calia noticed that the behemoths that had accompanied them had all but faded into the background. If she concentrated, she could pick out their outlines as they crept through the undergrowth to either side of the hill. Despite having seen their natural camouflage in action before, it was still a chilling sight.

It took only a minute for them to crest the hill, and Calia looked down in horror as she realized that she was right. The "pack" that Banin had referred to was a small town. Small cookfires burned outside what looked like temporary dwellings of hide stretched over wooden frames. She could see men, women, and children going about their daily tasks with no idea of what was about to happen to them. *Valesa was right*, Calia thought.

She was about to turn back down the hill when the first villager noticed them. A cry went up, and the village flew into a frenzy. Women scooped up children and dashed into the largest tent in the middle of camp, while most of the men jumped up to grab whatever weapons were at hand. This wasn't the first time they'd weathered this. Within moments there was a wall of spears arrayed around the central tent with several archers arranged behind them.

Please, gods, Calia prayed, *let them kill the behemoths*. She could see that they were already looking for them, their heads swiveling as their eyes swept back and forth. Only a stray glance or two was spared for the group on the hill. No, this wasn't the first time Anson had brought one of his sick hunts to their home.

"Many of the other gods come here to hunt," Anson said in a nonchalant tone, his eyes never wavering from the village.

"Certainly, there must be less...dangerous prey," Vibius replied.

"Of course." Anson waved the idea away like it was an annoying fly. "But this doubles as training. And it's necessary for the packs of Sanctuary."

"Necessary!" Calia blurted out before her hand darted over her mouth.

"In many ways. Much like any other population, the population of Sanctuary must be controlled so that it doesn't ruin the island or threaten anyone else."

Calia almost couldn't believe her ears. Anson was casually discussing the massacre of human beings as if he was a game warden talking about a population of pests that was getting out of hand. He continued before she could even think of anything to say in response.

"It also serves to prevent any one pack from gaining too much power over the others."

"Why haven't you or the other gods taken care of the problem in its entirety?" Vibius asked. Despite knowing that Vibius was putting on a show for their captor, it sickened Calia to hear him speaking this way about human lives. *He must do what he thinks will keep us alive and in the good graces of Anson*, Calia reminded herself.

"We've tried, a few times," Anson replied with a shrug. "But when we try, word gets around, and the packs band together. They are, if nothing else, clever and persistent beasts. I've no interest in losing several of my behemoths and soldiers to a guerrilla war that has no benefit to me. No, it's better to simply trim their numbers back from time to time. It benefits them as well. The packs have grown to consider these hunts as a part of a coming-of-age ritual. For a boy to be a man, he must first stand in the spear circle, or something along those lines."

Behind her hand, Calia's mouth was hanging wide open. What she was hearing beggared belief. It was horrific enough that the man believed that he had a right to "trim back" a human population, but to believe that he was helping *them* in the process was too much. She'd thought that Anson was eccentric before. Now Calia knew that the man was completely insane.

Now that Anson had mentioned it, Calia could see that many of the "men" she'd seen holding spears were little more than boys. They ranged in age from perhaps thirteen to sixteen, not even yet out of the awkward years. They stood shoulder to shoulder with men all the way up to the oldest, who looked to be about sixty.

Calia watched as the behemoths finally charged. They burst from the brush around the camp and galloped toward their prey. The spears held steady. Despite every fiber of her being wanting to look away from what was about to happen, Calia forced herself to hold steady. Willpower that she never knew she had steeled her heart even as the behemoths reached the ring of spears.

Despite the best efforts of the villagers, there was no stopping the charge of the behemoths. The monsters crashed through the forest of weapons as if they were made of paper rather than metal. Calia watched in horror as a man was torn to shreds by the claws of a behemoth, before his fellows could turn on it and force it back with all their combined strength. There was hardly anything left of the man except a gory lump of flesh and viscera that had been a living, breathing human mere seconds before.

The other behemoths had much the same effect. One managed to kill several men before being forced away, though when it was finally pushed back, it held the limp form of a boy in its unnaturally large jaws. Calia had to resist the urge to call out for this madness to stop. It would do no good. Even if the boy wasn't already dead, there was no way Anson would order the boy released for the sake of someone he thought nothing of.

A man who must have been the boy's father broke ranks and charged after the beast holding his son in its mouth. Another grabbed at him and tried to pull him back in line, but the man slipped his grasp and tried to stab the behemoth with his spear as it danced back. Within a few feet of the circle, another behemoth blindsided the man. A single swipe of its massive claws turned much of his torso into a fine red mist, and it scooped up the rest in its jaw before turning away.

The behemoths, satisfied with their assault, broke away and faded back into the brush. The only movement along the spear wall was to tighten ranks to account for their losses. It was faint, but in the distance Calia could hear the screams of a man who had been injured but not killed outright. Calia knew that the sound would haunt her in her dreams for some time to come, but she knew she had to listen.

The behemoths made their way back to the group, carrying their grisly prizes. Anson dismounted and handed his reins to Vibius. He walked up to the behemoths and took turns patting them on the heads as if they were loyal hounds returning to their master with a rabbit. The behemoths, for their part, looked the same as they always did. They didn't seem to have any feeling at all. If it wasn't for the fact that they were panting with exertion, Calia might have thought their gore-covered forms were oddly painted statues.

"A successful first night," Anson declared. "Each of my behemoths has returned with a prize, and only one major injury among them."

Calia wondered what the man was talking about. She couldn't see a single serious wound on any of them. They were scratched from the spears, but the wounds seemed shallow to her. She studied them further, and tried to convince herself to ignore the limp, bleeding forms that the creatures held in their jaws.

Her question was answered when one held up a clawed hand for inspection. Anson considered it for a moment and then withdrew the spearhead that had been snapped off in its flesh. The beast seemed to be in as much pain from the steel being removed from its hand as it might have been from a stiff breeze. It didn't so much as flinch. Anson wiped the deep red blood off the blade and then returned to the group.

Calia was surprised when he strode past Vibius and made his way straight to her. Every muscle in her body tensed as he stepped up beside her horse, and she knew that Valesa was calculating every way she could attempt to kill the man. Calia held up a finger from their white knuckled grip on the reins of her horse and hoped that Valesa understood.

Even if she could somehow kill Anson and not be torn apart by the behemoths in the process, they would be stuck on an unfamiliar island with no way off. Their only possible allies would have watched them stand idly by as their husbands, sons, and brothers were killed. Even if they still spoke a common language and hadn't developed their own, it would be hard to convince them to help. Calia knew that this was no place to begin their escape. Even if every fiber of her being wanted to see Valesa strangle the man to death right here.

"A souvenir," Anson said as he handed her the spearhead. "Careful, it's quite sharp."

"Thank you," Calia managed to say between gritted teeth.

Anson grinned at her, and she had to resist the urge to spit in his face or turn the weapon around and stab him with it. Calia knew that with her inexperience, she was more likely to hurt herself than she was to kill him. It was everything she could do to keep her hand from shaking as she returned it to the reins.

They returned to camp, Anson and his behemoths leading the way with their prizes dripping blood all the way down the hill. Calia felt her grip tighten on the spearhead. Anger, disgust, and sheer terror warred for her attention. Calia forced them away and tried to be rational. Being emotional wouldn't help her or anyone else escape this nightmare. There was nothing much she could do at this point to help, but there were plenty of things she could do to harm their chances of escape.

And Calia knew, now more than ever, that they had to escape. She would bring word of Anson and his atrocities back to the realm of man. Anson thought that he would descend upon the realm of man and take it over as his own, but Calia would make it her life's mission to rid the realms of him and his kind. She was no soldier, but she vowed to herself that she would do whatever it took to end this man's sick attempt at godhood.

Chapter 16

Akos rubbed at his temples, trying to will away the headache that was forming behind his eyes. He pushed away from the desk that had been set up in his room. It was the most spacious of any of the rooms that had been built by the shipyard so far. Even so, it was only slightly larger than his cabin aboard the *Mist Stalker*. The only other occupant of the room watched him with curious eyes.

It hadn't been so long ago that those same eyes had been filled with rage. After the slave crews had arrived to begin work on the foundation of the shipyard, Akos noticed that the same girl who had managed to look him in the eyes as they approached Ferundun was among those present. He didn't know if it was simple luck or fate, but Akos took it as a sign regardless. Using much the same ploy as he had in the keep, he'd ordered the guards to bring him the defiant slave so he could have his way with her.

Once again, no one questioned that order. Akos was beginning to wonder whether the men were as depraved as they acted, or if they were so certain of their superiority that they had no fear of treachery. Perhaps it was a mixture of both. They didn't seem to think of the slave as a real person, and that had to influence their thinking. Regardless of the reasoning, Akos wasn't about to miss any opportunity that was presented to him.

"If you plan to escape," the girl said, "why do you still work so hard to build his ships?"

Akos regarded the girl. She was much younger than he had thought at first. When he had first laid eyes on her, he'd assumed that she was at least an adult. But after questioning her, Akos came to realize that she was hardly sixteen, give or take a few years. It was always hard to know the true age of a slave since they were so frequently taken from their true parents. Akos gave his age as twenty-eight, but he knew that he could be off by as many as two years either way. Backbreaking labor in the elements had aged her beyond her years, and she looked to be twice her actual age.

"I have to keep up the lie," Akos replied. "Even if they know nothing of modern ships, these men know shipbuilding. If I lie to them about how to build the ships, they might get suspicious."

"So, you are willing to build him ships of war?"

"To an extent. I've got a plan to make sure he cannot use them. And the designs I've drawn up are not true warships. At least, nothing compared to what we have in the realm of man."

The girl didn't seem convinced, but she also didn't say anything more. It was nice. The first night he brought her to his room she fought and screamed so much that he thought he might have to knock her out and try again with a different girl. It took most of the night to convince her that he had no ill intentions, but not until after she'd managed to break his old chair over his shoulders. *I should have known better to turn my back to her*, Akos thought.

Still, the bruises had faded away and understanding had come, albeit far too slowly for Akos's liking. The girl's accent was thick, even worse than Anson's. And it seemed that the local slave dialect had become so bastardized that it was almost unrecognizable to him as common. It had taken him almost a full hour on the first night to learn her name, such as it was.

It turned out that the slaves on this island weren't even given the luxury of a name. Akos's name had been picked for him by an uncaring master, but at least it was a name. The girl was known as Thirteen-Thirty-Three. The only reason she even had that much of a name was because she was the thirteen hundred and thirty-third child born to a slave in the year she was born. It sickened Akos to think that tens of thousands of people lived on this island without so much as a name.

"You were telling me about the different gods," Akos reminded her, "and who their enemies are."

One thing that Akos knew from experience was that slaves always knew who their masters hated. News always had a way of trickling down. And that was true even here where the slaves thought their masters to be gods. Rather than petty squabbles among aristocrats that Akos had always learned of from the gossip of his peers, the feuds and fights among the lords here were treated with the same religious reverence a Hrothan monk might give to a discussion of his pantheon.

So far, Akos had found that he could replace the word "god" in his head with "king," and the squabbles were hardly any different than those of the nobles in the realm of man. Alliances shifted, formed, and broke the same as they did in any other form of politics. Still, he hadn't been able to convince Thirteen, as she like to be called, that neither Anson nor the others who claimed the title were true gods.

And there were several who claimed the title. It seemed that each island had at least one, and there were many islands in this realm. Only the center island, the hunting grounds, as Thirteen called them, had no ruler. From the way that she spoke of it, that seemed to be a combination of an agreement among the lords of the islands and the "demons" who lived there resisting their rule. It sounded as if none of them individually had the strength to claim it, and they had decided that if they couldn't have it, then no one else should either.

Akos continued to work on his drafts for a convincing war sloop as Thirteen talked. It seemed that Anson hadn't done himself many favors in the political arena. Sometime in the last century he had declared his intentions to be god over all the realm. Unsurprisingly, most of the other gods had ignored him when he demanded that they bend their knee to him or be destroyed. Though to hear Thirteen tell it, they were quivering in their fortresses, counting the moments until Anson arrived at the head of a grand army to crush them to dust. *At least now I know that no one will rush to his aid if he called for it*, Akos mused.

"You are a fool you, know?" Thirteen said.

"So I've been told," Akos said.

"Even if you get away from the island, there is nowhere to go. Every god will have you do this thing for them. And the demons of the hunting grounds will tear you apart as soon as look at you. What use is escape when you will only run yourself to death?"

"I've always thought of freedom as its own reward. And we won't go to any of the other islands; we will leave the realm entirely."

"Impossible."

"I thought so too, but a person much smarter than me found the way. We'll take that way out. You could always join us."

Thirteen did nothing but shake her head, lying back down on the rough bed. He'd made this offer several times, but every time she had refused it. Akos knew the mentality that had taken her. It was the same he had seen written across the faces of the slaves who had preferred to stay in their irons when he had attempted to break them free. It was simple resignation. Thirteen believed that there was no power in this world greater than Anson, and that there was nothing beyond the edge of the maps she had seen. It was Akos's word against something she had been taught as fact since birth.

If it came down to it, Akos would have to force her to come along. If he didn't, he might never be able to sleep well again. If Akos left her here, Anson or one of his lackeys would identify her as his helper soon enough. They would likely execute her out of hand for helping him escape, without sparing any more thought than they would before putting down a rabid dog.

"How fares the work on your project?" Akos asked, trying to change the subject.

Thirteen shrugged. "Digging ditches is not too difficult. Tunnels are a little harder, but not too much. We'll be done within a week or so."

By then the first of the keels would be laid. Akos was amazed by how fast the work was being done. The temporary housing for the guards and slaves had gone up in days. The buildings were not architectural marvels, but they were serviceable. The foundation and the facilities for the shipyard had taken a little longer, but only by a week or so. Some of the special equipment was still being crafted and arranged, but they would be ready to lay the first few keels within the next week or so.

Already the *Mist Stalker* had been brought around to the harbor to be used as an example for the shipwrights. The crew, of course, had not been kept with it. They had been moved to a temporary camp in a warehouse in Ferundun. By all accounts, they were doing fine. All their needs were being taken care of, and the only complaints Akos had received from his crew were those of boredom. Still, Akos had cursed his luck when he'd been told that they were moving them. It was already going to be difficult enough to get everyone in one place to make their escape, and this wasn't helping.

Fortunately, Leodysus was still with the crew. As long as he was there, whatever plan Akos managed to come up with would have a decent chance at success. The man's large and steady presence had helped the crew pull through several situations. Akos was sure that if he managed to get him a message, the message would make its way through the ranks without raising any suspicion.

The main issue was going to be getting a message there. It wasn't as if Akos could ask one of the guards here to deliver a letter without Lorantes going over it. And he didn't know any codes that he could use to hide such a message in plain sight.

That was a problem for another night, however. Akos rested his head against the back of the chair. At least that was comfortable enough. He'd taken to letting Thirteen sleep on his bed while he stayed in the chair. Though it was without a doubt the most comfort that Thirteen had ever experienced, Akos knew that it was a small payment considering the risk she was taking by helping him. Unfortunately, it was all he could do right now.

It felt as if he had barely closed his eyes when he was blinking awake to a new sun on the horizon. Akos tried to rub some of the sleep out while glancing around the room. Thirteen had already made her exit, going to rejoin her work gang before the day began.

Akos rose and tried to roll some of the stiffness out of his neck and back before getting dressed for the day. Before he left his room, he took a sword belt off the peg by the door and strapped it around his waist. It was a comforting feeling, even if it was a pointless one. The sword he had been given was a wooden training weapon. Still, the weight was familiar, and it helped soothe some of the nerves he had.

And it allowed him to work off some of the frustration that he had been feeling toward his situation.

As Akos made his way toward the shipyard, several men were already waiting for him. The soldiers stood in a loose circle, and they were all wearing the same wooden blades that he was. Even Lorantes had deigned to appear today, though it was clear that he had no interest in taking part in the training. Akos stepped into the center and drew his wooden blade, swinging it through a few drills to wake up his muscles.

Even though he knew he was training Anson's soldiers in modern sword drills, Akos had jumped at the chance to swing any blade again. For the first time in his life while overseeing the construction of the shipyard, he had started to get fat. *Probably a good thing Vibius wasn't around to see that*, Akos thought. The wayfarer would have never let him hear the end of it.

It had also helped him to keep his nerves from fraying. There had never been a time in Akos's life when he hadn't been physically active. Whether it was pulling an oar, climbing the ratlines to check on something, or fencing with the crew to keep his skills sharp, Akos had always gotten his exercise. Sitting in one place with nothing to do but pace and watch had taken its toll on his physique and his mental health.

Fortunately, Lorantes had seen the advantages to allowing him to drill his soldiers in modern sword forms. *Even if the crafty bastard tacked on one stipulation*, Akos mused. The count had, most likely at Anson's suggestion, demanded that he also train the men in the use of firearms.

That was one of the last things Akos wanted to do, but he had no choice. It was either that or put the count, and more importantly Anson, on alert that he was not dedicated to their cause. Akos had hoped that if he never brought up the weapons, Anson would forget about them. Unfortunately, that wasn't the case. Once the topic had been broached Akos had been left without any good excuses for why he couldn't teach them to use guns.

There were some mitigating factors that helped him to justify it to himself, however. Akos didn't know the secret to making gunpowder. He knew the basics, and most of the ingredients, but neither he nor anyone in his crew knew the whole process. That would take Anson's scholars some time to decipher and would cost a few of them some fingers in the meantime. And it wasn't as if the *Mist Stalker*'s powder reserves were infinite. Once they had burned through that, the guns would be intricate and inefficient clubs.

Being essentially a warship, however, the *Mist Stalker* had quite a bit of powder aboard. After they finished their blade work this morning, Akos would take several of Anson's brighter soldiers and teach them to use the muskets and pistols that once belonged to his crew. That was the real reason that Lorantes was here. The man looked as if he hadn't swung a blade in the better part of a decade, but a pistol might serve to make him dangerous. There was nothing Akos could do to help it, though he was making sure that they spent as much black powder during the training process as he could without making it obvious.

As soon as he was warm, Akos's thoughts shifted from intrigue and deception to attack and parry. It helped to clear his mind. Focusing on nothing but cut, parry, and counter put all his worries away for a while. They would still be there when he was done, but hopefully they wouldn't seem so large. The wooden sword in his hand was not weighted well, nor was it the style that he would have preferred, but it was good enough.

After leading the soldiers through some basic warm-ups, Akos had them pair off and spar. He moved between them watching for mistakes and correcting them before moving on to the next pair. It was a practice he had learned from Leo, and he had done the same with his own crew many times in the past. Even though these men were enemies who just didn't know it yet, Akos couldn't help but give constructive advice to each pair.

Fortunately, it didn't seem that there were any master swordsmen in their ranks. None who would win a bout with Leo, and not a one who could so much as touch Valesa. If they were fighting other armored soldiers or behemoths, their styles could have been better than anything Akos could teach them. But once they saw the effectiveness of guns against even their best armor, they would need to ditch the ineffectual armor for mobility as all the modern militaries in the other realms had.

Unless they didn't. Akos had noticed that the people of Logathia were resistant to change. It had taken the soldiers several beatings each before they'd admitted that they might have something to learn from him as far as swordplay went. He'd also noticed that not only were their ship designs ancient, but the architectural style and tools were far outdated as well. And even though their armor looked to be made of steel, Akos had noticed that it was of an ancient make, something that might have been hung in a museum or a noble's mansion as decoration.

Not that it mattered to him. If they didn't modernize, they would be an easier target for whoever attempted to take their island as their own. Akos had no interest in ever coming back here, but if he did, it would be as an enemy of at least one local ruler. If he ever had to cross blades with these men with blood on the line, he would hope that they had continued to hold to their stubborn refusal to assimilate better ideas.

After a while of watching and teaching, Akos called the session. Now came the part where he got his work in. The soldiers resumed their circle, a few of them stepping forward. Akos would spar with each of them in turn, and the first challenger today was a particularly nasty looking man with a jagged scar across the bridge of his nose and at least a full head of height on him.

The man launched a flurry of heavy blows, but Akos managed to turn them all aside without allowing any of them too close. He'd been working on his footwork since his bout with Valesa, and it was paying off. Akos was able to keep one step ahead of his opponent, taking much of the power out of his strikes. Eventually he parried and saw a chance to counter, launching a lightning strike to the man's gut that left him gasping for air in a heap on the dirt.

The next two men were much more measured in their approaches, but Akos had enough experience to change his style sufficiently to keep them guessing. With his second opponent he was much more aggressive, always pushing and probing for an opening. The moment one presented itself, he struck, repeating the process until the man bowed out with several fresh bruises across his arms and legs.

This went on for half an hour, and by the end, Akos was drenched with sweat. He'd managed to go without losing a single round today, though he would have a few tender spots tomorrow from glancing blows. As the session wound down, Akos caught Lorantes's eye and swept his blade out in invitation.

"Would you like to try your hand?" Akos asked loudly enough that all the men could hear.

"I think not," Lorantes replied, stroking his mustache with one hand.

"There's nothing to be afraid of. I'll take it easy on you."

"I've no fear. I simply do not wish to work up a sweat so early in the morning."

"Suit yourself." Akos smiled and sheathed his sword with a flourish.

Everyone present knew that Lorantes was lying. Akos had come to understand that he was a proud man, and he would rarely risk being embarrassed. Akos had to wonder whether the man knew how damaging his refusal to fight was to his men's opinions of him. Even if he'd lost, they would have respected his effort. No one expected a man of his age to hold his own against a man in his prime, but refusing to take his lumps with the rest of them would strip their respect away.

At this point, Akos hated the man. At first, undermining and insulting Lorantes had been a tactic designed to delay the shipbuilding process. Now that Akos had seen that the man was nothing but a blustering watchdog, he antagonized Lorantes out of spite.

As he had spent time with the count, he had come to understand him better. What Akos had learned was that Lorantes was a bitter and vindictive man. He was a belligerent drunk who abused those below his station and took all his frustration out on those helpless to oppose him. Akos had watched Lorantes have a slave flogged for failing to dig a ditch fast enough for his liking, only to later admit that he had only done it to get the other slaves to work faster. Akos despised him, but he couldn't let it show for now. He had to keep up the appearance that he was trying to work with Lorantes rather than against him.

"Good work today," Akos said to the rest of the men. "Let's head to the firing range to finish out today's practice."

• • •

"Cease-fire!" Akos roared above the din of firing muskets.

The straw men that had been set up down the short range were remarkably unscathed considering how much shot had been thrown their way. Some of them were missing tufts, but several of them were untouched. Akos knew that it wasn't entirely the fault of the score of soldiers who had volunteered to learn from him. The only thing they had ever shot was likely a crossbow. There was a great difference between the two of them, even if it was for the most part a mental difference.

Still, they had gone through almost two hundred rounds among the twenty of them, and the targets were only fifty yards away. His marksmen would have shredded all the targets in half the number of shots. Even his least experienced crewmen were held to a much higher standard than what was on display here. Despite himself, Akos couldn't help but sigh and shake his head. He was glad that he wasn't trying very hard to teach these men, or he might have to worry about his methods.

Fortunately, they were convinced that they had performed swimmingly. Akos wasn't going to say anything to dissuade them from that notion. If they thought that they were already the best marksmen the realms had ever seen, they were much less likely to practice. Only one of his students seemed to show any real interest in improving. And if they reported to Anson that guns were inaccurate weapons not worth wasting any effort on, all the better.

Lorantes had taken to practicing day and night. Anytime duty didn't require him somewhere else, the count was in front of the straw men, hammering away at them with shot after shot. Akos had noticed, with a great deal of annoyance, that the pistol he was using to practice with was one of his. Lorantes had taken to carrying one of the matching set of dueling pistols that Anastasia had gotten him as a secret present. They were of superb quality, rifled, and one of his most treasured possessions. Akos had considered strangling Lorantes for a moment the first time he'd seen the man wandering about the camp with it on his hip.

The men dispersed back toward the small armory that had been constructed, and Akos made his way toward the shipyard. The sound of pounding hammers had already filled the air, warring with the shouts of foremen as they directed the men. Carts full of seasoned timber were scheduled to arrive within the next few days, and then they could begin their work in earnest.

Akos stood at the door of his small office. The building was built on a rise so that he could overlook the entire operation. It was impressive how industrious the workers here were. Less so when Akos remembered that most of the work was done under the threat of death. The slave crews had been worked day and night to prepare the foundation, and to assemble many of the less important buildings. *I can only imagine how long Anson's been waiting for a chance like this*, Akos thought. *I might be a little anxious as well.*

Lorantes joined him as he looked over the yard. Akos did his best to keep the sigh in his head from escaping his lips. Not that there was much reason. Akos was sure that Lorantes already knew that he despised him. If Akos was right, wearing his pistol had been a crafted insult.

"I thought I'd let you know, we've been summoned back to the castle," Lorantes said.

"Now?" Akos said. "We're only days away from laying the first keels and assembling the skeletons. I'd like to be here to oversee that."

"No, but we will need to leave soon after the keels are laid."

"I thought Lord Anson was still away on his hunt."

"He is, but they are making the return trip soon. He sent a ship ahead. I must admit, I am anxious to return to the keep. I'm eager to show him the progress I've made here."

Akos considered correcting him but let the comment slide. None of this would have happened without his arrival. Even if he was nothing more than a catalyst, the entire yard had been of his design. In his mind, he knew that the yard was nothing to be proud of. Akos could never be proud of building something that required slave labor. What irked him was the idea of giving Lorantes any credit.

"Well," Akos finally replied, "we've still got a great deal of work to do."

"How are the designs faring?"

"Well enough, but it would be better if I could have my own shipwright here to help with the planning."

That was true. Old Haroln had been around ships so long that he knew everything there was to know about them. He could draw a draft from memory better than any university-taught engineer. And he'd been training Gasci to help him make repairs to the vessel. Either of the two of them would be a great help to the design process.

"Lord Anson declared that they were to be kept separate," Lorantes said with the trained swiftness of one who had been taught his entire life not to question Anson.

"So I've been told," Akos said dryly.

Lorantes decided not to reply. Akos didn't like the smug smirk that was splitting the count's face, but he shook the feeling away. Akos was sure that he was letting his disgust blind him. Everything the man did had taken on an annoying air in his eyes. The man was probably dreaming of the promotion and adulation that Anson would wreath around his shoulders.

"Regardless," Akos continued, "the plans should be done before the keels are laid. I'll be prepared to leave shortly after that."

Without waiting for Lorantes to reply, Akos turned and stepped into his office. He suppressed a curse as he immediately banged his knee against the desk. If he didn't know better, he'd have said that they'd placed the desk there and then built the room around it. Akos shimmied past the edge of the desk and stuffed himself into the chair behind it. Light poured in from the windows, and he immediately unrolled the schematics that he had been working on the day before, jotting down the notes he'd made in his room by memory.

Once he was sure that Lorantes had left, Akos put his head in his hands and sighed. Once the keels were laid, it would be only a matter of time before the ships were completed. He'd dragged his heels as much as he thought he could get away with, but it was like trying to stop a runaway horse. Akos was beginning to worry that he might have to complete the fleet before he was given enough freedom to get his crew together and escape.

There was always the possibility that he could grab whoever he could get his hands on and go. Akos dismissed the thought as quickly as it came. If the situation deteriorated to the point that he could not rescue everyone, he would have to live with doing as much as he could. But there was not a chance in the void that he would ever willingly leave behind any of his crew. They'd served him too loyally, and they deserved to have a better captain than that.

If only he could get a look at the forces who were guarding his men. That would change everything. If the soldiers there were as overconfident as the ones here, Leo and his men might be able to overpower them and escape. Or if there was only a small number of men watching over them. There were too many variables in play for Akos to be confident in a plan.

Well then, Akos thought with a grin, *I'll have to go look.*

Chapter 17

Akos wandered away from the middle of the shipyard. The keels had been laid, and the skeletons of ships were beginning to form. Soon enough, Anson would have a squadron of sloops to do his bidding. It wouldn't have been anything awe-inspiring in the realm of man, but here it would be an unstoppable force.

That was if they were outfitted properly, of course, which they wouldn't be. Anson could craft all the cannons he wanted. Their design wasn't exactly easy to replicate, but it wasn't beyond the skill of his craftsmen. But cannons were little more than deadweight unless you had the powder to fire them. Akos was sure that secret would elude Logathia's scholars for some time to come.

But not forever, Akos thought. If Anson ever did manage to puzzle out the recipe, he would likely have all the materials he needed. Even if he didn't, Akos had no doubt that Anson would have little trouble getting his hands on the ingredients he would need. Then there would be little contest between his forces and his rivals. Especially if they had built their fortresses as close to the water as Anson had. Even the undersized and undergunned sloops that Akos had designed would be able to pound such a fortress into rubble without being in any danger.

That was a worry for another day. And hopefully it would not happen before someone came back to the realm of behemoths to claim it for his own. Akos could only imagine the race that would begin the moment the *Mist Stalker* returned and Calia began to spread the news of her discovery. Macallia and Vanocia would be neck and neck, and even the conservative nation of Gellerit might try to extend their sphere of influence. They wouldn't come to the fight with just sloops.

Akos brought his attention back to the present. He was at the edge of the shipyard, looking out at where the slave crews were still toiling away.

Some were clearing back the jungle to make more room for the ever-expanding town around the yard. Anson had decided that a shipyard would need a town built up around it to function. Others were hammering together ramshackle buildings. Akos found that his attention was drawn toward those who were emerging from the ground carrying buckets of dirt and rocks.

There was no real way to tell, but the work on the drainage tunnels seemed to be going quite well. Lorantes had questioned the need for the tunnels, but Akos had convinced him that they would be necessary. Their little shacks were so rickety that they could be washed away if it rained too hard. This way the water would run away from their camp and back into the jungle.

Many of the guards overseeing the work were men he had beaten at this morning's sword practice, and one was even among his firearm students. When they noticed him watching, many of them smiled and waved. He returned both gestures. It had been hard for Akos to keep this version of his captain's mask up for so long, but he'd gotten quite good at it. He doubted that any of the men even knew that he hadn't bothered to commit any of their names to memory.

The one man that Akos had bothered to learn anything about waddled up beside him. Lorantes had a bad habit of showing up at his shoulder when he wanted time to himself to think. It was one of the man's few talents. Akos resisted the urge to sigh and drop his head, barely, and turned to face the man.

"How can I help you, Count?" Akos asked.

"The summons has come, and it is time for us to return home," Lorantes said.

"We'll leave in the morning."

Akos could see that his simple assumption of command had irked Lorantes, but he couldn't argue without seeming petty. That had likely been the plan anyway. Akos would be glad to have some time with company other than the count. He would be glad to see Vibius and Vibia. At this point he would even be glad to see Valesa. *I wonder if she's forgiven me for the little stunt with Calia,* Akos mused.

That ploy might be necessary again. Akos wondered how Calia had been holding up. She'd played her part well enough, but Akos didn't want to put any more pressure on her than he already had. Still, he would do whatever he needed to do to get them all out of this realm and worry about the stress later.

"It seems that these are almost done with your pet project," Lorantes said, gesturing to the slaves working on the tunnel.

"When they are finished," Akos said, "they'll need to begin work on the opposite side of the yard."

"At least the filthy things are in their natural habitat while they muck about in the dirt. I've half a mind to collapse the tunnels with them inside."

Akos didn't respond and had to fight with himself to keep his fists unclenched. If he struck Lorantes now, it would undermine everything he'd done so far. After a few breaths, he'd managed to regain control of his anger. If Lorantes had seen his struggle, he made no mention of it.

"I've still got some preparing to do before we leave for Ferundun," Akos said as an excuse. "I'll see you first thing in the morning."

• • •

The ride back to Ferundun was as dull as Akos had expected it to be. Days passed in the jungle that separated the burgeoning shipyards and the town without any incident. It was a small blessing, but Lorantes had avoided him for the duration of the trip. The quiet had been helpful, allowing Akos to plot out what he was about to do.

It wouldn't be long before they reached the crossroads at the edge of the jungle. One way would take them to Anson's keep, and the other would take them to the small town of Ferundun. Lorantes was sure to want to head toward the keep. Akos, however, planned to take the other road. Whether he got away with that or not would be a good indicator of where he stood in Anson's opinion.

The horse beneath him was restless, and Akos tried his best to remain calm. He told himself that the only reason he was nervous was because of the unfamiliar animal he rode and not because the guards that he was about to attempt to command held his life in their hands. Hands, he remembered, that had been all too eager to go into the slave camps to provide him with "entertainment." These were not men with scrupulous morals. He had no doubt that they would beat or even kill him at a moment's notice.

If, of course, Anson gave the order. If Akos had the measure of them, not even one would lay a finger on him unless Anson willed it. They all revered the man and feared him in equal measure. If he'd declared his future admiral off limits, they would most likely die themselves before risking hurting him. All Akos could do, however, was hope that Anson had ordered the men to accommodate *his* wishes rather than Lorantes's.

Confidence is the key, Akos reminded himself as he slipped into his captain's mask. He tried to remove all emotion from his face and sat straighter in the saddle. It would go better if he commanded rather than begged. At least, he hoped so. That had been his experience in the past. And despite the vastly different cultures of the realms, these were still humans after all.

A short half hour later, they emerged from the foliage to find the gentle hills that led to both the keep and the city. The crossroads was now yards rather than miles away. Akos steeled himself. If they refused to allow him to go, he would have to do what they said. But he wouldn't make it easy for them to refuse. He'd been weaving his way up the convoy until he was at its head, but not so quickly that it would have been obvious. Now would be when that patience paid off.

The crossroads appeared, and Akos continued down the right-hand path as if the left had never been an option. The first few soldiers followed him, and one of the carts bearing their baggage even made the turn. Akos didn't dare to glance over his shoulder. It wasn't the soldiers that he was worried about. Even if they noticed, they wouldn't have any authority to call him out on his actions. Lorantes on the other hand…

As if on cue, Akos heard a commotion from behind him. He didn't so much as twitch his head to the side until Lorantes was right behind him, shouting his name. The large man looked flustered, and Akos slowed his horse enough to allow him to catch up. But he didn't stop it. If Lorantes wanted to argue something with him, he could do it while they were on the move.

"Where are we going?" Lorantes asked as he finally drew even. "The keep is the other way."

"We're not going to the keep," Akos said. "We're going to Ferundun."

"Why in the realms would we go there?"

"It's been too long since I inspected my crew. I think it's time we remedied that."

"Your what?"

A look of genuine confusion crossed Lorantes's face for a moment before he realized what Akos was saying. His eyes narrowed, and his brow furrowed in thought. It wasn't anger. Akos had seen the man angry at the soldiers and slaves before. His face turned beet red and a vein popped out along his brow. This was something else. Consideration perhaps? Akos didn't know, and that worried him. He allowed nothing of what he was thinking to slip onto his face, though.

"Have you not been receiving the reports?" Lorantes asked. "I ordered that they be taken to you."

"Yes, I have," Akos said. "But there is almost always a difference between what you read in a report and the actual situation. I would like to see my men with my own eyes to make sure they are being adequately taken care of."

"I can assure you they are."

Akos ignored the comment and continued to ride. Lorantes wasn't going to get anywhere with weak protestations. Akos wondered how long it would take him to understand that. At this point, only a direct order to the soldiers behind them would stop Akos. Now they would find out whether Lorantes had the guts or authorization to issue that order.

"Very well then," Lorantes said with a huff. "But let's do hurry this visit along. I'd very much like to be in the keep before nightfall. Sleeping on a cot isn't doing my back any favors."

Akos nodded to let the man know he'd heard him but gave no such promises. They would spend as much time there as he pleased. He didn't think they would need long for him to make the arrangements he would need to make, but it depended on the quality of the guards who watched over his men. He wouldn't risk getting caught at this stage by rushing. Akos would be as patient as it took, to a point anyway.

The rest of the ride passed as uneventfully as the ride through the jungle. Within a few hours, Ferundun had come into view. The town was as dreary and drab as he remembered it. What few people there were moving in the streets stopped to stare as the men went riding through. They didn't hide, as they had the first time Anson had brought them through, but they weren't excited to see them. Akos hadn't been expecting a parade, but he hadn't prepared himself for the cold, glass-eyed stares he was receiving either.

Soon enough they were upon the docks, and one of the soldiers directed him to the warehouse that had been requisitioned for use as his crew's barracks. The building looked solid enough. It wasn't in any kind of disrepair, and it looked as if it might even have some offices that the officers who'd stayed with the crew could use as private rooms. The only guards present were the pair by the door, but Akos didn't doubt that there was a larger contingent waiting somewhere nearby.

"Who goes there?" one of the guards shouted as they approached.

"Captain Akos," he replied. "I've come to inspect my men."

"Was this approved by Lord Anson?"

"Of course it was." Akos handed his reins over to another soldier as he dismounted. He hoped that Lorantes wasn't within earshot. The man might try to dispute that. He might not have the courage to try to stop Akos himself, but he could always get someone else to do the dirty work for him. He seemed like the type to rely on the courage of others.

"Then right this way, sir."

The guard threw open the door, which Akos noted didn't appear to be locked, and stepped through. Akos glanced over his shoulder to see that Lorantes had assigned a pair of guards to him. They were dismounted as well, waiting for him to enter before following along. Akos had planned for this, of course, and it wouldn't adversely affect his plan.

They made their way through the poorly lit warehouse until they got to the main storage area. Akos blinked until he was used to the lantern light that filled the room. A hearty cheer went up from the assembled men as they recognized their captain. Despite trying to keep up appearances, Akos smiled. It was good to see the men again. He hadn't realized how much he missed them, and a great deal of tension he hadn't realized he'd been carrying drained out of him.

"How are you, Captain?" Old Haroln called from his lounging perch atop one of the crates.

"I've no complaints," Akos replied, clasping hands with the men and slapping shoulders as he moved between them. "How have they been treating you all?"

"Well, they won't play cards with us anymore," Gasci told him as they clasped hands. "But other than that, they've been all right."

"They've learned that you're all dirty cheats then?" Akos asked with a smile.

"Just unnaturally lucky, sir."

"Of course. Where is Leo? I'll get the full report from him."

"Leo has his own room, upstairs. First door on the left of the stairs."

Akos nodded and made his way up the stairs, with his shadows following him. As he topped the stairs Leo's dark head popped out from the door Gasci mentioned. His face split into a wide smile as he saw him. Akso returned the smile, and the pair slapped each other's backs as they clasped forearms.

"Good to see you, Captain," Leo boomed. "I'd begun to wonder if you'd forgotten about us."

"I tried," Akos replied, "but I could smell you all the way from the keep."

Akos joined Leo as he stepped up to the short railing that surrounded the small balcony. As usual, the man refused to wear a shirt. At least he seemed to be well fed and unharmed. That was a massive burden off Akos's mind.

"How are they treating you?" Akos asked, well aware that there were guards behind him listening in.

"Well enough," Leo said with a shrug. "They mostly leave us alone. They bring food a few times a day and lock the door when they leave."

Akos's eyebrow rose slightly as he looked at his big first mate. He was sure that Leo was trying to feed him information about the guards' routines without making it seem out of place. Most mistook Leo for a dumb man because of his size and violent abilities, but Akos knew he was anything but stupid.

"Hell, that's more than I eat most days," Akos replied. "Have you been keeping the men in line?"

"They're getting restless. None of us are used to sitting in one place without having something to do to fill the time. But they're nothing I can't handle."

"How are you and the other officers faring?"

"Well enough, I suppose. I must admit, it gets more than a little boring. I'm as patient as any other sailor, but I'd like to have a destination to look forward to."

"Hang in there. We'll be done with the ships soon enough, and then there will be plenty to do. In the meantime, would you like some…entertainment?"

"I wouldn't be opposed."

Akos motioned for one of the guards to step forward and gave him a short order. Within minutes he had returned from the caravan with Thirteen. Akos hadn't been sure how the girl would react to his ruse, but she'd agreed to play along. It was Leo's turn to look surprised as she was brought up to the balcony.

"This one has provided me with plenty of entertainment," Akos said. "But I've grown bored of her. Perhaps you would like to take her for a while?"

"Are you sure, Captain?" Leo asked.

"Of course."

Akos motioned for the guard to put Thirteen in Leo's room, and when the men turned to force her inside he winked at Leo. The man had to already be suspecting a ploy, but his slight nod told Akos he was sure of it now. *Good*, Akos thought. Now all he needed was for a few more pieces to fall into place before he could make good on his silent vows and free his crew from this place.

The pair continued to chat for a short time. Akos wanted nothing more than to try to break down the doors and escape right now, but he knew that wasn't going to happen. There were too many guards outside and a week's travel to the shipyard where the *Mist Stalker* was being held. Not to mention the fact that he would leave Vibius and the others in the grasp of Anson.

Thinking of his friend made Akos realize that he should return to the keep before he angered Anson too much. He didn't care at all about the other lords, but if he annoyed Anson with his little detour, it could place his entire plan in jeopardy. Akos knew that he might regret it down the line, but he also knew that he had to come see his men to ensure they were all right. Not to mention the fact that he had to find some way to plant Thirteen with Leo.

Akos hoped that the nights he'd spent leading up to their trip back to Ferundun trying to drill code words into Thirteen's head had stuck. The girl was quite intelligent, despite the lack of formal education. Akos knew from experience that could lead to men underestimating you. He didn't know how many hours she'd spent memorizing a list of phrases and words that he could send to Leo in a letter to give him signals without raising suspicions.

After making one more round through the crew, greeting everyone in turn, Akos said his farewells. He'd risked enough by coming here in the first place. He didn't need to risk any more by remaining. It was time to return to Lord Anson.

Chapter 18

The hunt had been very successful, according to Anson and his nobles. Calia hadn't been able to tell. All she'd been able to see were the faces of the young boys who had been carved to pieces by the behemoths. Fortunately, it hadn't taken long before the small tribes of the central island had spread the word of the hunt between them. They banded together, presenting a force that might have been able to fight Anson's party.

Despite knowing that she was a part of that group, Calia had almost wished they would attack. At least then she wouldn't have had to watch the callous killing any longer. No such thing had happened. They managed to kill one of the behemoths when it attacked. The beast had been left for them to tear apart and use for whatever they wanted. Anson seemed to have some perverse sense of honor as far as these hunts went. He'd stated that it was only right that they be entitled to the spoils of their victory.

Now that they were back on Logathia, Calia wanted nothing more than to sleep for a week and try to forget everything she had seen. Unfortunately, that didn't seem to be an option. Anson wanted an update on the progress of his shipyard, and he wanted to do it over dinner. Of course, all his "guests" were to attend.

At least the man would be distracted with Akos's report. With any luck, Calia would be able to make her excuses and leave dinner early. If Vibius did as well, they might be able to have a little time to themselves. During the hunt, they hadn't been able to spend more than a few moments together alone. Calia hadn't realized how much she had come to rely on their talks and nights together to keep her sanity in this situation. The stress she had been able to ignore before the hunt had all come crashing back down on her when she'd been unable to speak freely.

Even Valesa had been acting like she was feeling the effects of the situation. The unflappable maidservant was beginning to show a little bit of the tension Calia was sure she must be feeling. It wasn't much. A quick, angry word here or there that she never would have allowed to escape under normal circumstances. But Calia had known her for long enough to know when Valesa was trying to keep something from her.

Some of that tension was fading now that they weren't totally helpless. Valesa had taken the spearhead that Anson had given Calia as a trophy and wrapped enough cloth around the base to make it into a halfway serviceable knife. It wasn't much, but it still left her with enough sharpened steel to kill a man. How she managed to hide it beneath her dress without it showing was beyond Calia, but there was no doubt in her mind that Valesa always had it on her person.

Calia fell onto the bed in her room at the keep without so much as a word when they arrived. The ship ride back hadn't been horrible, but it had been difficult to sleep, nonetheless. Calia was grateful to have a solid bed beneath her, and the pounding of the drums was nowhere to be heard.

Unfortunately, her head had no sooner hit the pillow than Valesa was waking her to begin preparing for dinner. Calia sighed, cursing her luck as she pushed herself up. The sun had begun to set outside her window, so she knew that it had been several hours. They would be summoned when it was time for dinner, but it wouldn't be long now.

Calia couldn't help but wonder what Akos had managed to get done in their absence. Hopefully he was close to finishing his escape plan. It would take as long as it took, but Calia prayed that it wouldn't take much longer. She wasn't sure how much longer she could put up with the stress without saying or doing something stupid to jeopardize their chances. Her interactions with Lord Anson were limited, but still enough that she had to watch her words. She wasn't even sure what she could say to endanger their escape, since she knew next to nothing about what they were going to do. The fear hung over her head regardless. Even the knowledge that an escape was being planned would put their lives at risk.

It wasn't long before they were summoned for dinner, and Calia made her way with Valesa toward the dining room. Many of the others were already there. Vibius and Vibia were seated, discussing something. If Calia had to guess, he was telling her about their hunt in the most civil way that he could. Akos and the man who was set to watch him, Lorantes she believed, were there as well. Anson was standing at the stained-glass window to one side of the room, staring out of one of the few clear panels. Calia realized she had no idea how far above the ground the dining room was, but it had to be several stories.

The guards closed the door behind them, and Anson turned as the heavy wooden doors shut with a thud. He smiled his empty smile and rejoined the table, as they sat down. After everyone else was seated, he took his own seat, motioning for the servants to bring in the food. Calia could not wait for the meal to be over so she could rest.

• • •

Akos chewed his food without tasting it. It had been only a few hours since his group had returned from speaking with Leo and the rest of the crew. Anson had wasted no time in calling for them to come to the dining room, but then he'd insisted on waiting to hear their report until after they'd sat down to dinner. They'd come so quickly that Lorantes was still wearing Akos's pistol, which annoyed him to no end. He wore it like it was his own personal trophy that he'd won in battle, rather than stolen from Akos without so much as a please or thank-you.

Fortunately, for Akos anyway, Lorantes had been strangely quiet. He'd not spoken of the trip to the warehouse barracks where Anson was holding his men, though Akos had no doubt in his mind that Anson already knew. There was no indication of whether he approved or not. Though to be honest, Akos didn't think they would have allowed him to go if there was even a chance that Anson didn't approve of it.

Despite knowing that he needed to be present, Akos couldn't bring himself to focus on the food or the company. His mind was with his crew. Akos wondered if Thirteen had begun to speak with Leodysus about their codes yet. He'd instructed her not to waste any time, since he had no idea how soon they might need to utilize the code. It could even be tonight, though he doubted that it would be necessary for him to learn them that fast.

Akos couldn't help but wonder if the men weren't going a little bit stir-crazy by now. Even though the warehouse was much bigger than the *Mist Stalker*, there was much less to do. At least on a ship at sea, there was always some task to perform. Hundreds of things needed to be done to keep a vessel in top shape. Akos wouldn't be surprised if Leo had the men scrubbing the floors of the warehouse twice a day to keep them from getting restless.

Vibius asked some question of Anson regarding the dish they were eating, and Akos managed to drag himself back to the present. It was good to see that the wayfarer was healthy and whole. When Lorantes had told him that Vibius and the others were going on a hunt with Anson, Akos hadn't been able to keep from worrying about them. There were always things that could go wrong in a hunt even if you weren't hunting creatures that could hunt you back. The worry had only grown when Lorantes had let slip that the only thing to hunt where they were going were the tribes of humans who inhabited the island.

It didn't look as if any of them had suffered any physical trauma. There was something in their eyes, though, that Akos had seen before. It was the same blank stare men wore while they were trying to process the horror of their first battle. It was more prevalent in Calia, but he could see it on all of them. Vibius and Valesa had both seen death up close before, but the young scientist had never seen the callous brutality that he was sure Anson was capable of.

There was nothing to do for it now, however. Akos wondered exactly what the hunt had entailed. He was sure he'd get the story from Vibius later, if not Calia. He'd already planned to have her brought to his room to fill him in on what she'd learned and to inform the others of the details of his plot. Akos had to repress a shudder as he realized that their hunt had almost certainly involved the behemoths that Anson controlled.

"So, Captain," Anson said after another course, "what progress have you made on my fleet?"

"The foundations have been laid," Akos replied. "All that remains now is to finish building them. We have four slips at the present that can support shipbuilding and another four being prepared."

"Excellent. How much longer before we can outfit them?"

"I'd estimate another few months. After they are finished being built, we'll need to take them for a maiden voyage, and that will be no easy feat. Sailing a modern vessel is nothing like handling a galley. We'll need to start training sailors aboard the *Mist Stalker* to prepare them to sail on their own vessels."

"Well, we won't waste any time then. Lorantes tells me that you've begun training some of the men on those strange weapons your men carry. How does that go?"

"Some of your men are fair shots," Akos lied. "But it is an art that takes much practice."

"I don't see why you would replace a crossbow with a gun then." Anson said with a frown. "If it takes so much practice to use, it can't be very useful for the common soldier. Any man can learn to fire a crossbow. No matter, I'm sure the reasoning will soon become apparent."

"Indeed. In any case, we should be able to begin breaking in the ships within a few months."

"Excellent news."

Akos nodded as Anson smiled. It was true that this project was well ahead of where Akos had estimated they would be. But then again, he hadn't imagined that the people, both free and slave, would work so tirelessly to bring it about. He supposed that when one you believed to be a god walked among you, you heeded his orders with total abandon.

"I am afraid that it is not all good news," Lorantes said.

"Is something wrong with the shipyard?" Anson asked, his smile fading.

"No, that is all going well."

"Well, where does the problem lie then?"

"I'm afraid that the captain has not been truthful and forthright with us."

Akos felt his heart sink into his stomach even as his face hardened against betraying any emotion. His mind raced. How could Lorantes have found out? What could he do but listen to what the man had to say? They were in the heart of Anson's power, how in all the realms could they escape?

Four guards in the room, Akos counted. One at each of the corners and then another two outside the door, if memory served. And that didn't begin to consider the hundreds who were in the fortress, possibly thousands, if he counted the garrison of Ferundun.

Those present wore a simple arming sword. The best weapon Akos had available to him was a dinner knife. It was sharp enough to kill, but it wouldn't be much against an actual weapon and would be completely useless against anyone with armor on.

Anson was leaning on his elbows over the table, his face unreadable. His mouth was hidden behind laced fingers. Akos had to resist the urge to look away from his eyes. Instead, he met them steadily, though it was one of the most difficult things he'd ever done.

"And what makes you think this?" Anson asked, his voice devoid of any emotion.

"One night while looking for my cabin, I stumbled near Captain Akos's lodgings. I expected to hear him…entertaining himself with the slave he'd had us bring him, but instead I heard them talking."

"Looking for your cabin?" Akos said. "Drunk off your ass most likely…"

"Quiet," Anson commanded. There was no anger in his tone. He hadn't even raised his voice. Still, Akos could practice for the rest of his life and not put as much emphasis behind an order as Anson just had. Akos's mouth snapped shut despite itself. "Please continue, Lorantes, but mind yourself. I care not if he likes to get to know his playthings."

"Thank you, my lord," Lorantes said, emboldened. "I can assure you it's much more than that. After that night, I had my suspicions, so I had a few of my men with the sharpest ears go to his cabin every night after that. Every night, they discussed the local geography, the local customs, and most importantly, his escape plans."

There was no going back now. Akos could see the cold finality in Anson's eyes. Either Akos was going to die for this, or Lorantes was. There was no way that they were making it out of the situation. It might be a prolonged death, at least until Anson could figure out Calia's secret for transcending the void madness, but it would be death, nonetheless. Akos felt every muscle in his body tense.

"Have you anything to say for yourself, Captain?" Anson said.

"Lorantes is a liar," Akos said. He was amazed with himself that he managed to keep his voice even with his heart pounding so hard in his chest. "He is jealous that you chose me to lead your new navy when he believes the honor should be his."

"Of that," Anson said, leaning back in his chair, "I have no doubt. I've watched Lorantes since he was a simple sailor. He's always been a petty and jealous man. But the one thing he has never done is lie to me, even when it would have benefited him. It's one of the reasons I elevated him to his position as a count, though after tonight I think he might deserve a bit more than that. I must say, Captain Akos, I expected great things for you. I'm disappointed that you couldn't see what I was offering."

"I saw what you were offering," Akos growled. "A gilded collar. I've worn chains for far too long not to know what they look like when I see them."

"A pity. I'm sure that progress on the shipyard will take much longer without you."

Anson made a motion with one hand and the guards began to close in.

"Try not to harm him," Anson ordered. "But do what you must to get him to the dungeon."

Well, Akos thought, *so much for subtlety.*

Chapter 19

Everything seemed to explode into motion all at once. Akos rose from the table fast enough to knock his chair over backward. Following his motion, Lorantes rose as well. Soon enough everyone but Anson was moving. He sat and serenely watched the chaos unfold from his seat at the head of the table.

Akos gambled on being faster than Lorantes and had the advantage of action rather than reaction. He reached down and yanked the pistol out of the holster on the fat man's hip. Lorantes didn't even have time to get a hand over it before Akos had wrenched the gun free with one hand and cocked the hammer with the other. The second part of Akos's gamble was that the man always kept it loaded.

Akos jammed the barrel into Lorantes's chest hard enough to shove him back into his chair. The man grunted in pain, eyes widening as he realized what he had done. Akos pulled the trigger, barrel still touching Lorantes's sternum. The spark found powder, and the crack was loud enough to force one of the guards back a hesitant half step.

Lorantes, for his part, looked confused. His eyes tore away from the smoking pistol in Akos's hand and slid down toward his chest. A large plume of blood was already beginning to form from the charred hole in his sternum. His eyes glazed over as his mind caught up to his body, and he slumped over in his chair.

The moment Akos had pulled the trigger and been rewarded with a shot, he'd been moving. He'd placed the weapon over Lorantes's heart, a sure kill shot at any range. Akos was already looking for other threats. The guards by the door had begun to close in on him, but one was already lying on the floor. Akos wondered what had happened to him, but then saw Valesa charge the other with what looked to be a knife in her hand. Akos wondered where she had managed to get that but decided that it was a question better left for another time.

Vibius had stood up almost as soon as Akos moved and was shepherding Vibia and Calia behind him. He'd armed himself with a dinner knife, though he wasn't trying to do much more with it than protect himself as a last resort. That was fine. Vibius had never had a fighting spirit. Akos turned his attention to the guards, who had recovered from their shock at the sound of the pistol.

He turned almost too late. Anson had risen from his seat without so much as a noise and was attempting to attack Akos with his own dinner knife. The serrated blade passed a few inches from Akos's throat as he dodged backward. There was no time for thought. It was all he could do to keep in front of the blade, but as soon as he saw an opening he lashed out with his own weapon.

The barrel of the pistol connected with Anson's temple. Akos hadn't been able to put everything into his swing or it might have killed the man. Still, the force was enough to crumple him to the ground, unconscious. Before Akos could finish the job he'd started, the guards leaped for him with swords drawn. Akos was forced to retreat before a flurry of swings.

One of the soldiers dropped his sword to drag Anson back and out of harm's way. Akos glanced back in time to see the door burst inward and the guards from outside rush in. As he'd guessed, there were two of them. Their eyes swept the room and gravitated toward him. That was a fatal mistake. Valesa caught one in the neck with her dagger, felling him instantly. The other managed to dodge away, using his superior reach to keep her at bay.

Akos turned back to focus on the man in front of him, but the guard seemed more concerned with keeping him away from Anson rather than pushing his advantage. Why should he? His only job was to keep his god from physical harm. There were more than enough soldiers in the keep to finish off Akos and his crew.

As that thought crossed his mind, a shadow passed in front of the stained-glass window. Before Akos had time to shout a warning, the window exploded inward. Akos had to shield his eyes from the flying shards of glass, feeling them dig into his skin in several places. Still, he could see the massive black form that had burst into the dining hall. Somehow a behemoth had crashed through the window.

Vibius and the others were moving toward the door. Akos was prepared to sacrifice himself to keep them safe, even as he backpedaled toward the door. *I wish I'd been more religious in my life*, Akos thought. *Now would be a good time for a little divine intervention.*

Akos was certain that the gray mountain of muscle and death would make a beeline straight for him. To his surprise it bounded toward where the guard had pulled Anson. With a flash of motion, it eviscerated the man. Blood sprayed the walls. Akos impacted the door near the wall as he continued to backpedal. He couldn't tear his eyes away from the ferocious creature. He knew that if he did for even a moment, it could cover the distance between them and end his life in a heartbeat.

The second guard didn't fare much better. He managed to turn and see the creature, throwing up his blade as its clawed hand arced toward him. The steel managed to cut deep into the creature's massive paw, turning aside its razor-sharp talons. But the force of the blow spun the soldier around, and the creature bit down. Neither the steel chest plate nor the flesh and bone underneath slowed its jaws.

Akos risked a glance to the side to see that Valesa had finished off the other guard and scooped up both of their swords. The others were dashing through the now open door.

"Go!" Akos shouted.

Valesa didn't need any more encouragement. She ducked through the door. Akos turned back to see that his shout had drawn the attention of the creature. It lunged for him, and he rolled along the wall to the door. He leaped through right before the behemoth could reach him. He felt the air in front of its claws as they passed mere inches above his back. He rolled to his feet, turning to see that the behemoth was stuck in the door. He took a few involuntary steps backward as the creature made another vain reach for him, knocking dust off the masonry as it impacted the wall.

Fortunately, the door was too small, and the walls too thick. The behemoth gave up after a moment, glaring at the group with its dull eyes before ducking back into the room. Akos felt his heart hammering in his chest, but there was no time for him to process the fact that he'd passed within inches of death, several times. They needed to move, before more guards could arrive and find out what happened.

Valesa handed him one of the swords, and Akos took it with a nod of thanks. The group was waiting for his orders. Akos took a moment to collect his thoughts. He wasn't sure what to do from here. All his plans had revolved around Anson allowing his crew to join him to train the others, and then somehow getting the others there to leave. He never imagined that Lorantes of all people would stumble upon his plans and reveal them.

"What now?" Vibius asked.

"We get outside," Akos decided. "We have some advantages."

"Do we?" Valesa asked. "Two swords and an empty pistol?"

"No one knows what actually happened yet," Akos replied. "Follow my lead."

Akos began to lead the group at a jog down the halls. If the gunshot hadn't been enough to draw the attention of everyone in the keep, the behemoth crashing through the glass was certain to. Soon enough they reached a group of soldiers moving in the opposite direction, toward the dining hall. They tensed when they saw Akos running toward them with a sword, but he acted as though relief washed over him.

"Thank the gods," Akos shouted. "Lord Anson is injured in the dining hall."

"What happened?" the lead soldier asked.

"I don't know. We were talking and then Lorantes went on a rant before attacking Anson. I think there's a rival god here. A behemoth is in there attacking everyone but Lorantes."

"Move men, we have to protect Lord Anson!"

Akos grabbed the arm of one of the last soldiers before he could rush off.

"Before the attack," Akos said, "Lord Anson told me to have someone rush an order down to the docks."

"The docks?"

"Yes, the docks! Pay attention, man."

Akos gave the soldier one of the code phrases that he'd taught Thirteen. The man was very confused, but Akos made him repeat it back several times before he was content. The urgency on his face must have convinced him of the importance of this mission. Akos set the soldier loose, and he sprinted off down the hall. Akos gave him several moments before leading their group after him toward the exit.

"What was that all about?" Vibius asked.

"I want to give Leo a fighting chance," Akos responded, praying that the soldier reached them before any other word could.

• • •

The crew played cards, but there was none of the usual banter. Leo had watched as the boredom set in over the past few months, driving them insane. It had been enough to cause a few fights among the men, though he had put an end to that. They had enough to worry about without having to worry about infighting as well.

Captain Akos's visit had helped some to relieve the tension that the men were feeling. Just knowing that he was working toward their escape was comforting to Leo. Akos was not the best at everything he put his mind to, but he was persistent and unrelenting once he'd made a decision. If he said that he was going to get them home, he would. It was as simple as that.

Leo had spent all afternoon and most of the evening with the slave girl that Akos had brought with him. He had to wonder how long the captain had spent with her, trying to drill the various code phrases and combinations into her head. It must have taken quite some time. Leo was still turning the words she'd given him over in his head, trying to remember what each phrase meant.

Now that Leo believed he knew enough to get by, he'd sent her down the hall to the next officer. The guards didn't watch them all the time, so he didn't have to use the pretenses that Akos had when he'd dropped her here. He'd simply told her to go introduce herself and let the rest of the crew know what they needed to know. The guards came only to bring them meals and to make sure that none of them had died of boredom. Otherwise, they kept the doors closed and locked.

Into the Void

It was shaping up to be another long evening. Leo leaned on the railing of the balcony, pretending to watch the men play cards. He was there only to make sure that none of the men got too aggressive. He'd already had to break up Kerel and Jav twice this week, and he didn't think that the men had gotten over whatever slight had caused them to fight in the first place. But neither man wanted a beating, so they were keeping to opposite sides of the warehouse, at least while Leo was watching.

Leo was so far gone into his own thoughts that it took him a moment to register that his name was being called from below. He blinked and looked over the railing, where one of the guards was looking around while shouting for him. Leo frowned. There was no reason that they should be here. They'd already dropped off the meal for tonight, a bland soup that Remford had scoffed at as he'd ladled it out to the waiting men. One of the men indicated him, and Leo stood to his full height as the man craned his neck to peer up at him.

Though he would never admit it aloud, Leo always enjoyed the way men's eyes widened when they saw how large he was. He knew that the gods had blessed him, not to mention his orc father. It was more fun when they pretended not to be intimidated, which was what the man who made his way up the stairs was trying to do. The soldier was a full head and a half smaller than he, and at least a hundred pounds of muscle lighter, but he still held his chin up and addressed Leo as if he were an inferior. *Must be an officer*, Leo mused.

"Are you the first mate?" the man asked.

"Aye," Leo said. "That would be me."

"I've a message from Lord Anson. He says, ah…to watch for sails on the horizon?"

The man said the last part of the sentence as if it were a question. Leo rubbed at the stubble that had overtaken his chin. That didn't make any sense at all. It was almost as if he were trying to sprout one of Akos's code phrases, but he'd heard it only from afar.

"Are you sure Lord Anson didn't say that there was a sail on the horizon?" Leo prodded helpfully.

"No, no," the man said emboldened. "He said there were two sails upon the horizon."

"You're sure he said two?"

"Yes, I'm quite sure."

"Good, that means that we get to leave."

"It...what?"

Leo reached up under the man's chest plate with one hand while the other clamped down on the collar. Before he could so much as begin to protest, Leo had picked him up and thrown him over the railing of the warehouse. The man flew fifteen feet down and out into the middle of the warehouse, where he landed with a sickening crack. The men playing cards jumped back at the sudden corpse that had interrupted their game, cursing as they went. All eyes were riveted on Leo as he dusted his hands off.

"Captain says it's time to leave this port, lads," Leo said. "All hands make ready."

The men scrambled to carry out their orders. Leo had not been idle the entire time he'd been stuck in this warehouse. Men pulled the heads off the mops they'd been given to scrub the warehouse with to reveal sharpened stakes. Others overturned crates to hand out the sharpened bits of metal they'd found and wrapped in cloth to form makeshift knives. Those who didn't receive one of those weapons were handed sturdy pieces of wood that could be used as cudgels in an emergency.

Leo wasted no time going room to room, informing everyone who warranted a room of his own that it was time to go. They joined him as he made his way downstairs. Leo walked over to the man he'd thrown and relieved him of his blade. It was a one-handed arming sword, made for someone who had much smaller hands than he did. Leo's pinky struggled to find purchase on the pommel, but it would have to do for now until he could find a proper blade.

The men were soon formed up into several crews, and he inspected each for a half second before nodding to himself. They looked pitiful. There hadn't been space in the warehouse to drill anything properly. Half the men had started to go from lean muscle to fat. They looked more like a roving band of vagabonds than they did the crew of a proper fighting vessel. Still, they hadn't lost their fighting spirit. Leo could see it in their eyes; they were hungry for freedom and willing to kill anything that got in their way. *I wonder if that will survive an encounter with one of those behemoths*, Leo thought.

Nothing would be able to answer that question save firsthand experience, Leo supposed. There was no time for doubts. He did his best impression of Captain Akos as he stood ramrod straight before them. They were looking to him for their orders. Leo wondered if Akos felt this same nervousness in his stomach whenever he ordered them into battle.

"We break through those doors and make for the west," Leo said. "If we can make it to the jungle outside of town, we have a chance. The captain will find us there. Cause as much chaos as you can on the way out of town. Knock over lanterns, kill any armed man who stands in the way. Understood?"

There was a chorus of ayes, and Leo nodded once before turning down the hallway to the outside of the warehouse. The men rushed to follow him. They crowded the double doors that led to outside. Hopefully, they would lead to freedom as well. Leo waited until they were all ready, and then braced himself next to the door.

There was no bar over the door. He'd noticed that when they'd moved the crew into this warehouse. It was a simple iron latch. The doors were sturdy, but he was sturdier, and with a war cry he started forward. At the last moment he turned his headlong charge sideways and impacted above the latch with his shoulder. The momentum of his charge carried him through the shower of splinters and onto the street.

Leo rolled onto his back in time to see the stunned door guards be overwhelmed by his crew. They were armed and armored, but that stood no chance against the fury of the *Mist Stalker*'s crew. They went down beneath a barrage of fists, cudgels, and knives. Still, one of them screamed into the night, and that meant that more of them would be on their way soon. If enough of them could present a united front to Leo's crew, they would stand no chance. They had to keep moving.

Leo leaped to his feet, waving for the men to follow him as he took off at a jog down the streets. The evening lanterns had already been lit, and his men were knocking them down and swinging them into buildings as they went. With any luck one of those would catch and the town would have bigger problems on its hand than a few escaped prisoners. That was the idea at least, but Leo knew what could happen to a plan in the face of the enemy.

Rather than concentrate on what was happening behind him, Leo forced his attention forward. In the dark, in a strange city, it was hard to know which direction he was leading his men. Akos had ordered them to get into the jungle west of town, and that he'd find them from there, but west was hard to judge without a sun to go by. Leo turned straight away from where he knew the docks to be and kept that as his bearing.

Soon enough they came upon a squad of soldiers patrolling the street, moving toward the commotion they were making. Leo was among them in a moment. Their complete surprise was his advantage. He'd bowled over a pair of them with his initial charge, and he made quick work of another pair with his sword. By the time they'd begun to turn to face him, his crew was upon them as well. They were all experienced fighters, and though they were not well armed, they had the advantage of numbers and surprise.

They'd taken care of them within moments, and Leo continued to move. Several of his crew were considerably better armed at this point, and his confidence was growing by the minute. Ferundun wasn't a very large town. It wouldn't be long before they reached the outskirts if they kept going in one direction. Once they were there they would be able to orient themselves and find their way.

Leo looked behind him only twice, once when his men shouted at some curious civilians to get back inside, and again when a triumphant shout went up from his crew. They had been tossing lanterns as they went, and it seemed that one of them had caught. The blaze was visible over the rooftops behind them, an orange haze against the black sky. Soon enough they would have to choose whether to deal with the escapees or with the raging fire. Leo hoped that they picked the fire.

They quickly made their way to the outskirts of the small town. In the distance, Leo could see the outline of the trees that marked their escape route. He had to resist the urge to bellow in triumph. From here on, they would need to be much quieter than they had been in town. Still, he pumped a fist toward the air. Finally, he turned back around, making sure that the crew was still there.

A quick head count revealed that they were down a trio of men. A few quick questions revealed that they had been killed by the guards they'd run into. Leo cursed their foe, but inside his heart he knew that it was a light price to pay for the freedom of over a hundred men. He'd mourn his brothers later. For now, they had to move.

As they marched toward the jungle, Leo could not help but glance toward the mountain that he knew disguised Anson's keep. He could just pick out the shadow of the mountain against the night sky. The rest of their crew was somewhere. Leo sent a silent prayer to the gods that his captain and his friends would make it to their rendezvous safely. It frustrated him, but it was all he could do for them.

Prayers and hope were weak weapons in the face of the behemoths he'd seen on the beach so many months ago, but they were all he had.

Chapter 20

The night was chaos. Men screamed and yelled for direction as Akos led his small group out of the gates of the fortress. Most of the soldiers had ignored them. The false report he'd told the first group of soldiers about Lorantes's coup had spread like wildfire, and everyone was rushing to their god's aid. There hadn't even been another fight as they'd made their way through the gates. The jungle stretched out before them, a looming beacon of relative safety in the nighttime.

The good news was that it seemed that there were no behemoths tight on their trail. Akos had been casting nervous glances over his shoulder the entire time they'd been on their escape. Not that he was likely to be able to see one in the dark. Akos couldn't imagine that they would have gotten far if the beasts were hunting them.

It hadn't taken very long before the jungle was looming before them. Once they were within the relative safety of the trees, Akos allowed the group to rest. They were all winded from their escape, and Akos was starting to feel the aftereffects of his adrenaline rush as well. His hands were shaking, and he leaned against the trunk of a tree as he panted into the night air.

"What do we do now?" Calia asked suddenly.

It was a fair question, and Akos only had part of an answer. He'd hoped to be able to get his crew to the shipyards without raising an alarm. But at least he'd planned a little something for this. The "drainage tunnels" he'd ordered the slave crews to begin digging led to the center of the dockyards. From there they could use the rowboats that he'd stashed along the docks to get to the *Mist Stalker* and to freedom. The only problem was they had a long distance to go through unfamiliar jungle to even reach the tunnels. He'd had them dug as a last-ditch plan, but now it seemed that it was his only option.

"We keep moving," Akos said, pushing himself away from the tree. "Leo should have gotten the message. If he did, he'll be making his way to the jungle now." *Assuming they can escape.* "If we can meet up with him our chances go up drastically."

"Where will they be?" Vibius asked.

"South of here. I told him to meet us near the crossroads."

Akos was close enough that he could see the question that Vibius wasn't asking. His eyes darted between Akos and the rest of them. His eyes lingered on Calia and Vibia. Valesa was in good enough physical condition to make a miles-long hike through the jungle, but were the other two? And for that matter, was Vibius? Even at the best of times he spent most of his day reading rather than working as Akos and Valesa did.

To answer him, Akos shrugged. They would simply have to find the endurance to make it. If they couldn't, then they would all be doomed. Akos wasn't going to go anywhere without them. If he had to carry one of them he would, but they needed to keep moving. Akos knew that he had to lead by example, so he put one foot in front of the other and started marching south along the tree line.

The sun was coming up before they reached the spot where Akos told Thirteen to take Leo. All that he could think of at this point was that he was glad he had eaten something before their fight with Anson. Vibius and the others collapsed against various trees when Akos called the halt. Akos stayed on his feet, but only by strength of willpower. He'd been awake almost a day and a half straight now and moving for most of that. But there was no time to rest. Someone had to go and find out if the others had made it.

"Valesa," Akos whispered to the only member of the group still standing.

The bodyguard joined him at his perch overlooking the road. She looked tired, but she was much more used to physical labor than the others. She'd made a makeshift baldric for her sword out of the bottom part of her skirt. Akos was glad she was here. It was nice to have one other steady hand with them, in case they couldn't find Leo.

"I'm going to look for Leodysus and the others," Akos said. "They might not have been able to find the crossroads in the dark. If I'm not back by sunset, take the group along this road by night. It's about three days to the shipyard. You'll be able to find a way aboard the *Mist Stalker* from there."

"Four people can't sail a boat," Valesa pointed out.

"All the more reason to hope I find Leo."

"Good luck."

Akos nodded and set out through the jungle.

• • •

The trunk of the tree was the most uncomfortable thing that Calia had ever slept on, but she'd still managed to doze through half the day against it. Their escape from the keep and the hike through the jungle had been draining, far more draining than she'd expected. But every time Calia had thought of stopping, she'd found the will to take one more step. After what felt like an eternity of hiking, she'd been able to rest.

Now Calia almost wished she hadn't. Every part of her hurt. She tried to stretch away the pain, but it didn't seem to be going anywhere. She wondered how Valesa and Akos had continued to be mobile after they had called their halt.

Calia's heart skipped a beat when she couldn't see the captain or her handmaid. She was about to yell when she saw Vibius dozing against the tree next to her. She stifled her shout at the last moment. Calia didn't want to wake either him or Vibia. They needed their rest as much as she had. Instead, she rose to her feet to try to get her bearings.

Instant regret flowed through Calia as her legs resisted every motion. She had to brace herself against the tree to keep from sinking right back to the ground. Somehow she managed to stay standing, and after a few shaky steps her legs stopped hurting quite so much. She moved to the edge of the small clearing they'd sheltered in for the night to see what was around them. Valesa appeared in front of her so suddenly that she almost screamed in surprise. Calia managed to contain herself, but only just.

"Sorry," Valesa whispered. "I didn't think you'd be up."

"I wish I wasn't," Calia responded. "Have you rested yet?"

"Haven't had time. I was looking for fresh water."

"You need to sleep."

"I needed to find water first or we wouldn't be doing much of anything for long."

Calia had to admit that she was dying of thirst. She hadn't realized it until Valesa had said something, but now it was all she could think about. She didn't think she'd make it another mile if she didn't have something to drink soon.

Fortunately, Valesa had been successful in her hunt. The handmaid led her to a creek a few hundred yards away from their resting place. Calia leaned down and drank deeply, before splashing the cool water over her face. It was the most refreshing water she'd ever tasted. After she'd drank her fill, she returned to the clearing.

Valesa sat down against a tree, glancing up to see if she could spot the sun between the leaves of the canopy. It seemed to be around noon, though Calia had no real way of telling. Calia sat next to her bodyguard, glad to be off her feet again.

"You need to rest," Calia said. "Who knows when we'll get another chance?"

"Someone has to stand watch," Valesa replied, but there was no real fight in her voice.

"I'll stand watch. As long as I can do it sitting down."

That drew a slight chuckle from her guard, and Valesa nodded as she leaned back against the tree.

"That shouldn't be a problem," Valesa said. "Take this."

Valesa handed her the sword she had taken from one of the guards she'd killed. Calia was careful with it, unsure of what to do. She'd handled only very dull ceremonial weapons before. This one didn't even have a sheath to keep her from cutting herself.

"You might want to cut your skirt down," Valesa said as she faded off to sleep. "It'll help you get around in the jungle."

Calia rested the blade across her lap as Valesa drifted off to sleep. She looked down at the hem of her dress. It was a full-length skirt, one that she'd brought from home. Even stained brown and green from her trek through the jungle, her dress was still worth more than some people made in a month. Unlike some of her peers, Calia's father had taught her the value of money and that not everyone was as fortunate as she was.

Even while he was teaching her, though, Lord Hailko had lavished gifts upon her. This dress had been one of those gifts, right before he had passed away. The thought made Calia hesitate. There were many other reasons she didn't want to cut the bottom off her skirt. It would be improper and immodest, especially for a woman of her station. Valesa could get away with it, but she was a warrior, not a noblewoman.

Calia glanced over at Vibius and blushed. Of course, he had seen her legs by now, but this was different. Akos and the rest of the crew would as well. Manners and etiquette had been as important a part of her upbringing as her schooling, and it was not something that a proper lady did.

That thought made Calia wonder what a proper lady might do in this situation. If the novels she'd read were any indication, a proper lady would sit and wait to be rescued. They'd languish in the top of their tower and wait for their knight to ride up and defeat the villain. But there were no knights here. There was no one to rescue her if she waited. She had no doubt that Akos would never leave them behind, but if she slowed them down too much, she would doom them all. Calia doubted that someone like Anson would let them have another chance at escaping.

Calia grabbed a handful of her skirt, just below the knee, and brought it toward the edge of the sword. Still she hesitated. The dress was a gift from her father. How could she destroy something like that?

Father would rather I have my freedom than a pretty dress, Calia realized. The choice wasn't much of a choice at all. She couldn't wait for someone else to rescue her. Calia had already promised to herself that she would do anything necessary to get herself out of this situation. Even if that meant a bit of impropriety.

Calia dragged the material over the blade. It cut easily enough, and with a little fidgeting she managed to shorten her skirt from floor length to knee length. It almost made her feel nude, but it was liberating all the same. It was such a simple thing, but Calia knew that if she could do that, she could do whatever else it would take to escape.

The sun was beginning to set before Vibius and Vibia woke. Vibius raised his eyebrow when he saw what she'd done but didn't say anything. Calia told them where to find water, and they set off. The movement woke Valesa, who groaned and stretched. She looked to the sun and frowned as she saw the lengthening shadows.

"Akos told me to leave if he wasn't back by nightfall," Valesa explained.

"I'm sure he'll be here," Calia said.

Valesa grunted in response, folding her arms across her chest. Calia returned the blade, and Valesa nodded silent approval at her now significantly shorter skirt. The pair waited impatiently with Vibius and Vibia for nightfall to come and decide whether they would be moving with or without the others.

It was getting close to the evening when the first of the search parties went by. Several riders passed by, and Valesa made Calia and the others hide deeper in the jungle while she watched the group pass. Fortunately, it didn't seem that they were looking for them in the jungle. They were scouring the road, and within a few moments they had passed by, completely unaware of the presence of their quarry a scant hundred yards away.

"Odd," Valesa muttered to herself as Calia and the twins emerged from the trees.

"What's wrong?" Calia asked.

"They didn't even bother to check the jungle around the road."

"Perhaps they think we are taking the path straight to the shipyard."

"Could be, but it seems odd to me."

Before Calia could respond, there was another rustling in the trees, and without a word she scrambled for cover again. Soon enough, their fears were banished as Akos led a weary-looking band of sailors across the path through the jungle and toward their clearing. Calia didn't know the exact number of crew, but it appeared that they were almost all there. Even if the giant Leo was carrying Old Haroln over one shoulder like a sack of potatoes.

"I was beginning to wonder if you were going to make it," Valesa said as Akos stumbled into the clearing.

Calia had to wonder if the man had rested at all since the night before. It didn't look as if he had. His eyes were hardly focused, and his walk was unsure. His hair was plastered to his face, and Calia noticed with a start the blood that stained his shirt. From the way he was moving, she guessed that it was someone else's blood, but it still showed that he'd been in another fight since they'd last seen him.

"Lucky for me," Akos said, "Leo is relentless."

"Run into any trouble?" Valesa asked, eyeing the bloody shirt.

"There was a small patrol. It won't be long before Anson knows they're missing. We need to get moving before he sends his behemoths into the jungle."

Just the thought of being hunted through the trees by those grinning monstrosities sent a shiver down Calia's spine. They would never survive a night in the jungle with those creatures stalking them. She remembered the way they had seemed to materialize out of the trees around her that first day on the beach, and the thought made her glance around apprehensively.

But it didn't seem like the crew of the *Mist Stalker* was in any shape to keep going. Akos looked as though he could fall asleep on his feet at any moment. The only one who seemed unfazed by the full day and night of forced march through dense jungle was Leodysus, who was grinning as he went from man to man, speaking shortly with each of them.

"We need to rest, and then we need to move north," Akos declared. "Anson won't miss the patrol until at least nightfall, and we'll have a head start on them by then."

"Won't north take us farther inland?" Vibius asked.

"It will, but it will take us to as safe a place as we'll find on this island. And it's actually a shortcut."

"How does that work?" Valesa asked.

Instead of answering, Akos gestured at someone near Leo. Calia looked over to see that there was a slender girl with him and wondered how she'd gotten there. The group turned questioning eyes back toward Akos, who was sinking to a seat next to a tree. He shrugged.

"Thirteen says that neither the behemoths nor Anson's men will go to a certain area in the north, and that it leads close enough to the shipyards that we can risk a dash for the tunnels."

"Why won't they go to this area?" Valesa asked. "Is it dangerous?"

"She says that it's haunted."

"Haunted." Vibius repeated dryly.

"It doesn't matter if we believe it," Akos said with a shrug. "All that matters is that Anson's men believe it. She calls it 'the boneyard.' If we can get there ahead of Anson's creatures, she's assured me they won't look for us there. Now give me a little time to rest, and we'll depart."

Calia exchanged a glance with Vibius, who looked as incredulous as she felt. It seemed preposterous that anyone would avoid a whole section of an island for something as silly as the belief that it was haunted. *This is a place where they worship an ancient madman as a god*, Calia reminded herself.

Still if that was their ticket to freedom, Calia hoped that they were as superstitious as Thirteen claimed.

Chapter 21

Navigating a jungle at night was no easy feat. Akos wasn't sure that they'd have been able to do it without Thirteen. She knew the tricks for finding her way on the island. If it had been a vessel at sea, Akos would have almost instinctively known how to find north in any realm, but here he was lost. He let the annoyance he felt at being all but helpless fuel him for one more step.

Despite the short rest they'd gotten in the clearing, Akos felt as though he hadn't slept in days. His legs protested every movement, and the sword that he wore in a makeshift sheath on his hip felt as though it weighed fifty pounds rather than two. Akos knew he couldn't let any hint of his discomfort slip through, however, for the sake of his men. So, he stumbled on without complaint, allowing Thirteen to guide them to the fabled boneyard.

The place had come up as he'd studied maps of the island in preparation for their escape. It was a blank space on every map. At first he thought it was some impossible area that the cartographers hadn't bothered to include on their sketches, but after noticing the same spot on several maps, Akos had brought the question to Thirteen.

She'd informed him that it was the graveyard of ancient behemoths. All the behemoths that were killed in battle or died of natural causes were heaped there to rot away until the hills were made of bone. It wasn't a frequent occurrence outside a war between gods, but the islands had been around for a very long time.

Thirteen told him that the bones of the behemoths were still possessed by their spirits. She told him that the site was a holy place to Anson and that he dared not trespass there lest he anger the behemoths under his control. What might happen to a group of outsiders who entered the boneyard, Thirteen didn't know. Akos was more than

INTO THE VOID

willing to chance it. He didn't believe in ghosts, nor did he fear the wrath of dead behemoths. He was much more worried about the living ones.

The sun was beginning to peak over the horizon when the jungle began to thin out somewhat. Akos was grateful. The undergrowth had made it difficult for them to make good time as they trudged toward their destination. Fortunately, it seemed that the behemoths had long since hunted all wild animals into extinction, so Akos and his men had not been forced to deal with hostile wildlife in addition to the jungle itself.

It was a small blessing, but Akos was willing to take anything he could get right now. The odds were stacking against him with every passing second. There was no way to know that for a fact, but Akos was certain of it, nevertheless. Their window for escape from this island was slowly closing.

Valesa had informed him of the party that had ridden toward the shipyards without so much as looking for them in the trees. That worried him more than he was willing to admit. If Akos were in Anson's shoes, the first thing he would have done once he regained his wits was have a party go to scupper the *Mist Stalker*. If that were the case, they could still steal a galley to escape, but it would be much more difficult. Not to mention the fact that the only experience he had with a galley was as an oarsman.

They would cross that bridge when they came to it. For now, they had to reach the shipyard. That alone would be no easy task.

The main thing that worried Akos was food. His stomach growled as if to prove his point. His men were going to need sustenance to retain their strength for the trip home. Water was easy enough to find in the jungle; there were several clear streams, and it rained regularly. But they were surviving on what little fruit they could forage as they walked. Hopefully, whatever vessel they ended up taking had a stocked galley. If not, they would be forced to go ashore somewhere and try to find enough food to get them home. Akos didn't like the odds of that.

Reaching the shipyard should be simple enough, though far from easy. If he recalled his maps correctly, the westernmost edge of the boneyard would bring him within a day or so of the shipyard.

From there they would be able to find the tunnels he'd instructed the slaves working there to build. That would put them near to the docks where they would be able to get to the *Mist Stalker*, or whatever ship they could find.

It sounded simple enough, but Akos knew that it would be a difficult task. The shipyard would be on high alert. Anson was no fool. He knew the *Mist Stalker* was Akos's best ticket off the island. If he took that option away, he would be forced to scramble for something else, and Anson would have the advantage.

There was no helping that now. Akos's own carelessness had put them in this situation. He'd been so sure of himself that he hadn't considered the idea that Lorantes of all people would stumble on to his plot. There was nothing to do for it now but push forward, but Akos cursed himself all the same. He'd have to prove, once again, that all the disadvantages in the world wouldn't stop him.

Akos was about to call for another rest when Thirteen waved him down. He moved forward enough that he could see what she was pointing to. The jungle parted, and Akos could see the mountain that Anson made his home in the distance, rising above the canopy. He walked to join their guide.

"We are here," Thirteen said as he approached.

Akos looked around in disbelief. They appeared to be in the foothills of whatever mountain range led toward Ferundun. The trees didn't seem to want to grow on the rocky white hills that rolled out toward the west.

"You're sure?" Akos asked.

"Look closer."

Akos peered toward the hills, and then almost recoiled in shock. What he'd thought at first blush to be stony hillsides were mounds of bone, bleached white by the sun. It was too far to see much detail, but Akos could make out skulls, claws, and ribcages poking out from the mound. It seemed that they had found the boneyard that Thirteen had spoken of.

"Let's keep going," Akos shouted to his men. "I'd like to get out of sight of the tree line before we rest for a bit."

Akos started walking but paused when he realized that Thirteen was rooted in place. She had a look of pure terror on her face. This was a place of legend to her, and all the legends were bad. Akos remembered her telling him that no one who set foot in the boneyard ever made it out again. He'd discounted it as propaganda spread by Anson to keep people out, but to her it was truth handed down by a god himself.

"Are you coming?" Akos asked. He dreaded the answer. He already knew that if she said no, he would have his men subdue her and bring her along. It might not be the most gentlemanly thing to do, but there was no way that Akos was going to leave her to the mercy of Anson when he'd dragged her, unwilling, into his schemes in the first place.

"Yes," Thirteen replied, taking a shaky step toward the hills of bone. "Better dead behemoths than living ones, I suppose."

"That's the spirit," Akos replied.

Akos did have to admit that there was something unnerving about the place. Seeing the monstrous behemoths rendered down to so much bone was unsettling. Akos would bet that much of the chalky dirt they were walking on was bone that had been worn away by the elements over time. Still, if it was a place of safety, he would welcome the eeriness of the surroundings.

Relief washed over Akos as the last of his men managed to get hidden from view of the trees within the mounds of bone. It might not be much, but at least they were unlikely to be detected here. Hopefully that would last all the way until they reached the shipyard. There was no way that they would make it if Anson could force them to fight through his forces.

Akos dropped to a soft spot in the field and lay down. The bone chips and dust that made up the ground wasn't much different than a rocky hillside. He'd slept on worse. Within a few moments, the warmth of the sun had lulled him to a dreamless sleep.

• • •

Calia knew that she should be resting for the march ahead, but she couldn't help herself. The bones around her were too interesting for her to even think about sleeping. Calia regretted that she didn't have a journal to record her theories about the different bone structures she was seeing.

The skulls were the most interesting of the bunch. They were thick and had small spaces for the eyes that she knew surrounded the crown. Cracks ran down a few, and Calia had to wonder what would be strong enough to crack the dense bone that surrounded the behemoths' brains.

Even with the variety of bone that she was finding as she wandered about their surroundings, none of the teeth she found were cracked, split, or broken in any way. Calia found bone that was halfway ground to dust by the elements, split by some force, and broken in dozens of places. But she didn't find so much as a chipped tooth. *Their fangs must be made of something much stronger than human teeth*, Calia mused to herself.

"This is fascinating," Calia murmured to herself.

"This is terrifying."

The voice nearly made her leap out of her skin. Calia whirled about to see the slim slave girl who had been leading them nearby. Arms wrapped around herself, Thirteen glanced about the boneyard as if she expected the skeletons to come to life at any moment.

"Sorry to startle you," Thirteen said.

"It's quite all right," Calia replied. "I just didn't realize there was anyone else here."

Thirteen moved to stand with Calia as she examined the bones. Calia continued to lean over the various interesting-looking skeletons and try to commit as much of the detail to memory as she could. Hopefully there was still some paper and ink on the ship that she could record some of this with. Otherwise, it would have to wait until they'd made the long trip all the way back to Macallia. As great as her memory was, Calia didn't think she'd remember the details very well over that length of time without some way to jot it down.

"What are you searching for?" Thirteen asked after a moment.

"Nothing in particular," Calia responded. "I just enjoy puzzles."

"What do you mean?"

"Well, everything is a puzzle. Things don't come to be for no reason. It makes me ask, why are things the way they are? Why do behemoths have such thick skulls? What are their teeth made from? Why is there only one burial site for them on this entire island?"

"Because the gods commanded it to be so," Thirteen replied. Her brow was furrowed, but there wasn't much conviction in her voice. Calia realized that there was probably no such thing as the scientific process in this realm. Thirteen had likely been taught that the answer to every question of the natural world was Anson.

"Maybe originally," Calia agreed. "But I think we both know that Anson is no god."

Thirteen flinched when Calia said his name. It was a small thing, but it was enough to make Calia wonder whether she should keep pressing. *If she's going to come with us*, Calia reasoned, *she's going to need to hear this eventually*. Otherwise, the shock of seeing the way things were in another realm might be enough to drive her catatonic.

"He's nothing but a man," Calia said. "Somehow he has deciphered eternal youth, and how to control those behemoths, but that doesn't change the fact that he is a man."

"But he eats the fruit of the gods," Thirteen said.

"The what?"

"All the slaves tell the tale. There is a secret place where only a few people can tread, deep within his fortress. Any slave taken there is never seen again. It's where he grows the fruit of the gods."

"Why does he eat this fruit?"

"No one knows. But no one wants to be taken for the duty of caring for the fruit."

"Why is that?"

"The elders say that several generations ago, one of the slaves damaged the fruit while he was carrying it to Lord Anson. It touched the ground and was stepped on. They say that Anson picked one out of every three slaves on the island and set his behemoths on them as a lesson."

Calia shivered at the thought. "How horrible."

"It was a long time ago." Thirteen shrugged.

Calia turned back toward the bones, but her mind was some distance away. Perhaps this fruit was the secret to his godlike powers. It seemed as if he was protective of it. It amazed her that Anson let the secret to it be so public, but she supposed that it was difficult to cover up a secret that had killed a third of the island's slaves some time ago.

"I've been wondering," Calia said finally, "how many behemoths are on Logathia? And people, for that matter?"

"Well, no one knows for sure," Thirteen answered. "Tales say he used to have thousands of behemoths, but then the gods conferred and decided that they would keep their numbers much lower. Perhaps a hundred? Less? No one is sure. As far as people go, Logathia is home to around twenty thousand free men and a quarter of that in slaves."

"That few?"

Thirteen looked at her quizzically, and Calia realized that for the realm of behemoths, that might be a huge number. Geralis was home to five times that number of people on its own, however, and it wasn't even the largest city in the realm of man. Calia was trying to think of a way to explain that to Thirteen when a familiar voice called out from behind her.

"My lady."

Calia turned to see that Vibius was waving to her from some distance away. She smiled and walked to join him. Thirteen followed along behind her, not wanting to be left alone among the bones. Calia didn't mind. After everything they'd been through, keeping her feelings hidden was the least of her concerns.

"I thought you might like to see this," Vibius said.

"What is it?" Calia asked.

Rather than answer, Vibius gestured at the next hill over. Calia wondered what exactly she was supposed to be looking at. She shielded her eyes from the sun and leaned forward for a better view. It didn't take long for her to realize what it was. A gasp escaped her lips as she realized that the hill wasn't made of an amalgamation of skeletons like the other were.

This one was one large skeleton filled with smaller ones.

It had to be at least twenty times larger than any of the others. Calia spotted the outline of a rib and traced it with her eyes until it broke away. Even with part of it missing it had to be at least twenty feet long. Calia searched until she'd found the skull and saw that the fangs were just as solid as their smaller counterparts. They looked to be at least as tall as Leodysus, and possibly larger. She would have to see if the man was available for comparison.

"An ancient behemoth," Thirteen muttered to herself.

"How ancient?" Calia asked.

"No one knows exactly. All that anyone knows is that the gods used to wage war with these monsters. They could tear down entire castles with their claws and swallow soldiers whole, armor and all."

"What made them stop?"

"They agreed among themselves that they would no longer use them. Eventually they wasted away here."

"Fascinating," Calia and Vibius said at the same time.

The pair exchanged a brief glance and a smile. Calia reached down and intertwined her fingers with his and leaned against his shoulder. They stood there like that for some time, each doing nothing but admiring the great beast and enjoying the other's company. They were interrupted only when someone cleared his throat obnoxiously behind them.

"If it's quite all right with you, master wayfarer," Akos said. "I think we should get moving again."

"No, I think we'll wait a few more minutes," Vibius replied over his shoulder with a grin.

Akos looked as if he were trying to keep a sour face, but he couldn't help grinning himself. Vibius earned an eye roll, and then Akos was off stomping to wake the others.

"You have until everyone is up," Akos called. "And then I swear on the gods, I'm leaving you here."

"Good luck with that," Vibius replied. "You wouldn't last a day without me."

"Well," Calia said once Akos was gone. "You may stay as long as you like. I think I've had enough of this island."

"A few more moments won't hurt, as long as I'm sharing them with you."

Calia wanted to argue, but that was the sweetest thing anyone had ever said to her.

"I suppose I can stand a few more."

Chapter 22

The tunnels led out into the jungle, just as Akos had planned. The slaves must have been busy. The entrance was little more than a hole in the side of a hill, propped up by wooden timbers. But it was wide enough for two men to pass through at the same time, and tall enough that only Leo and Vibius would have to stoop.

There were still a few hours until dusk, and Akos didn't want to move until nightfall. They would come up toward the center of camp, and from there they would be able to find their way to the skiffs and galleys that could take them out to the ship. Hopefully, the guards would be so focused outward, watching for their approach from the forest that they wouldn't be patrolling the interior of the camp.

Akos doubted they would get that lucky. They would have to strike hard and fast, relying on the surprise to carry them through the other side. It wasn't that much different than the dozens of times his crew had taken a ship by surprise in the mist between realms. The only difference was that the enemy was alert that there was a possibility they might be there. *That*, Akos thought, *and their pet monsters*.

There wasn't much they could do if there were behemoths present. With the proper preparation, Akos was sure that he could defeat one, or even a few. But his men were exhausted. Half of them weren't even armed, and the arms they had were up-close-and-personal weapons. Akos didn't want to get any closer to a behemoth than he had to. They would have to make their dash to the boats and hope Anson hadn't sent any along.

The men were all resting around him, but Akos found that he couldn't get any sleep. Despite the bone-deep exhaustion, his mind would not let him rest. Instead, he paced around the makeshift camp, giving his men a once over. Akos didn't want to disturb anyone's rest, so he passed through and tried to judge their mental and physical state with a glance.

Most of them looked better than he had expected. Akos hadn't known whether to believe the reports from Leo that the crew had been well taken care of and well fed during their time under guard. Now he could see that they had been. The ordeal of the previous few days had started to wear on them, but they were much better rested to start with than Akos had been.

Leo, as usual, was entirely unperturbed. Akos passed him as he slept like a baby against the bole of a tree. It must have been some of the orc blood running through his veins. Akos couldn't recall a time he'd seen the man worried or tired. Even after the worst storms and the toughest fights, when Akos had wanted nothing more than to collapse and sleep through a week, Leo had been on his feet and cheery as ever. On more than one occasion, Akos had wondered if the tattoos that covered his body were magic.

Vibia dozed next to Valesa, who was checking over the blades that she had managed to acquire. As a wayfarer, Akos knew that Vibia was able to sleep at a moment's notice. It was a skill they all seemed to pick up as they plied their trade. Wayfaring exhausted the wayfarer, and most people wanted to spend as little time between realms as possible. Wayfarers had to get their rest when they could.

Valesa glanced up as he passed and gave him a brief nod. Akos swallowed his shock and returned the gesture. It wasn't much, as far as gestures went, but it meant more than it implied. Akos believed that Valesa held him directly accountable for everything that was happening to them, and he hadn't thought she'd forgiven him for the stunt he'd pulled with Calia.

It seemed that they at least had an understanding now. Akos doubted that all was forgiven, or that it would be if everything worked out and they made it home. But at least she seemed to know now that he wasn't about to throw them to the wolves at his earliest convenience. That was enough for now. Akos didn't need her to like him, as long as she would do what he said when he said to do it.

Satisfied that her equipment was in order, Valesa returned to a resting position against the tree. Even as she tried to sleep, it seemed that she was coiled and ready to spring into action. Not for the first time, Akos wondered where the Hailkos had found her. There was no doubt in Akos's mind that she wasn't some self-taught bodyguard. He'd known that the moment he'd sparred with her. Valesa likely had been born with a great amount of natural talent, but she'd been honed into a weapon by someone.

The memory of her tearing through Anson's personal guard with nothing more than a spearhead she'd fashioned into a makeshift dagger flashed through Akos's mind. He knew that he was a match for most swordsmen, but even though he'd taken a point off her in their friendly sparring match, he didn't think he could do anything against her if there was murder on her mind. Akos was glad that she was on their side.

The next pair he came across were Vibius and Calia. They sat against the same tree, holding hands as they rested up for the coming night. Akos moved on past them without slowing his stride. A smile creased his lips. Though they were not bound by blood, Vibius was his brother. The man was the most selfless person Akos had ever met. He'd risked his life to help Akos free of his chains. He'd spent almost every penny to buy the *Mist Stalker*. When no one would look twice at issuing a letter to a privateer with the last name Freedman, Vibius had lent them credibility.

It warmed Akos's heart that Vibius had finally found some of the happiness he deserved. Calia was a kindhearted and genuine person. And she was one of the few he'd ever met who matched his friend in intellect. They were a perfect fit for each other. Akos wondered how long it would take them before they married when they returned to Macallia.

They would have to plan around each other's wedding's, Akos realized. For the first time since he began his planning, Akos allowed himself to consider life once they returned to the realm of man. Visions of Anastasia danced through his head. She would be waiting for him, and he would finally have the dowry prepared. Even if he gave the remaining sailors in his crew a sizable bonus, the amount that Hailko had offered him would more than cover the remainder. He could settle down with his new wife and find some way with Calia to monetize their discovery in the void.

It was odd to even consider a life without the *Mist Stalker* or her crew. Akos had never thought of privateering as anything other than a profession, a means to an end, but there were certain perks to living a life on the seas. He was his own master. Akos considered that to be priceless.

The lifestyle also never lacked excitement. Sure, there were long stretches at sea where there was nothing to do but pray for an enemy to raid, but for the most part there was always something to do. Akos knew that he would have to find some other form of excitement to fill his days once he was no longer plying the ways looking for ships to capture. It was a sacrifice he would make without a second thought to spend the rest of his days beside his Anastasia, though.

Akos shook his mind to clear her image away. He still had several hurdles to clear before any of this became certain. Things could still go south, and he had to have his mind clear so that he could prevent that.

The march through the boneyard had taken two days, and along the way, Akos had sent foraging parties out into the jungle to find what little food they could. Fortunately, the trees had been heavy with fruit, and they had found more than enough to sustain their march. Akos had even had them form makeshift bags out of their clothes to carry some along with them onto the ship. It would do little good to get aboard the *Mist Stalker* if they all starved to death before they could make it halfway home.

If there weren't supplies aboard the ship, Akos knew that they would have to put ashore on the central island of the realm and attempt to resupply there before they left. That would be risky. Not only would they have to contend with Anson sending his forces after them, but they would also have to worry about the other gods finding out about their presence and doing the same thing.

The natives of the central island would also be a threat. They most likely wouldn't be able to tell the difference between them and their oppressors. Akos wouldn't be able to trade with them for supplies. They would have to forage and hunt for enough food, and while his crew were veteran sailors, they were not experienced hunters. There was no telling how long it would take to resupply, and every moment spent in this realm was another minute that Anson had a chance to find them and destroy them.

Akos wouldn't be able to do anything about that until they were sure that it was an issue. If they had water, he knew his men could go for some time without food. Not long enough to make it all the way home, but long enough to find a different solution. They could also fish until they reached the ways, but that was only a stopgap solution.

Fortunately, Akos knew that their black powder and cannons were still on the *Mist Stalker*. He'd seen the men carrying it ashore a barrel at a time as they needed it for marksmanship practice. That meant that if Anson sent his ships after them, they could pound them into splinters. Akos almost hoped that they would. It would be a satisfying conclusion to his time here. With any luck, the man had left some of their small arms as well, but that wasn't nearly as important as the long guns.

Akos finally finished the circuit through his men. They looked tired, but they also looked anxious. He remembered that while he had been running himself ragged trying to plan their escape, they had been forced to sit and wait for their chance. It was a look he'd seen many times before as they came upon a ship in the mists. They were ready for whatever was ahead, and Akos sent a silent prayer of thanks to the gods for blessing him with such a crew.

The sun had dipped farther toward the horizon, but still not low enough for his liking. Akos settled in to wait for dusk, but his own anxiety kept him from getting any real rest. The tunnel was only half a mile long but leading his crew through it would likely take some time. If they left at dusk, it would be good and dark before they were ready to emerge in the camp.

As the sun finally dipped down to touch the horizon, Akos rose and stretched some of the exhaustion out of his limbs. With a nod to Leo, they began to rouse the crew and give them last-minute instructions. They all knew the plan, but Akos wanted to make sure they knew their priorities. He wanted to sow as much chaos as they could once they were among the ships, but that was a secondary goal to getting out to the *Mist Stalker*. If he was of a mind to be spiteful, once they were aboard he could turn the ship and fire upon the shipyard.

That would be a decision for later. Akos rallied the crew around the mouth of the tunnel. He glanced over the assembled men. Most captains believed that their crews would follow them into the void, but his men had done it. *Time to return the favor*, Akos thought, *and lead them back out*. The men sorted themselves into a single-file line. Akos and Leo would lead the line, with the wayfarers and guests in the middle.

Akos did a quick headcount to make sure everyone was there and then turned and made his way into the tunnel. Once inside, he stopped and lit the torch they had prepared along the way. Akos didn't want to draw attention to the edge of the jungle so he'd ordered his men not to light them until they were well within the tunnel. Fire flickering and illuminating the uneven floor, Akos began to creep forward.

The trek took even longer than he'd thought. The slaves had dug the tunnel, but they hadn't bothered to smooth out the floor. Rocks jutted out from the floor and walls at odd angles, and Akos had to keep his pace slow so that he didn't trip or turn an ankle. More than once his arm grazed against a rock jutting from the walls, and he had to bite back a curse as he bounced his head off a low-hanging rock as he looked down at the floor. Behind him, Leo stifled a laugh and word was passed along the line to be on the lookout for that rock. Akos rubbed his head and swallowed a few choice words as he continued.

After what felt like an eternity, they reached the edge of the grate that they had covered the exit of the tunnel with. Under Akos's orders, they had done nothing more than hammer out a crude iron grate and then drop it over the hole. His excuse had been expedience. Fortunately, no one had questioned him, and it appeared that the grate still rested against the ground without anything to bolt it down. Stars and lanterns cast their shadows into the tunnel, and Akos snuffed his own torch against the ground before getting too close.

There was a small clearing around the exit of the tunnel, and he waited until the word had been passed along the line to stop before inching forward. Akos's heart pounded in his chest. This was the most delicate part of this plan. If someone noticed their presence now, they would be done for. They would have to retreat down the tunnel and back into the forest, and their plans would be shot. Not to mention the fact that since he was going first, Akos would likely be captured or killed before his sailors could start on their way back down the tunnel.

Akos ignored the fear building in his chest and continued to inch forward. He could see up through the grate at enough of an angle to know that there was no one immediately around it. He gestured for Leo to come forward, and together they quietly lifted the grate free and slid it along the ground and out of the way. The entire time, Akos held his breath, waiting for a shout of alarm or even someone to wonder what was going on.

After the grate was clear, Akos waited several tense moments before motioning for Leo to give him a boost. The big man laced his fingers and Akos planted a boot in them, slowly lifting himself up to the edge of the tunnel, just far enough to peer over the edge.

The buildings around them were quiet and the streets that had begun to form between them were empty. Akos didn't see any signs of guards, and he couldn't hear anything other than the sound of his own heartbeat in his ears. That wouldn't last long. Some lucky guard would wander by eventually. They didn't have long. Akos nodded down to Leo, and the man hefted him up, helping him scramble over the edge of the tunnel and out into the street.

Akos moved away from the street and toward one of the buildings as Leo helped the next sailor up. Within moments, dozens of them were posted around the tunnel, watching for any incoming guards. Akos watched the way that led down toward the shipyard but didn't see any signs of life anywhere. It was making the hairs on the back of his neck stand up. Hopefully, the guards were too focused outward to worry about anyone rising from the midst of their camp, but Akos couldn't shake the feeling that something was wrong.

It didn't take long before Leo, with the help of a pair of sailors, pulled himself up through the hole and returned the grate. Akos did another quick headcount before gathering the men and making their way down to the shipyard. There didn't seem to be a single soul in the entire town. The feeling that something was wrong built in Akos's chest until they reached the entrance to the shipyard. A slight palisade had been built around the yard, but the gate was still open.

As Akos peered out from between buildings, he noted a pair of guardsmen at the gate, chatting the night away. Some of the tension began to drain out of him. It was possible that he was being overly cautious. Anson's forces hadn't shown a great deal of competence yet, so expecting them to post interior guards might have been expecting a little too much from them. Akos pulled his sword from its makeshift sheath, and he heard the men around him do the same.

This was the decisive moment. They would charge the guards and take the shipyard. Akos had stored all the dinghies and longboats for the sloops he was preparing in the northwest corner of the yard, near the water. If they'd moved them or put them aboard the half-completed ships that he could see rising above the palisade, they might be in trouble. There could also be an entire company of armored soldiers in the yard, complete with arbalests and their stolen firearms.

Akos would have liked some more time to scout out the yard, but there wasn't any. If the sun came up and they were still there, they would be discovered, surrounded, and destroyed. They had to move now, before any kind of alarm could be raised. With that, Akos rose from his half crouch and sprinted as quietly as he could toward the pair of guards.

The men were so entranced with their conversation that the crew was almost on them before they noticed them. The sound of someone's feet falling was too heavy to ignore, though, and they turned in time to curse before the charging sailors were upon them. Akos took the man on the left, a tall and stocky man who had just enough time to take a step back and reach for his blade before Akos pounced on him.

The man's chest was armored with a breastplate, so Akos ducked low and drove the point of his blade upward. The tip hit the man square in the groin, and the force of the blow was enough to lift the man off the ground. Akos pushed the blade upward until he felt it grate against the inside of the bones of the man's ribcage. He let out a high-pitched scream, and Akos whipped the blade out to slice across his throat turning the scream into a gurgle. But the damage was already done. Leo had finished with the other guard, and already ducked inside with several other crewmen.

Akos glanced back at the town, and within moments he saw several lights flick to life. He cursed himself for not going for the throat the first time, but if he'd missed or bounced the blade off the man's gorget, the result would have been the same. Akos waited until his whole crew had passed through the simple gate before stepping through himself. He gathered several of his crewmen and helped them to force the heavy wooden gate closed before dropping the massive iron bar that held it in place.

Fortunately for him, there hadn't been a company of armored soldiers waiting for them in the shipyard. Leo and his men were clearing what few guards there were, while another party was sprinting to find the dinghies. Akos made his way toward the docks and looked out over the water, seeing the lanterns of the *Mist Stalker* in the distance. He sighed with relief. Akos hadn't wanted to have to take a galley.

"Captain," one of the men called.

Akos made his way to the corner of the yard and saw to even greater relief that the longboats were still there. The men were beginning to push them out into the surf. Akos took a moment to allow the relief to wash over him before taking command of the situation.

"Everyone aboard," Akos called into the yard. "We're leaving."

The men leaped to obey. The guests and Vibius were bundled onto one longboat, and Leo took command of another. Akos took a place next to Vibia in the third, preventing the chance that a single capsizing would take out their entire command structure. Soon enough they fell into a rhythm, rowing out to sea toward their salvation. There would almost certainly be a skeleton crew aboard the ship to deal with, but they had managed to maintain their element of surprise. Dealing with the last few guards wouldn't be anything to worry about.

It felt like an eternity, but they finally pulled up alongside the *Mist Stalker*. Akos took hold of one of the ladders carved into the side of the ship, pulling himself up with caution. Once he was aboard, he glanced at the deck. *Deserted?* Akos wondered why there weren't at least a few guards. Instead of dwelling on it, he grabbed a nearby rope ladder and tossed it over the side. Leo was doing the same a few yards away, and Akos could see the same confusion on his face. Akos waited until most of his men were aboard before he began to give orders.

"Leo, take a squad and make sure the holds are cleared," Akos barked. "The rest of you make ready to sail."

The door underneath the aft castle sprang open and stopped Akos in his tracks. Anson strode out with several men flanking him, swords already drawn. The crew stood in stunned silence. The tarps that they'd assumed covered their longboats flew away to reveal soldiers lying in wait. The grate that covered the hold and the door to the crew quarters flung open, and soldiers began to spill out. Fortunately, there didn't appear to be any behemoths among them. *Thank the gods for small blessings*, Akos thought, his body already in motion.

Akos strode toward the grinning god with his blade already in hand. He heard his men begin to engage the soldiers spilling forth from the hold, but he already knew that there were too many of them. In the tight quarters of the deck, their armor would give them an enormous advantage. The math was already piling up in their enemy's favor, but Akos didn't care. If he could end Anson, their resolve would break. He knew it. It was their only chance.

Anson seemed to read his mind. He stepped forward and slid his own blade from its sheath. It was a long dueling blade, almost like the rapiers the noblemen in Vanocia had begun to wear but thicker. It whipped through the air as he stepped toward Akos.

"Come try it," Anson said simply.

Akos was happy to oblige.

Chapter 23

Chaos swirled around him as Akos tried to close with his foe. For his part, Anson simply sent his blade through a few test strokes to warm up. Out of the corner of his eye, Akos saw Leo toss a soldier clear of the ship and into the sea before ripping his blade free of its scabbard and skewering another through his breastplate. Valesa fought by his side, darting out and stabbing through the defenses of some unfortunate soldier before backing behind the massive sailor.

Vibius had a blade in hand, but he looked none too eager to join the fray. Instead, he stayed behind the other two and let them handle the fighting. Akos was glad. Vibius could guard Calia and Vibia in a pinch, but he'd prefer the wayfarer keep himself out of physical danger. It seemed the soldiers had similar orders, as they ignored the trio entirely.

Sailors were falling before the steady onslaught of soldiers. They were at least even as far as numbers went, but the soldiers were armored. The sailors were fighting like demons, but there was only so much they could do. Perhaps at sea, with the deck pitching beneath them, they would hold an advantage. But with the anchor dropped and calm seas, their opponents held the upper hand.

Akos knew in his heart that if he were to get to Anson and end him, he would break the foes' spirit. If they didn't surrender, they would at least be so dismayed that they would be easy to mop up. Without thinking, his sword flashed out midstride and knocked away a blade that flashed toward him. Akos returned an instinctive counterstroke and bit deep into a man's unarmored arm, forcing him to drop his sword and back away.

There was enough of a break in the conflict that Akos could get through and meet his foe face-to-face. Anson waited for him, his guardsmen having already joined the fray. The god was grinning like a madman. It would have been enough to unnerve a less experienced opponent, but Akos had faced down far more terrifying challengers. Without his behemoths, Anson was no better than any other man. And Akos had killed more than a fair share of men in his lifetime.

"I have to admit," Anson said as they began to circle each other. "I am quite surprised that you made it this far without raising any alarm. I've had my behemoths scouring the jungle in every direction for the last two days, and they've seen no trace of you."

Akos ignored the man and looked for any opening in his defenses. It seemed that he was far more skilled with this blade than he was with his dinner knife. Akos sent a few probing strikes forward, but they were swatted away with practiced ease. Anson returned in kind, and there was a surprising strength behind his swings. It was nothing Akos couldn't handle, and he parried well enough. They fell into a rhythm of observe, strike, counter, reset. Anson continued to talk as they did so.

"I would have let you get this far anyway," Anson said. "I hoped that seeing me at the last moment, when you thought you'd finally found sanctuary, would break you mentally. Another part of me hoped that you would fight, so I could have the pleasure of killing you myself."

Akos slipped his blade through the defenses and scored a weak cut down the man's side. If it hadn't been for the gasp of pain from Anson, he wouldn't have thought it cut anything but cloth. Akos grinned and pressed the attack. But to his frustration none of his strikes after that landed. Instead of fear, he thought he saw something like delight in Anson's eyes. That was much more unnerving than the grin that he'd worn earlier, but Akos ignored it and kept fighting.

The pair broke for a second, separated by the body of a man being flung between them. Akos panted as he leaped backward. This fight was taking far too long. His men were fighting and dying by the moment. Akos knew that he was their only hope. Anson darted back in as soon as his feet were back underneath him, pressing him with a speed and a ferocity that Akos wouldn't have thought the man was capable of before.

"I want you to know that I will kill everyone on this vessel," Anson hissed as they locked blades again.

"You'll kill your only chance of ever seeing the other realms again," Akos grunted in reply.

"Oh, I'll spare the wayfarer. Maybe even his sister. If any of the rest survive, I'll put them in chains and allow them to work the rest of their days for me."

Akos didn't respond, and he didn't give Anson any more time to speak. With a wordless battle cry, Akos began to press the man back until his back was to the aft castle. He'd never fought this hard in his life. His blood sang with the exhilaration of combat, and he could see the feeling mirrored in his opponent's gaze. Steel flew, independent of any of his own thoughts, turning away Anson's blade and seeking further hits.

Sharp pain flared up his arm as Anson scored his own blow, but Akos didn't care. The only thing that mattered in the world was killing Anson. He'd deal with the pain afterward. Akos landed the tip of his blade against the man's thigh, but the strike didn't have enough weight behind it to do much more than stagger the god. In that moment, Akos had all the opportunity he needed.

Desperation added strength to Anson's blows, but it was too little too late. Akos had him on the backfoot now, and he wasn't letting up the pressure. Anson tried for one last lunge, trying to catch the captain in the chest. Akos slid past the blade, allowing it to jab into his left shoulder in exchange for slicing along Anson's wrist, severing tendons in a spray of crimson blood. The blow was almost enough to sever the man's hand, and Anson fell backward to the deck with shock written across his face.

The blade that had embedded itself in Akos's shoulder clattered to the deck and Anson scurried back until his back hit the aft castle. Akos stepped forward to pursue. His breath came in huge ragged swallows, but he had never felt so alive. The pain in his shoulder and arm were all but forgotten.

For the first time since they'd met, Anson had nothing to say. Akos thought that the man would attempt to beg for his life. It wouldn't have mattered. Akos did not intend to leave such a powerful enemy at his back. But Anson merely glared up at him, hate and pain written across his face. There was something else there too. *Triumph?* Akos wondered. He didn't let the curiosity give him pause. His sword rose for the coup de grâce.

...

Calia watched the battle with barely restrained fear. She'd considered jumping back over the side, but the water below didn't look very inviting. Vibius had swept her behind him when the fighting started, and Valesa and Leo had done their best to steer it away from them. Vibius had been forced only to chop at a pair of men, but as soon as they'd realized who he was, they'd backed away. Clearly Anson had given orders to leave the wayfarer unharmed.

The noise and fury of the fight was enough to make her want to curl into a ball and sob until it was all over. But much as she had when Anson had invited them along on his hunt, she forced herself to watch. These men were dying to protect her. The least she could do was keep her eyes open and observe their sacrifice.

Soon enough she heard a wordless yell rise above the general din of combat. Calia sought out the source of the shout and saw that Akos and Anson were locked in single combat. Anson must have ordered his own guards to stay out of it, as they pressed farther up and kept the *Mist Stalker*'s crew from joining their captain. The battle seemed evenly matched, though Akos was driving back the god with the strength of his blows.

Calia let out a slight shout when she saw Anson's blade tear a bloody streak down Akos's forearm, but he seemed to pay the wound no mind, immediately responding with a stab into Anson's thigh. That seemed to be enough to cause the man to lose his footing in the duel. Akos pressed his advantage, further staggering Anson until the god made one final, desperate lunge at his opponent.

Vibius had noted the fight as well and had begun to inch toward it. Calia placed her hand on his back to let him know they were following, and the group made their way along the railing toward the duel. Vibius cried out when lunge connected with Akos's shoulder, but the captain paid that blow no mind either. Instead, he reached up and *pulled* the strike farther in to carry his opponent off balance and then struck the man's wrist once he was overextended.

Calia watched with elation as Anson's blade clattered to the deck, and the man along with it. He backed away from Akos as far as he could, until there was no more room for him to run. Calia wanted to drop down to her knees with joy. It was almost over. Akos raised his blade to deliver the final blow.

The elation turned to panic in a heartbeat as Calia noticed the behemoth swinging itself down from the ratlines on the other side of the ship, kicking directly at Akos. Her voice joined Vibius's in a shouted warning, but the creature was moving too fast. It had swung itself feet first at the captain, and he noticed it at the last second, trying to dive away.

No man would have been fast enough to move out of the way, however, and the creature's massive feet impacted his side. Akos was thrown from his feet and into the railing not far from her. The wood cracked, but fortunately it did not send him tumbling into the water below. Calia put her hands over her mouth as the behemoth followed its own momentum, bounding to stand over Akos with its claws poised for the killing blow the way his sword had been over its master mere moments before.

But within the space of a heartbeat there was another in front of the crumpled form of the captain, and both Calia and Vibia gasped as they realized that it was Vibius. The wayfarer snatched something up from Akos and planted himself in the path of the beast's claws before it could strike. The creature hesitated, and Vibius voice rang across the deck.

"Stop!"

•••

Akos crawled back to his senses. He'd had just enough time to see the behemoth before it blindsided him. The pain running down his left side where it had hit him was almost enough to knock him unconscious. When he tried to push himself up, he blacked out, though only for a moment. He contented himself with lolling his head around to see what was happening around him.

Much to his surprise, Vibius was standing above him. The behemoth that had tried to kill him was towering over the wayfarer, glaring down at the pair as if wondering what to do. Vibius had guessed that Anson wouldn't risk injuring or killing him and placed himself in harm's way to protect Akos.

Trying to move his left arm sent a fresh wave of red-hot agony through his body, and Akos could only watch as the behemoth took a half step back, allowing the pair to see Anson struggle to his feet, holding his jacket against the bleeding ruin of his wrist. Akos gritted his teeth and focused through the pain, realizing that the fighting all along the deck had stopped. He saw Vibia and Calia several yards away staring at Vibius in shock and horror.

Akos returned his gaze to his friend and realized why they were so worried. A ball of ice formed in his stomach, and his mind was suddenly clear despite the pain coursing through him. Vibius had gotten a pistol from somewhere, and he had the cocked weapon pressed against his temple. Akos glanced down and felt some of the fear fade away. Vibius had taken it from his belt, and Akos knew it was unloaded. He'd put the only shot he had into Lorantes back in the citadel.

Anson didn't know that, though, and he stumbled over to be within speaking distance. Akos had to wonder if Vibius knew, or if he thought he was holding his own life in his hands. Akos tried to force himself up one more time and rose a few inches before his strength gave out, and he collapsed back down to the deck.

"Don't do anything hasty, wayfarer," Anson was saying. For the first time since he'd met the god, Akos thought there was a hint of fear in his voice.

"I'd give you the same advice," Vibius said, without a hint of fear in his voice. "Have your beast back away."

Without a word, the behemoth took several steps back. It was the two of them now, with Anson edging about as close as he dared. Akos almost wished the pistol was loaded. Vibius could have turned the weapon on Anson and ended the whole ordeal right here. *There is the little issue of the rogue behemoth that would leave on the deck*, Akos reminded himself.

"So, how do we proceed from this impasse?" Anson asked.

Akos wondered how he was keeping his tone so even with the wound in his wrist. Anson must be much tougher than he'd given him credit for.

"You let us leave," Vibius said.

"No," Anson replied flatly. "I'd rather we all die than let you leave. You understand that you are the key, don't you? You must, otherwise this little ploy would not have entered your mind."

"In that case...you let the others leave, and I will remain behind with you."

Akos tried to argue but he could only manage a weak gasp. Calia and Vibia shouted their protestations for him and the pair tried to rush forward, but Valesa appeared in front of them to keep them back. Akos tried to rise and almost managed to get a knee underneath him before the sharp, shooting pain along his entire left side forced him back down.

"And, how do you propose we accomplish this?" Anson asked.

"Two of my crew will row me ashore," Vibius said. "Once there, you and your men will return to shore, and you'll allow my men to return to the ship."

Anson looked as if he was considering the plan, but Akos saw that there was no doubt left in his eye. Akos reached up and grabbed the railing, gasping and ignoring the pain as he dragged himself to his feet. He almost collapsed right back down, but he managed to keep his balance long enough to prop himself up against the cracked railing.

"Done," Anson said.

"You...can't..." Akos managed to gasp between the flares of fire in his side.

"Leo," Vibius said before he began to descend to the lifeboat with his hand-picked men. "Keep Akos from doing anything stupid."

"Aye." The big man nodded.

Akos couldn't believe it. There was no way in all the realms and the void that he would allow his friend to remain behind like this. Not in exchange for his life. He glanced to the side to see that Valesa was having to physically restrain Calia, while Leo kept Vibia back. No one had bothered to restrain him, but Akos didn't think he was in much of a shape to do anything about it.

"One condition," Anson said before Vibius could swing over the side and scurry down to the longboat. "Once this trade has been made, your friends must leave. If I catch them around Logathia after this point, their lives are forfeit."

"Fine," Vibius replied, looking Akos dead in the eye as he said it. The message was clearly meant for him. Akos tried to stumble after the wayfarer, but he tripped on his own feet and fell hard onto the deck. The pain forced him unconscious. When he came to, Anson's men were loading into the spare longboats, taking their dead along with them.

Akos groggily motioned for a man to help him up. It was Gasci. The young man had a ragged cut along his jaw, but it wasn't deep enough to be dangerous. Still, his cheek and neck were soaked in bright red blood. He reached down and bodily hauled Akos to his feet, remaining under his arm to keep him from collapsing right back down.

The pain nearly knocked him out once more. Akos's breath was short and ragged. Breathing deep caused a sharp pain in his side, and his left arm hung limp at his side. He ignored the pain as best he could.

"Where..." Akos managed.

"He's ashore," Gasci confirmed his worst fear. "Anson's going to join him."

"Stop...them."

"Sorry, Captain," Gasci couldn't meet his eyes. "Leo told us not to listen to you until you came to your senses. We need to get you to the sawbones anyway."

Gasci began to half-help, half-drag Akos toward the hold. Akos fought back with all his strength, but he didn't even slow his crewmen. Inside he was fuming. *How dare Leo give that kind of order*, Akos roared in his mind. *I'm the captain of this gods damned vessel.*

But try as he might, Akos could not remain angry at his first mate. He would have given the same order had the roles been reversed. It was simple math. One man for one hundred, or whatever was left after that fight. Vibia was almost as skilled a wayfarer as her twin and could more than handle the task of bringing them home.

Akos quit fighting and allowed Gasci to carry him away. Just before the man ducked below deck, Akos held up his hand. He steadied himself as much as he could and drew in as deep a breath as he dared.

"Take me to the aft castle," Akos ordered.

"Captain, you're barely on your…"

"That was an order, Gasci."

For a moment, Akos thought that the man might ignore the command and take him to the ship's surgeon anyway. But his demeanor wavered, and Akos gave him his best smile.

"I won't do anything stupid," Akos assured him. "But I need to see this."

"Aye, aye, Captain," Gasci replied.

Akos attempted to help as much as he could, but it was all he could do to stay upright. The pair reached his usual place next to the helm, where he could see the shore. Akos thanked the sailor and leaned against the railing, but Gasci didn't go anywhere. That was probably a good thing. Akos could already feel that he was going to need someone to carry him back down those stairs.

It wasn't long before the longboats bearing Anson's force reached the shore and the men began to offload, surrounding the lone figure already standing there. The two waiting in their own longboat left the shore, and Akos watched his friend wait patiently with an unloaded pistol to his temple until the crew had begun to haul the longboat aboard.

The figure of Vibius was joined by another, most likely Anson. Akos watched as Vibius finally turned away from his friends and toward Anson. The pistol left his temple and shot out toward the god. The guards around him jumped for a moment, but nothing happened.

Despite the distance, Akos heard a deep laughter roll over the waves, and Vibius threw the weapon down on the ground between the two men. The guards surrounded him and bundled him off. Even through the pain and sorrow that was filling him, Akos felt the corner of his mouth twitch upward. He would have paid to see the look on

Anson's face when the hammer fell, and then again when he realized that the weapon wasn't loaded.

"Captain," Leodysus said.

Akos turned his head to regard the first mate. The big man had acquired a half dozen cuts across his torso, but none of them looked dangerous. There was a look of concern in Leo's eyes. Akos sighed, wincing as the motion sent fresh waves of pain through him.

"Get the ship underway," Akos said. "Bear west for now, toward the mist. Get me a report of what supplies we have."

"Aye, aye, Captain." Leo relaxed at the lack of anger in his captain's tones.

"Watch for anyone following. Even watch for shapes in the water. That behemoth got onboard, and I'll bet it swam out. Load the guns with grapeshot if we have any, and be ready for them. I'll be in the infirmary."

With a nod Gasci helped him down the stairs and into the infirmary. The ship's surgeon was already there going through all his supplies to see if anything was missing. The short round man hurried back and forth between the cabinets, glancing through them and muttering to himself. When he saw Akos he rolled his eyes and gestured to a bed, and Gasci helped him into it before Akos dismissed him.

"I should have known," Krallek said, "that you'd be the first one in here."

"Take care of the others first," Akos said. "There were a few wounded on deck."

"Walking wounded. I did triage before I left the deck. You're the worst wounded who might pull through."

Akos grunted. The dwarf had never sugarcoated his analysis of anything before. Krallek was one of his oldest hands, both in time spent aboard the *Mist Stalker*, and in general. But dwarfs lived two to three times as long as humans and were loyal to a fault, so that was unsurprising. He pulled up a stool and cut away Akos's shirt without even asking.

"How many dead?" Akos asked.

"Two dozen," Krallek said, his eyes sweeping over Akos's side. Akos didn't dare to look down at himself and instead fixed his gaze on a knot in the wood of the ceiling. "Another seven are going to die of their wounds. I made them as comfortable as I could. The rest are walking wounded. They can bandage one another up."

Akos's heart fell as he heard the news. Over thirty of his men dead or dying, and another being left behind. It wasn't the worst battle they'd ever been through, from a casualty standpoint. Perhaps it was the loss of Vibius that made him feel as though it was the end of the world. Akos glanced down to see that Krallek was offering him a thick strip of leather.

"You're going to want to bite down on this," Krallek said. His tone was much more sympathetic than it had been mere moments before. "This is going to hurt like fire, but I have to find out what's broken, and I think the bastards took all the whiskey."

Chapter 24

Calia looked out over the rails and into the mist. The journey back to the mist had taken a few days, and they'd not seen hide nor hair of any of Anson's forces following them. *A pity*, Calia thought. After being forced to watch, helpless, as Vibius was taken away, she had hoped for the chance for the crew to end the lives of a few more of his lackeys.

A heavy sigh escaped her lips, and Calia pulled herself away from the railing. She was at the very back of the ship, watching their wake for as far as she could see it before it disappeared into the mist. Calia felt as if there were a hole in her heart. Currently that hole was being filled with rage, but she was managing to keep that contained. For now.

A quick glance over the deck showed that the crew was going about its business as if nothing had happened. *How can they go along that way?* Calia had asked herself that question many times over the course of the last few days. She knew the answer of course, in her mind. But her heart couldn't help but tell her that the world had ended, and this was nothing more than the vain attempts of men trying to convince themselves that it hadn't.

The only thing out of ordinary on the deck were the two people occupying the captain's and wayfarer's spots. Rather than Akos and Vibius, Leo and Vibia had taken control. Akos was still on bedrest, by order of the ship's surgeon, though he hadn't let his injuries get the best of him. He'd still been issuing orders from the belly of the ship.

"Lady Hailko," Old Haroln said with a slight bow as he approached her and Valesa.

"After everything we've been through," Calia responded with a kind smile she didn't feel, "I think you can all call me Calia."

"Aye, well, Calia. Ahem, the captain has asked to see you at your earliest convenience."

Calia looked over to Valesa with a raised eyebrow, but her bodyguard shrugged. She couldn't imagine what the captain could want to talk to them about right now. There didn't seem to be anything to say that couldn't wait until he was no longer bedridden.

"We'll make our way to him shortly," Calia replied.

"Of course, Lady Hai…Calia."

Calia and Valesa made their way below deck and found the infirmary. They'd buried their dead at sea once they'd been away from Logathia, and it had been the only time that Akos had come above deck for the last few days. Fortunately, no one else was injured enough to require significant treatment, and the infirmary was bare except for the dwarf surgeon and Akos propped up in his bed.

The captain looked far worse for wear. His entire left side seemed to be wrapped in bandages, and his arm was in a sling. His right forearm had a tight bandage wrapped around it as well. There was a massive bruise spreading out from beneath the edge of his bandages across his chest. How he had survived the blow from the behemoth was anyone's guess, but his eyes hadn't lost any of their sharpness.

"Thank you for coming," Akos said as they entered the room.

"Of course," Calia said.

"Krallek, could you give us the room?"

The dwarf lifted an eyebrow but didn't say anything as he stomped out. Akos waited until the door to the infirmary had closed behind him before his eyes swiveled back to Calia. There was an odd light in them that she'd never seen before, and it made her a little curious.

"Do you love Vibius?" Akos asked suddenly.

The question took Calia aback. Whatever she'd been expecting the captain to ask her, this had most certainly not been it. She considered walking out right there. This was no proper question to ask a lady right to her face.

Without being bid to do so, Calia's mind flashed to the night in the jungle when she'd decided that she would no longer let propriety hold her back. Akos was waiting patiently for an answer, and Calia let him wait as she made her way over to a stool that was next to his bed and sat on it. In truth, she needed a moment to compose her answer more than she needed a seat.

It didn't take much consideration to know how she felt. Of course, Calia loved Vibius. No other man had ever made her feel the way he had, simply with his presence. She'd had crushes before, of course, on classmates and peers. But this was something else. It went beyond butterflies in her stomach. Vibius engaged her mentally, and she'd rarely met a man who could keep up with her in that arena.

"I do," Calia finally said, more to the floor than to Akos. It was a simpler reply than she felt the question warranted, but she supposed it hadn't been a complex question.

"What would you be willing to do to get him back?" Akos asked.

Calia's head snapped up, and she saw Valesa's eyes narrow. Was he asking her to return to the void to rescue Vibius? There was no way that they were in any shape to do so. The crew was exhausted and depleted. Akos was physically broken. If they so much as attempted a rescue they would be dead within days.

Even knowing that, Calia realized that if he asked her to help him right now she would turn around and do it. And she could see it in his eyes as well. Akos wanted nothing more than to turn and go to his friend.

"Anything," Calia answered.

"Wait a minute," Valesa interjected. "I think we all know that we wouldn't last another week in the void. We can't go back."

"Not right away," Akos agreed.

"What are you proposing?" Calia asked, intrigued.

"I plan to return to the void, once I've recovered. Anson won't dare risk Vibius's life, regardless of what he does. That means we have time on our side."

"Then return," Valesa said. "What does that have to do with us?"

"I'll need a great deal more firepower than the *Mist Stalker* can manage, and more men than it can hold to free Vibius. I have a decent personal fortune, but I don't think it will get me everything I need."

"You need a financier?" Calia asked.

Akos nodded.

Calia glanced at Valesa. Clearly the woman was against the idea of doing any more to help than they had to. But her face softened a little when she saw Calia's gaze. She knew her handmaid wanted only what she believed was best for her, but if Valesa got her way, then Calia would be locked in a tower for the rest of her life.

"How much will you need?" Calia asked.

"I don't honestly know," Akos replied.

"I'm sure that I could get brother to fund another 'expedition' into the void."

"Even if you get your men and materiel, what is your plan?" Valesa asked. "Sail up and ask nicely?"

"That's the first step," Akos said. "If that doesn't work, I plan on showing up with a warship and blowing his citadel back into the last century where it belongs, and then ask again."

"And if he flees inland and refuses?"

"Then I'll have to figure something else out."

"I'll do everything I can," Calia said, rising to her feet. "On one condition."

"What?" Akos asked.

"I come with you."

Valesa immediately opened her mouth to argue, but Calia held up a hand. Regardless of what her bodyguard thought, she was the one in charge of her own person. And she was tired of watching others take risks for her. If this was going to happen, she was at least going to share as much risk as she could and help however she could as well. Valesa stopped herself, but Calia could tell that there would be an argument later, when they were alone. *That's fine*, Calia thought to herself, *but this is happening.*

"There will be no guarantee of safety," Akos warned. "And once I come back to the void, I'm not leaving without Vibius."

"Then we are of the same mind." Calia smiled, and for the first time in days, it was genuine.

A matching smile split Akos's face, and he held out his right hand. Calia shook it firmly. Without another word, she turned and left the room for her own, Valesa hot on her heels. *Good*, Calia mused, *let's get this argument over with as quickly as possible.*

Into the Void

• • •

Krallek took his time making his way back into the infirmary. Akos had to wonder if the man had taken a circuit of the entire ship before making his way back around. There wasn't much for Akos to do while he was recovering but sit and suffer. His entire body seemed to hurt, but his left side seemed to be in constant agony.

The dwarf surgeon had given Akos something to chew on that helped to numb the pain, but he'd been right about the Logathians taking all the alcohol off the ship. Fortunately, they'd been planning to use the *Mist Stalker* as their training vessel, so they'd had it somewhat stocked. It would be enough to get them back to Macallia if they rationed it well enough. By the time Krallek returned, Akos had popped a handful of the root that had been left in easy reach into his mouth.

"You're going to get addicted if you keep going through the stuff like that," Krallek admonished as he stomped past.

Akos didn't respond, but he spat the wad of root out of his mouth. Within moments he was already longing for the spreading numbness.

Not for the first time, Akos wondered if he didn't want the mental fog that the root provided as much as the physical relief. There wasn't much to do in the infirmary but sit and stare at the ceiling. He supposed that he could read but holding up a book was difficult and painful considering the amount of bandages he was swathed in and the size of his bruises. And though she'd offered, he wasn't going to ask Vibia to waste her valuable resting time in the infirmary to keep him company.

And all that doesn't even come close to the real reason that you don't want to be in your right mind at the moment, Akos admonished himself. He'd lost men before. Men he considered very good friends. This was something different.

Vibius might come from an entirely different life, but he'd been Akos's brother as surely as if they'd been born to the same mother. A not insignificant portion of the pain that he felt in his chest had nothing to do with his broken ribs.

What had to be the worst part was that Akos was sure that he was solely to blame for Vibius's recapture. Sure, the wayfarer might have made the ultimate decision, but if Akos hadn't been so careless he would have never been able to make that choice. If he'd planned for a few more eventualities, or if he'd not involved Thirteen in his plot, Akos might have avoided this entire problem.

Akos sighed and tried to put his mind past all that. It was in the past now, and all he could do was move forward with the conviction that Vibius would not remain a prisoner for long. Now that Calia was involved, he might stand a chance of succeeding. As great a ship the *Mist Stalker* was, it didn't have the firepower or the crew capacity to support what he would need to retrieve his friend. Fortunately, he knew several people who might be able to help in that regard, though convincing them to aid him would be difficult, to say the least.

That was a problem for another day, though, and Akos needed something to distract his mind in the present. Krallek sat and cleaned his various tools in one corner of the small infirmary. The dwarf was not very talkative, but Akos knew that he was the only option if he wanted to make some conversation.

"You never told me," Akos said after a moment of thought, "what the extent of my injuries are."

"I didn't want you thinking you were well enough to turn the ship around to sail back to Logathia," Krallek said without looking up.

"So, they aren't as bad as I thought?"

"No, they're much worse. If you were a southpaw, I would warn you against ever picking up a blade again. Your shoulder will heal up well enough. But you broke your humerus and your ulna. The breaks were clean though, and simple, and they should heal up well enough if I can keep you from moving them too much for a while. You broke three ribs, and one of those punctured your lung. Honestly, it was nothing short of a miracle that you were able to stand, even assisted, so soon after your injuries."

"But everything will heal? Will I be able to fight again?"

"It will, if you don't move too much. You're going to lose some dexterity in your left side, though. I'd say your days of climbing mansion walls are over. But, you won't be a cripple. You will be able to wield a sword, but not for several months."

"That's good."

Krallek snorted.

"It's nothing short of a miracle. I was watching your fight. You spun in the air and impacted the railing on the same side that the behemoth hit you from. If you'd turned just a little less, you would have hit your spine. And we might not have been having this conversation if you'd done that."

"I've never been in a short supply of luck."

"You've an odd definition of luck, Captain."

Akos started to laugh and immediately regretted the act. Krallek winced and rose from his chair to fetch Akos some more of the numbing root. Akos allowed him to set it next to his bed but did not grab any. Even though his body ached for the relief it would provide. Krallek was right, he needed to slow down, or he would be no good to anyone once they returned to port. It was bad enough that he was going to be laid up for the near future; he didn't also need to be off his mind on narcotics.

"Already planning your return?" Krallek asked after a moment.

"What?" Akos raised his head to look at the dwarf.

"It's the only reason I can think why you might want to speak to Lady Hailko alone."

Akos thought for a long time before answering. The word was going to get out soon enough, but he had conflicting feelings about that. His crew had more than earned a lengthy leave, but Akos couldn't give them that. He already planned on divvying out a significant bonus for every man aboard from his own personal fortune. But Akos knew that he would need men he trusted to return to the void with him once they were prepared.

The thing that made Akos hesitate was the fact that even with all the preparation in the world, returning would mean no certain victory. No matter how many extra hands he hired, they would still be outnumbered by the tens of thousands. And that was just the one island. If Anson managed to conquer more while they were away, or if he somehow cemented alliances with the other gods, they would have even longer odds.

Much like Vibius, they would be free to make their own choice. But it weighed on Akos that the choice was necessary only because of his mistakes. There was little doubt in his mind that many of them would choose to stay with him. If they died, the blood would be on his hands.

Akos knew that wasn't far removed from the everyday life of privateering. The men knew they might die when they signed on to his ship, but they were doing that for profit. This was Akos's personal vendetta. Somehow that made it feel different. It made him feel as if there were more responsibility on his shoulders.

A long sigh escaped Akos's lips as he realized that he would have to bear that responsibility as best he could. There was nothing he could do to stop them if they wanted to join, short of going alone. And that would be true suicide.

"I am," Akos finally answered.

"You seem conflicted about that," Krallek noted.

"Not about returning. I am conflicted about asking the men to return with me."

"We already sailed into the void once for you, Captain."

"It's not that I'm worried the men won't go. I'm worried that they will and won't return again."

"We all know the risks. Some men will decide that you and Vibius aren't worth it. Personally, I know that you'd risk your life for any one of us, and I'd do the same."

"I'm glad to hear it." Akos said with a smile. "I might need a doctor again before this is all over."

"With your 'luck,' you'll definitely be needing a doctor again." Krallek snorted again and rolled his eyes. This time Akos laughed, ignoring the pain. Even Krallek gave a chuckle.

Chapter 25

The docks of Geralis bustled with activity. After seeing so many cities that were practically ghost towns, this was a welcome sight. Calia was somewhat surprised to realize that she had begun to think she might never see her home again. It was the first sight in a while to make her heart swell, even if the smell was still nothing to write home about. It had been a lifetime since they'd been on these docks, when it had been less than a year.

Leo descended the ramp first to deal with the dockmaster, and then Valesa helped Calia down the gangplank. Akos wasn't far behind, declining the helping hand even though he was still heavily bandaged, and his left arm was splinted and in a sling. Calia made her way down to the end of the wharf they stood on and hired a carriage to take them back to her estate.

The ride was quiet. Each person was lost in thought, and Calia wasn't about to break the silence. She had too many things on her own mind. She wondered what Halis would say. *Will he even believe me?* It was a question that had begun to plague her as they'd neared Macallia.

When she'd left for her expedition, Calia had assumed that people would take her word for the results. As they'd made their way back, she'd realized that there was nothing to prove that they hadn't simply been traveling for a year. Her peers would be just as resistant to the idea as they had before she'd left. There was nothing she could do about that now.

For now, Calia needed only Halis to believe her. With his support, the rest of the world could be damned for all she cared. Halis was the one that would help them get back to the void and her love. Calia prayed that he would believe her.

The seasons had turned while they were away. The road was littered in red, brown, and yellow leaves as the carriage churned along. After so long in the mist, it still felt warm to Calia. Their return trip hadn't been as fast as the first, with only one wayfarer propelling them along. Hopefully they would be able to outfit and leave before it got truly cold. Every moment they wasted here was another moment that something might happen to Vibius. And *that* was a risk that Calia wanted to minimize.

Soon enough, the Hailko estate loomed in the distance. The sight brought a rush of emotions to Calia's heart. Relief warred with sadness. She wished she could have brought Vibius back with her. The estate was so beautiful in the fall, and he would have loved the library. Still, the sight of her childhood home warmed her heart.

Even with the warmth spreading through her, Calia made a solemn mental note to visit her father's gravestone before she left again. She wished he would be waiting for her when she reached the front door with an embrace and a solution. But she knew that it was a childish wish and that he wouldn't be. This would be on her, for better or for worse.

Calia wondered if he would be proud of her. She decided that he would have been proud of the way she'd decided to take control of her life. He would have believed her regardless of what she'd told him of the void. Halis would be a little more skeptical.

The carriage ground to a halt in the driveway, and they dismounted. Calia could always hear the calls that accompanied any unannounced visitor to the estate. Servants would be rushing to let everyone know that there was someone there. Already she could see familiar faces descending the steps to greet them.

"Lady Hailko?" The surprised doorman gasped as Valesa helped her down from the carriage.

"How are you, Jevis?" Calia asked.

"Wonderful now that you have returned. There is so much to tell you, but your brother will want to see you first."

"Can you take me to him?"

"He's out riding now, but I will send someone to fetch him immediately. If you'd like to come in out of the chill?"

They were ushered inside, and Calia had to deal with a whirlwind of servants greeting her and inquiring after her. She exchanged pleasantries with all of them but didn't tell them much about what they'd been through. Calia had decided with Akos that it would be better to tell only the bare minimum of their exploits for now. Having a thousand explorers and adventurers rushing to the void might be a good thing for their cause, but it could also endanger everything they needed to do. Either way, it was a wild card that they didn't need to shuffle into the deck for the time being.

Soon enough they found themselves in the library. The servants seemed content to gossip with each other while they fetched them refreshments. Calia sat down, trying not to be overwhelmed by the entire situation. The conflict in her heart had only grown. It was wonderful seeing all her old friends and servants, but a pall hung over the happy greetings. During the long trip back, Calia had wondered if distance and time would dull her feelings toward Vibius, but they had served only to heighten them.

Akos sat down next to her, but Valesa remained at her shoulder. They hadn't agreed about going back, but in the end Calia had won the argument. It hadn't been easy. She'd had to play a little dirty, guilting Valesa about putting her in a gilded cage. But in the end, Valesa had agreed to go along with her plan. *Now to get Halis on board*, Calia thought.

As if summoned by her thoughts, the doors to the library were thrown open, and her brother strode through. Beralin and Lusalin were at either elbow as he walked in. His face lit up when he saw her, though she thought that she could see some surprise there as well. She didn't blame him. They'd planned for an expedition of a few months, not over half a year. He must have begun to worry at some point.

"Sister!" Halis crossed to her and embraced her in a hug as she rose. "I must confess I'd begun to lose hope that I'd see you again."

"I have to confess to the same," Calia agreed.

Halis held her at arm's length as if to examine her, and Calia did the same. He didn't look good. There were slight bags under his eyes that hadn't been there when she'd left, and several more strands of gray in his hair. His eyes looked tired, though that could be for any number of reasons. Calia put all of that out of her mind as she sat back down with him across from her.

"Captain Akos," Halis greeted. "Thank you for bringing my sister home to me."

"Of course," Akos inclined his head in a small bow.

"Brother," Calia interjected, "you might want to settle in. I have so much to tell you."

END

Made in the USA
Columbia, SC
24 September 2019